# Tackling Temptations on the Line

## Dev Hahn

Fox Arrow Publishing

CONTENT WARNING: There are references to a predatory character, potential sexual assault, and instances of bullying in regards to the FMC's size. If these may be triggering, do not go forward. Your mental well being is far more important. Due to it's sexual content, bad language, and possible triggers, this book is suitable for readers age 16+. Reader discretion is advised.

eBook Edition ISBN-13: 979-8-9896823-6-2

Paperback ISBN-13: 979-8-9896823-7-9

Cover design by Black Widow Designs.

Editing services by Dee Houpt of Dee's Notes. https://www.deesnoteseditingservices.com/

# Also By Dev Hahn

**Standalones**
Beyond Broken Colors


**Bellwood Lady Baller Series**
Coming Out on the Sidelines
Catching Feelings in the End Zone
Tackling Temptations on the Line
Opposing Hearts on the Field, *Coming Fall 2025*

**For every soul who's ever measured their worth in mirrors—**
*May you know, without question, that your body is not a problem to be*
*fixed,*
*but a story to be honored, a vessel worthy of love,*
*just as it is, just as you are.*
*You are beautiful.*
*It's the standards that are broken, not you.*

# Contents


Prologue ............ 1

Chapter 1 ............ 9

Chapter 2 ............ 19

Chapter 3 ............ 27

Chapter 4 ............ 37

Chapter 5 ............ 47

Chapter 6 ............ 59

Chapter 7 ............ 71

Chapter 8 ............ 81

Chapter 9 ............ 89

Chapter 10 ............ 99

Chapter 11 ............ 113

Chapter 12 ............ 123

Chapter 13 ............ 133

Chapter 14 ............ 143

Chapter 15 ............ 151

Chapter 16     161

Chapter 17     172

Chapter 18     179

Chapter 19     189

Chapter 20     201

Chapter 21     211

Chapter 22     223

Chapter 23     235

Chapter 24     245

Chapter 25     257

Epilogue     271

Acknowledgements     281

About the Author     283

Also By Dev Hahn     285

Connect With Me     287

# Prologue

## Maisie ~ 6 Years Old

"**G**et the hell out of my house, you worthless piece of shit!"

*Smash!*

What was that? Sounded like a plate. Or maybe a coffee cup? Mommy always makes sure the breakable cups and plates are not near the edge so Sissy doesn't pull them down and break them. I wonder if she forgot to move something when Daddy got home before the fighting started. She's been screaming and yelling at Daddy since he got home. I don't know what he did, but it made Mommy really mad. She's been crying too.

"How could you do this to us?! To me? Your daughters? You fucking ruined our family!" Mommy yells before I hear another smash. Mommy really should make sure the breakable stuff is out of reach.

"No, no. You see, that's where you're wrong. *You* ruined this family, Clara!" Daddy yells back at Mommy.

"Oh, I ruined this family? Really?" Mommy laughs, but she is mad. I'm so confused. "Please, tell me, Gabriel, how I'm the one who ruined our family. The last I checked, I'm not the one who stepped out on our marriage. I'm not the one who has been sleeping around with their coworker while their spouse is at home, tending to the house and making sure the kids are cared for from the time they open their eyes until they go to sleep. You did!"

Mommy laughs again. "I knew I couldn't trust that skank, Deanna. You always told me there was nothing to worry about, and look where we're at!"

"Well, if you had taken better care of yourself, I wouldn't have found her so alluring and given in to temptation!" Daddy yells back.

It goes quiet, and I hope Mommy and Daddy are done fighting because Sissy is napping down the hall, and I don't want them to wake her up. She will be very cranky if she doesn't get her full nap.

"What the hell is that supposed to mean?"

Ugh! Please, please stop arguing soon! I don't like it. It makes me super sad, and I want to run away from the fighting. Maybe I should go down and ask them to stop fighting so they don't wake up sissy.

I grab onto the wooden railing and take a step at a time. One time, I tumbled down the stairs, so now I'm extra cautious. I walk into the dining room and head to the kitchen, where I hear Mommy's and Daddy's voices.

"Since you gave birth to Josie, you've put on some weight. You lounge around in nothing but sweats and do nothing about your appearance. I mean, would it kill you to do your hair and get dolled up for me before I come home from work? Then I would have looked forward to coming home to you instead of finding someone else who appeases my desires."

"Wow ... you're so unbelievable! You know that? Tell me, Gabriel. When do you expect me to find time to work out around tending to our girls, cooking all the meals, cleaning the house, doing the laundry, washing dishes, running errands, and everything else in between?"

"As if you actually do all of that in a day. I have yet to come home to a clean house. There are always toys lying about, a dirty dish or two in the sink. The one work shirt I needed today was still in the dryer!"

"Excuse me, I thought you were a grown-ass man who could do his own laundry, and not some petulant child. In case you forgot, I am not your mother; I am your wife!"

"A wife is supposed to do those things, especially when the husband is the one who goes to work. I'm the one who wakes up at the crack of dawn to go to my job to provide the money for you to take care of our home and our children. Not for you to sit around on your fat ass and munch on snacks and do the bare minimum!"

Mommy grabs her big, heavy frying pan and chucks it at Daddy. With a loud thump, the pan hits Daddy, and Daddy falls to the floor.

"Mommy! Daddy! Stop it!" I scream. My voice catches Mommy's attention. I see anger on her face, then her eyes go all big when she spots me.

"Maisie!" She walks toward me, but I turn and run away from her, making my way to the front door.

"Ow!" I screech, feeling something sharp in my foot, but I keep going. I need to get to my quiet space.

"Maisie, please wait!"

"Mama!" The sound of my baby sister crying upstairs makes Mommy stop. I know she will go to sissy. She needs to because sissy is younger than me and needs her more.

Out the green front door I go. Hopping down the stairs, I do my best to stay off my one foot, which is hurting really badly. I head around the side of my house to the big bush that sits between my house and the neighbor's house. It has a big hole in it toward the back that you don't notice from the front. It's my secret hiding space my older neighbors helped me make.

I wanted my own little fairy house, like Tinkerbell, so I could play fairies with my friend Charmaine and her sister, Corrine. Daddy wouldn't make me one, but the nice grandparents next door said they could. The grandpa used his bush scissors to make the hole, and the grandma planted pretty flowers around it to make it more like a fairy house.

Mommy and Daddy don't know about this spot. It's where I have been coming when they get into their fights. It's quiet, and I can make my heart stop beating super fast.

I crawl into the dark hole, pull my knees to my chest, and let the tears fall down my face. I hate Mommy and Daddy arguing. I hate their yelling. I'm worried about Daddy and hope he is okay. He was mean to Mommy, but he didn't need to get hurt.

I sob into my hands, my foot hurting and stinging with so much pain.

"Are you okay?"

I lift my head and see a boy with brown hair and pretty blue eyes. A boy I've never seen before. How did he find my hiding spot?

"N-n-nno. My parents ... are fighting, and my ... foot hurts. Really, really bad," I sob.

"Oh. I'm sorry. That sounds bad," the boy says. "Do you want me to look at your foot?"

He seems nice. I'm not sure I can look at it, but I know I want it to stop hurting, so I nod, giving him permission to check.

His hands feel warm when they grab onto my ankle, and he carefully lifts my foot.

"You've got something in your foot. And it's bleeding. You're going to need to get it out before it gets an infection. You don't want that."

"Why? Is that bad?"

"It's something that happens when you get a cut. If it doesn't get cleaned, it can turn green. And if green turns to black, they cut it off."

My eyes widen in terror. I can't have them cut off my foot! I need my foot.

I start to cry even harder.

"Hey! Hey! Don't worry. I can help! My mom's a school nurse. She knows what to do. She can help you!"

"R-r-really?" I sob out.

The boy reaches his hand out toward me. "C'mon. I'll take you to her, and she will make you all better."

"B-b-but I don't know you. And my mama said I shouldn't leave with people I don't know."

"I'm Dylan. I live next door."

"Next door?" It's an old grandma and grandpa who live next door. And most mommies and daddies aren't wrinkly like they are.

"Yeah. We just moved in," Dylan tells me. "What's your name?"

"Maisie Janine Jorgensen."

"That's a big name. It is pretty but too big for me to remember. How about I call you …" He taps his finger to his chin. "How about … Freckles?"

"Freckles?" That's a weird name.

"Yeah. Your face and skin are covered in all those brown dots. I've got a cousin with dots like those, and my mom says they are called freckles."

"Freckles sounds weird. I don't really like it." I stick my tongue out and scrunch my face. "You can call me just Maisie. Or MJ. Some family call me that."

"Okay, MJ. Let's take you to my mom so you don't need your foot cut off."

Dylan and I crawl out of the bush. He lays my arm across his shoulders, and his arm goes behind my back.

"Keep your hurt foot off the ground so you don't get dirt in it."

"That's kind of hard to do. It's a long way to your house!"

"Hmm." He taps his chin. "I know! I'll give you a piggyback!"

"Okay. If you are sure you can carry me," I say.

"I'm strong, just like my dad. Don't worry. I got you!"

I hop on Dylan's back, and he carries me all the way to his house, then helps me sit on the step of his front porch.

"Stay here! I'm going to get my mom so she can get her kit."

Dylan rushes into his house, leaving me to sit on his porch step by myself. For a little moment, everything is quiet. I look over at my house next door, wondering if the fighting has stopped yet. Did Daddy get up off the floor? Is baby sister calmed down? Has Mommy stopped crying?

"Hello," a gentle voice comes from a pretty woman with brown hair, the same color as Dylan's, and she sits beside me. "I hear you have a hurt foot."

"Mama, you need to tell her who you are first. She isn't allowed to talk to people she doesn't know. Her mommy said so."

Lips painted soft pink and teeth white like pearls smile back at me. "Hello, sweet girl. My name is Nora Myers, and I'm a school nurse, so I know all about boo-boos and how to fix them. Can you tell me your name?"

"Maisie. Maisie Jorgensen."

"What a beautiful name."

"Thank you," I say, giving her my best smile.

"Do you mind if I look at your foot and see if I can make it all better?"

"Yes, ma'am. I would 'preciate it very much."

"Oh, what lovely manners you have. You could teach Dylan and Carver a thing or two."

"Carver?" I ask.

"He's my older brother. Sometimes, he can be a pain in my ass."

"Dylan Beckett Myers!" His mom scolds him. "Language, young man! What have I told you? You do not have permission to use adult words. That's money for the swear jar."

"But Mommy! He is!" Dylan whines back, and his mommy doesn't look too happy with his tantrum.

"You should say 'Sorry, ma'am' and not say it again. It's the proper way." It's what my mommy always tells me.

"Sorry, ma'am," Dylan says, looking down at the ground.

"Wow." Nora looks from Dylan to me. "You made that look as easy as pie. Miss Maisie, I think I'm going to like you being friends with my son. You seem to have a good influence on him." She looks back at her son. "This one's a keeper, Dylan. Don't let this one go."

Nora grabs her little kit and pulls out some rubber gloves, like the ones they use at the doctor's office, before facing me.

"Let me take a look at your foot, sweetie." She gently grabs my hurt foot and places it on her lap.

"Oh, my goodness!"

"What is it?" I ask, and Dylan's mom's eyes go big.

"There's a piece of broken glass stuck in your foot. I bet that doesn't feel too good, does it?"

I shake my head. "It hurts really bad."

"It looks like it hurts. May I ask how this happened?"

"My mommy and daddy were fighting, and I think one of them dropped something. I didn't see any broken glass when I ran outside. That's when it hurt."

She has a weird look on her face before she speaks to me. "Do they always fight?"

"They've been fighting more and more each day. I wish they would get along. It's not nice to fight. They are supposed to love each other."

"I agree. It is not nice to fight. Do your mommy and daddy fights ever get ... harmful?"

"Harmful?" I'm not sure what she means.

"Never mind. Let's focus on getting your foot better. Shall we?" She takes another look. "I know just how to fix this and make it all better." She goes back in her kit and brings out what looks like tiny tongs.

"W-w-what's that?" I ask, nervous what she will do with those.

"These are called tweezers. They are going to help me grab onto that piece of glass and pull it out so I can clean up your foot and put a bandage on it."

"W-w-will it hurt?" I ask.

"It might for a little second, but then you'll feel so much better. I promise!"

Dylan bumps into my back as he sits behind me, his hand reaching for mine. "Take my hand. You can hold onto it and squeeze it if you need to. It's okay to be scared."

"I'm not scared!" I try to say in my biggest, bravest voice, but the moment his mommy places the tweezers near my foot, I shut my eyes, not wanting to look.

Dylan lowers his head so it's next to my face. "Don't worry, Freckles. I've got you."

# Chapter 1

**Maisie – Present Day**

"Where do you want to meet up? The library?"

"Mmm ... how about the new coffee shop on Main? The town has been raving about them, and honestly, I really could go for an iced mocha latte right now."

"Are you talking about the Rustic Mug?"

Admiring my reflection in my floor-length mirror, I ensure my bra straps are hidden beneath my floral tank top straps. I adjust the olive-green miniskirt, making sure it's not riding too far up and my ass isn't hanging out of the bottom. My mother would have a heart attack before lecturing me about how I should dress for my "body type."

"Yep. It's right across the street from the art therapy studio. See you there in twenty minutes?" Alora asks, her gorgeous face taking up my cell phone screen.

Glancing at the clock on my side table, I note the time. "Give me thirty minutes? I got to drop Josie off to her ballet class first."

"Sounds good. Mirko and I will grab a table if we get there before you. See you soon! Bye, girl!" Alora finger-waves before hanging up our FaceTime.

A moment later, the slightest jingling of a bell rings before soft fur brushes against my leg.

"Meow."

"Morning, Jinxy." I pick up my fluffy cat and nuzzle her little pink nose. Her big sapphire-blue eyes surrounded by a gorgeous gray mask stare up at me. "I'd love to lay down and cuddle with you, but I have plans today. Maybe later. Okay?"

Jinxy jumps out of my arms and flicks her bushy tail as she sashays her way out of my room, unhappy with what I said. She loves when we get to lounge around and cuddle, especially since it's still summer break.

"The diva attitude is unwarranted," I yell after her before muttering, "Should have named you Sassafras."

Turning back to my mirror, I apply another layer of pink lip gloss and ensure no baby hairs are out of place before making my way down the hall to my little sister's door, the sound of a Taylor Swift song blasting from the other side.

"Josie Mae!" I bang on her door, hoping she can hear me over the music. "We're leaving in fifteen minutes, so you better be ready!"

"I'm moving as fast as I can!" she shouts, full of fourteen-year-old attitude. Josie and I have always been close, but lately, her moods roll in like summer storms—loud, sudden, and gone before I can catch my breath. I know it's the hormones, those wild teenage chemicals stirring everything up and throwing her off balance. You know, the classic mood swings.

*Lord, help me.*

I do my best to remind myself she needs me now more than ever to help guide her through this stage of her life. Especially since Mom is barely around, with working her job during the days and hitting up pilates in the evenings. Weekends, she designates to going out to local bars or a club in the next town over, trying to find the next Mr. Right.

I roll my eyes at the thought as I make my way downstairs to gather my things to meet up with my friends. I'm working on my portfolio for the fashion school I'm applying to in Boston. I desperately want my friends' input on which of my pieces I should include. It's the school of my dreams, so my picks need to be the best of the best if I want to get in. No one's input matters more than Alora's and Mirko's.

"What on God's green earth are you wearing?" My mother's voice breaks through my train of thought. I didn't notice her sitting at the dining table drinking coffee in her pink bathrobe while scrolling through her phone. If I had to guess, she's probably going through her dating apps to pick her male choice of company for the evening.

I glance down at my appearance before making eye contact with my mother, giving her my smuggest smile. "Clothes, of course. Going out in public in your birthday suit is frowned upon in this country."

My mother rolls her eyes. "Clearly," she responds. "What I mean is, it doesn't suit you."

*Annnddd ... here we go.*

"They cover everything that needs to be covered," I retort. "Besides, I happen to love it and how I look in it, and Alora has already given her stamp of approval."

"Alora has the figure to pull something like that off."

*Ouch.*

Sadly, this isn't the first time my mom's made this sort of comment regarding my outfits or size. I'm not a size two or petite like my little sister. I fit in a size ten, twelve when it's that time of the month, and let's not forget I have a big ass along with a nice pair of double D's. Where most girls my age may be self-conscious with this figure, I embrace mine. I love my curves. I'll proudly wear what I want to wear, and I'll be damned if I allow the opinion of others or this skinny-obsessed society to tear me down.

"My body doesn't need to be a certain way for me to wear the clothes I want to wear. You may not be comfortable with my size, but I am, and that's all that should matter."

"I'm not uncomfortable with your size, MJ. I just think if you want to wear stuff like that, you should work on shedding a couple of pounds. I could help you. We can go to my pilates classes together and be workout partners. I mean, how else are you going to attract a man—"

"I'm nearly eighteen years old! I'm about to start my final year of high school and preparing for the future I have dreamed about since I was five. Looking for attention or affection from a man isn't at the top of my priorities like it is for you!"

"What the hell is that supposed to mean?"

"It means I don't need some validation from the male species to feel good about myself. That sort of thing starts from within, Mother. If you would just go to therapy to work through your trauma and your self-confidence, you would see that you never need a man to complete you."

My mom glares at me as Josie stampedes down the stairs before coming to a halt beside me. Her long strawberry-blonde hair is up in a tight bun. A dance bag lays across her leotard-clothed torso, and a pair of baby-pink Crocs are on her feet.

"What did I miss?" Josie asks, looking from me to our mother, not missing the staredown between us.

My mom shakes her head, breaking the tension, and turns toward Josie, giving her a warm smile. "Nothing, honey. Why don't I make you something healthy to eat before you leave?"

"Sorry, Mom, but we really should get going. I don't want to be late for ballet." Josie turns and heads out of the dining room.

"Well, then you should at least take a protein shake and drink it on your way. You don't want to dance on an empty stomach." Our mother disappears into the kitchen and returns in seconds with a vanilla protein shake in hand.

"Ugh, whatever," Josie relents, rolling her eyes before taking the beverage. "Got to go! Love you! Bye!"

Josie dashes out the front door, and I follow after her, wanting nothing more than to put some space between our mother and me. I could not be more grateful to be going to spend time with my friends.

Using my key fob, I unlock my lime-green Honda Civic and remote-start it, giving Josie time to toss her bag in the back seat and crank the AC before she starts complaining about the humidity ruining her perfect ballerina bun.

As I approach my car, my phone buzzes in my hand.

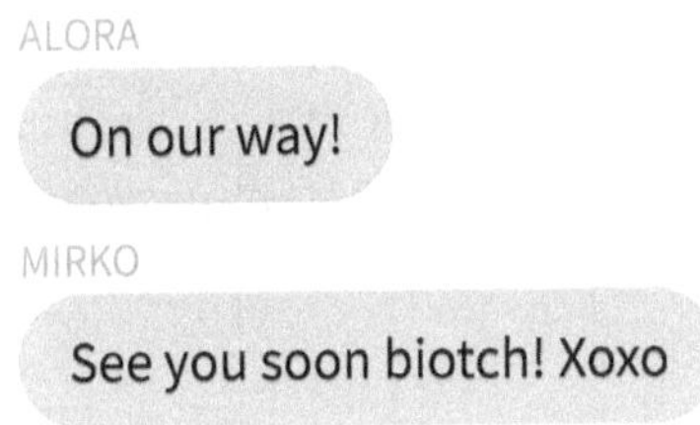


I'm about to reply when I collide with something hard, and two strong arms catch me, preventing my ass from making impact with the sidewalk.

"Whoa! Easy there, Freckles! Wouldn't want you to hurt yourself."

*Oh, that voice.* That deep timbre of a grown man I would recognize in any crowd.

My eyes slowly drift from the hands gripping my bare skin up the tan, defined arms attached to the glistening chiseled chest, and a jawline that could cut diamonds, before stopping to peer into the most gorgeous icy-blue eyes.

Dylan Myers.

My next-door neighbor and best friend since I was six years old. The guy I may have developed a teeny, tiny crush on since the eighth grade, but I refuse to acknowledge those feelings because ... well ... he's my best friend.

That, and he has a girlfriend.

"What have I told you about calling me that?" I tease, gently pulling myself from his hold. Not that I want to, but I need to put some space between us. Having my body flush against his does things to me, especially since he is wearing athletic shorts without a shirt, sweat glistening down his washboard abs.

"Sorry. I can't help it. I like the way your nose scrunches up when I call you that. It's cute." He chuckles, and my god if it isn't the sexiest sound in the world. I could get lost in the way his eyes sparkle, or when his mouth lifts on one side, showing off his pearly white teeth, and that one dimple makes an appearance. "Are you in a hurry to get somewhere?"

"I got to drop Josie off to ballet, then I'm meeting up with Alora and Mirko in town." I do my best not to ogle the living fuck out of him. The last thing I want to do is make him uncomfortable that his best friend is salivating at the sight of him shirtless. "Sorry for interrupting your run."

"It's fine. Not like I had that much farther to go." He nods toward his house that is a few feet away from mine.

"Still, I feel terrible for—"

*Honk! Honk!*

I look past Dylan to see Josie aggressively tapping her wrist, letting me know we need to get going.

"Seems like I'm holding you ladies up. I won't keep you any longer. It was nice bumping into you, Freckles. I hope you enjoy the rest of your Saturday." Dylan gives me a wink before jogging off toward his house.

I stare after him, admiring his backside, then another honk brings me back to reality.

"Yes, yes. I'm coming," I mutter before getting in my car.

"What was that all about with you and Mom?"

"It was nothing." I smile at her, keeping my eyes on the road ahead.

"She was giving you crap about your weight again, wasn't she?"

"She didn't like my outfit. That's all."

"Which means she was talking about your weight. I'm not stupid, big sis. Anytime it's about your clothes, it's always in reference to your weight, and I just don't get why she cares so much."

If I weren't driving, I would bear-hug the living shit out of my little sister. It warms my heart that she is on my side.

"She cares because she loves us. It's what moms do."

Josie rolls her eyes before looking out the passenger window as we approach downtown. "She should love you just as you are."

*I agree with you, little sis.*

I turn into the alley that runs alongside Beyond Broken Colors and pull into the parking lot behind the row of shops on Main Street. It's a better spot, especially on weekends and during the holidays when all of Bellwood seems to be out and about—more so on warm, sunny days like today.

After I walk Josie to Roots and Rhythm Dance Studio for her ballet class, I head across the street to Rustic Mug. I spot Alora and Mirko sitting at a small square table outside the coffee shop—Alora, tan and radiant, her big curls pulled back into a high puff, scrolling through her phone, and Mirko beside her, icy-blond hair perfectly styled, tapping his nails impatiently against the table like the barista is personally offending him by being slow.

"Hey guys!" I singsong, and squeeze them both.

"I went ahead and placed your drink order with ours," Alora informs me.

"Oh, you're the best!"

"Hey! I made sure she included a strawberry cream cheese danish for you. Where's my love at?" Mirko fake whines.

"You're the bestest," I say, blowing two air kisses his way.

"And you better never forget it," he replies.

The three of us laugh, and I'm reminded how grateful I am for these two. "Seriously, you guys, I'm so glad we are hanging out, because after this morning, I needed this."

"Uh-oh. What shitfiasco happened now?" Mirko asks, resting his chin onto his hands.

"Shitfiasco isn't a real word," Alora informs him.

"Maybe not in the English language, but in Mirko's world, it is," he snarks back. "So ... spill it, Red."

"Nothing other than my mom bitched about my outfit, saying Alora is better at pulling this off than I am, and that happened before I accidentally ran into a near half-naked Dylan because I wasn't paying attention."

"Okay, I cannot believe your mother compared the two of us with your outfit, which, by the way, you're killing it. I mean, hello? Hot stuff right there!" Alora says this too loudly, causing people to pause and look our way.

"Ssshhh … do you need to draw attention our way?" I admonish my beautiful friend.

"Your mom's a mega bitch."

My jaw drops as I stare at my other best friend. "Mirko!"

"What? She is. I'm just calling it like I see it. Now … what's this about a half-naked Dylan?"

"Those words would be the ones to grab your attention." I shake my head and laugh. "Do I need to remind you that you have a boyfriend?"

"Need I remind you that Andrew and I are very secure in our relationship. Besides, you're more obsessed about Dylan than anyone."

"I am not! Dylan is just a friend."

"A friend you want to fuck," Mirko says, waggling his eyebrows.

At that very moment, one of the guys working at the coffee shop delivers us our drinks and treats, glancing at my friends, then me. He's tall, with golden-blond hair that catches the light, bright-blue eyes, and a small silver hoop in his right ear. A devilish smirk flashes my way, and I feel my cheeks warm.

"Enjoy," he says, his gaze lingering on me for a moment before he heads back inside the coffee shop.

"Um … okay. That guy was definitely checking you out," Alora says, taking a sip of her drink.

"No, he wasn't." I quickly take a bite of my Danish and moan at how delicious it is. The flaky golden pastry crumbles around my teeth, revealing a soft, smooth filling that's both rich and tangy. The buttery layers contrast perfectly with the creamy interior, and the strawberry adds a sweet, fruity touch of summer.

"Girl, the way your boobs look in your top had his baby-blue eyes laser focused. It's a good thing he didn't hear you moan like that, or he would be sporting a boner the rest of his shift."

I nearly choke at Mirko's statement. "Mirko!"

"Just telling you like it is, as I always do."

"Can we please redirect our conversations to why we are here in the first place? I need you guys to help me get this portfolio in order so I can send it to Harborview School of Fashion soon. The sooner I get this sent in, the sooner I'll be able to breathe."

"Don't stress it, girl. You've got this whole thing in the bag. Your designs are killer, and it would be their loss not to accept you." Alora reaches across the table and squeezes my hand for added support.

"Thanks, Lor." I squeeze her hand in return, grateful for her unwavering support.

After almost two hours, I have my designs selected and a portfolio I am about ninety percent confident with.

Mirko and I hand Alora money for a tip, as we always want to show our support for our local businesses. A few moments later, she returns with a mischievous smile on her gorgeous face.

"Here," she says, handing me a piece of white paper.

"What's this?" I ask, hesitantly taking it from her.

"The handsome gentleman who eye-fucked you earlier wanted me to give you his number. He said he hopes to have a text by the time he gets off."

"You're lying," I state, opening the note and reading the handwriting that is definitely not my friend's.

***Brock***
***555-213-7842***
***Hope you'll text me later, beautiful. My shift ends at 5.***

"Sooo ... are you going to message the hot Adonis later? See where things go?" Mirko taunts me. "Or are you going to ogle Dylan Myers through your bedroom window."

I nearly drop the note at the mention of Dylan's name. I'm unsure why having another guy's number feels wrong. Dylan isn't my boyfriend and never will be. It stings every time I remind myself of that fact, yet my heart never wants to listen. I need to get over this incessant crush and move forward.

I look up at my friends and shrug. "Guess you'll just have to find out later."

# Chapter 2

**Dylan**

Fuzzy puppies. Naked mole-rats. That time a cow gave birth right in front of us on our field trip to the dairy farm back in second grade. A shiver runs through me as I remember how my classmates and I were witnesses to seeing something most people deemed beautiful. I beg to differ. At eight years old, nothing left me traumatized like seeing a whole baby cow covered in blood and fluids come out of its mother, but the memory served its purpose. The last thing I wanted to do was enter the house sporting a boner, unsure if my parents were up yet. Not something I would like to explain to them about why I'm pitching a tent after going for a run. How embarrassing would that be?

I'm just grateful her eyes didn't look down before we parted ways.

Colliding into Maisie and having her glorious curves pressed against my skin, sent little sparks of energy throughout my body, causing my dick to swell.

Seeing her in that outfit, the way her clothes accentuated every glorious dip and swell of her body, I had to choke back the groan that tempted to slip past my lips.

Should I be having this kind of reaction to my childhood best friend?

Maisie Jorgensen has been pretty since I saw her for the first time. My family was moving things into our new home that day. I was running out of the house for another box to bring in when I saw her running from hers. She seemed upset, and that had bothered my six-year-old heart. She ran to the bush that separates our yards and disappeared inside. My childish mind instantly thought of *Alice in Wonderland*. I'd worried she'd fallen into a deep hole that led to a trippy drug-hallucinate world, so I crossed the front yard to follow her.

I was grateful there was no endless rabbit hole to fall through when I entered, but the sight of her sitting there squeezing her legs with her head buried was cause for concern. She was crying for reasons I didn't know, then I noticed her foot was bleeding. I introduced myself so I could get her to my mom, who can fix any boo-boos. Maisie's head popped up when I spoke, and seeing her face for the first time left me in awe. I quickly pushed whatever that was aside because helping her was more important.

Six-year-old me had never been interested in girls. It was as if a worldwide boy code made all girls off-limits as friends because "girls are gross and don't like to get messy," but Maisie was different. She enjoyed wrestling around and getting dirty, playing along with whatever games my friends and I wanted to. Never once did she complain.

Then puberty hit and my feelings began to change, as did Maisie's body. I started viewing her not just as a friend but as someone I was becoming attracted to. Many nights had me dreaming of more sinister things that left me with damp bed sheets and morning wood. How can I not, though?

Her coppery-red hair that falls in waves, like fiery waterfalls surrounding her gorgeous face. Eyes that shimmer blue under bright sunlight and fade to gray on a cloudy day, as if they've learned to mirror the sky. Freckles pepper her face and arms, a constellation of tiny golden dots, each unique and imperfect like little kisses from the sun. A body so voluptuous it exemplifies strength and softness in perfect harmony. Maisie is more than her curves. It's the confidence in who she is and not giving a damn what other people think or say about her that make her alluring—a temptation.

Fuck, I'm not helping myself.

I make my way into the kitchen, grab a bottle of water from the fridge, and guzzle almost all its contents before my phone rings with an incoming video call.

"Hey, shithead. How's the Army life treating you?"

My older brother, Carver, is stationed at Fort Campbell and is a member of the Army's 160th Special Ops Aviation Regiment, the Night Stalkers. From what Carver has told us, they are a unit who provide helicopter support for special forces operations. They are skilled to fly helicopters at night with the help of night vision equipment to insert and extract special forces, conduct aerial surveillance, and provide air assault capabilities when needed. He does a lot of secret missions he's restricted from discussing with anyone, family included.

"It's kicking my ass but keeping me in line. How's Bellwood?"

"Same old, same old." It's a small town, so nothing exciting ever truly happens here.

"You just get back from running?" he asks.

"Yeah. I just finished three miles today. Trying to get right for football season."

Football conditioning is around the corner, and shortly after, the new season begins. I'm more than ready to take my place as the starting quarterback for the Bellwood High Eagles. I rode the bench most of last year as a backup to Payson Moore and Brady Thomas. It's hard to get any play time when you have two incredible quarterbacks who dominate their positions despite the intense turmoil between them. When Brady couldn't finish the season due to an injury and Payson took charge, there were a few times she feigned needing to sit out. I'm certain it was so I could play during my junior year. The girl is athletic as hell and takes her health seriously, there was no way she needed those breaks, but Payson was the epitome of a leader. She cared for all her teammates, ensuring our coaches let everyone have their moment to shine—even the backups. I respected the hell out of her and what she did for our team, and I plan to do the same.

This year, it's my turn to lead us to the championship game and make us repeat winners.

"Just make sure you hydrate and get your electrolytes. I remember how humid those South Carolina summers are."

"That's why I run early in the mornings."

"How are the college applications coming along? Still applying to Harvard?"

"You know I am."

"Have you thought of applying to other colleges? You know, just in case."

In case I'm not good enough to get into the one I want.

Harvard Law is where I plan to go after graduation. Dad's a lawyer with his own law firm, and since Carver went military, it's been left to me to follow in Dad's footsteps so I can take over the firm when he retires.

I know my brother means well. Sure, there are other colleges I could apply to, but if I'm going to be a good ass lawyer like my dad, I need to go to the best law school in the country, and that's Harvard, Dad's alma mater.

To avoid getting into an argument, I change the subject. "So, what's with the call? Shouldn't you be sleeping or playing soldier on that big ass base?"

"Can't a big brother check in?" He laughs. "Actually, I am about to head to do some training, but … "

"But what?" My heart beats slightly faster, an uneasiness settling over me that whatever my brother is about to tell me will not be good.

"There's a reason I'm calling you first because I'm not ready to share with Mom and Dad yet and deal with their emotions or barrage of questions." Mom tends to get extremely emotional, but Dad, the lawyer that he is, starts rapping off any question that comes to mind. I can't blame Carver for holding out.

"You're being deployed to another secret mission?" Every time he makes these check-in calls, he informs us of his previous missions, except he usually finds a time to tell us all at once.

"Yeah. We will deploy next month, but this one ..."

"Just spit it out, Carv." My anxiety has my stomach twisted in knots.

"You know I can't tell you anything about my missions, but I need you to understand this one isn't like the previous ones. Where we're going is extremely dangerous. I need you guys to try to stay optimistic, all right? I need all the good energy and prayers to make it out of this one alive."

"Fuck!"

"That sounds like a dollar for the swear jar," Mom calls from somewhere in the house. I guess that wasn't in my head like I thought it was.

"Shit. Listen, I got to get to training. Do me a favor and keep this between us until I get a moment to talk to Mom and Dad? Got to go. Love you, bro!"

Before I get the chance to say anything, his face disappears. *Chicken shit.*

My mom, still dressed in her purple flannel pajamas, appears in the kitchen and goes straight for the coffee maker. "Was that Carver's voice I heard?"

"Yeah. He was just checking in, wanting to see how I'm doing with college applications."

"Have you been applying to other colleges?"

I shake my head.

"Sweetheart, I know you have your heart set on Harvard, but at least think about applying to other colleges. It's good to have options."

"Carver was saying something similar. I guess it wouldn't hurt to check out other programs." I walk over to my mother and place a kiss on her cheek. "Sorry for cursing. I'll be sure to put a dollar in the jar before I head out later. I'm going to go take a shower and wash off the sweat."

"Yeah, please do. You stink." She holds her nose before returning to make her and Dad's coffee.

I head upstairs to my bedroom, tossing my AirPods and cell phone on my dresser before I head into my ensuite. After the water is a temperature I'm comfortable with, I strip down and get to work scrubbing away all the sweat from my run.

My thoughts drift to my conversation with Carver and his new deployment. My brother and I were never super close since there is a four-year age gap, but the day he left for boot camp, something changed. I never realized how much I would miss having him at home. Miss his presence. Every time he comes home on leave, our family makes the most of it. Every deployment, we hope and pray he comes back to us, forever fearing the worst until we receive that phone call he made it back, then we are able to breathe a sigh of relief. This next mission, I'll be praying like hell we get the same call.

Anxiety makes her presence known, as my heart starts to race and my stomach forms those familiar knots. Damn, I need to focus on something else. Something more positive. Uplifting. I think of football, but then my brain goes left to my encounter with Maisie earlier, and my dick twitches back to life as I recollect that moment.

Jesus.

Quickly, I turn the water from warm to freezing cold, hoping the temperature change will help it go away. No way in hell am I going to jerk off and risk my parents overhearing me.

I grit my teeth, trying to withstand the cold as I make work of rinsing myself off, waiting for my dick to go limp, but I give up and shut the water off.

After drying myself off, I wrap the towel around my waist, my hard-on clearly visible, and head into my bedroom. Using my phone, I browse the internet for colleges with programs similar to Harvard's, anything to take my mind off Maisie and my ... problem.

"Hey, Dylan." My mother's voice comes from the other side of my closed bedroom door. "Charmaine's downstairs in the living room."

At the mention of my girlfriend's name, my hard-on goes away.

"Tell her I will be down in a little bit."

I have no idea why Charmaine's here. We're supposed to meet up later for the party, and of course, I'll put on the usual smile and act like I'm glad to be with her. That's what I do. But honestly, the thought of another night like that just feels exhausting. Maybe it's time I finally stop pretending—for good this time.

*And see where things go with Maisie.*

I glance out my bedroom window to Maisie's bedroom window. Is there a possibility of us as a couple? I mean, she is fun to be around, and we get along amazingly. Not to mention, there seems to be chemistry there. Would it be so wrong?

*What if we don't work out?*

There's the angel on my shoulder, the voice of reason, and the thought that sends cold chills down my spine.

There's a reason I try to keep whatever thoughts and feelings of being something more than a friendship with Maisie at bay. We could end up with broken hearts, and she could simply walk out of my life for good. That's the very reason I don't want to take that chance, to risk what we have, because a life without Maisie is not something I want.

# Chapter 3

## Maisie

"You're awfully peppy." Josie smirks from the passenger seat. After spending almost three hours with Alora and Mirko helping me with my portfolio, I had to leave to get Josie from the dance studio.

I glance at my little sister and give her a smile. "Is that supposed to mean something?"

"I'm just saying, for someone who just went to have coffee with her friends, you can't be that"—she makes a circular motion with her hand toward my face—"giddy."

"Hanging with my friends always makes me happy. I can't help that."

"Right, right. So it has nothing to do with a cute guy giving you his number?" She arches one of her brows.

My jaw drops. "Okay, how the hell do you know that?"

"Mirko texted me about it. He said to make sure you text the guy at five o'clock and that he wants an update if anything transpires."

"Freaking Mirko," I mutter. "Always trying to play matchmaker."

"So, are you going to message him?"

"Mirko?" I feign stupidity, knowing she's referring to Brock.

"No! Hot coffee-shop guy! I think you should."

"Why?"

"Because he gave you his number, which means he's interested in you. It will be nice for you to try dating someone so you're not so hung up on Dylan."

"What!? I am not hung up on Dylan. He and I are just *friends*, Josie."

She scoffs. "Yeah, keep telling yourself that. I'm not blind, big sis. I see the way you look at him when you don't think anyone is noticing. And who knows? Maybe if you date this dude, it might make Dylan jealous and he'll finally see what's in front of him."

Now I'm confused. "Please. As if Dylan would ever have feelings for me and get jealous if I date somebody. He only sees me as a friend, nothing more. Plus, he's with Charmaine, remember?"

"Speaking of the devil herself," Josie mutters as I park in front of our house. Dylan and Charmaine are standing outside of Dylan's house. Judging from their body language, it looks like whatever they're discussing is intense.

There's a reason for Josie's comment. Charmaine and I were best friends, once upon a time. We were practically inseparable throughout elementary school, but that all changed in middle school. Our friendship began to taper as puberty hit us, and she was drawn into the popular-girls circle with her cousin Lydia. That's when the bullying began.

They started calling me names like "Miss Piggy" and "Porkenstein" all because I was chubby and hadn't "thinned out yet," according to my mother. For two years, I had hoped all my fat would go to my boobs and butt, giving me the curvy hourglass figure like the models boys in my grade were obsessing over in those magazines they would sneak in. The ones that are not appropriate for children.

Eighth grade year, I finally began to blossom into myself. I gained the curves, but the thin part missed the memo. My mother seemed disappointed but held out hope. I didn't understand her reasons for wanting me to be thin. I still don't to this day.

That was also the year I started developing a crush on Dylan. While many boys and most of the popular kids made fun of my size or avoided me due to ugly rumors, Dylan was one of the few people who stuck by me. I will never forget the day he showed me a magazine on their coffee table with a gorgeous woman on the cover; one who wasn't stick thin. She had this aura you could feel from the image that exuberated confidence.

*"I told my mom not to throw this away."*

*"Why?"*

*"Because I wanted you to see that not all those women in magazines are small, and that's okay."*

I instantly opened the magazine to read her interview about being a plus-size model and how she was tired of the skinny culture norms. It resonated with something in me, and that was the day I told myself I would love myself more and appreciate the body I was blessed with. That day also sparked my love of designing clothes for people of all sizes, especially the bigger girls. Why should certain clothes be worn because you look a certain way?

I used to always hang out at Dylan's house after school until my mom got home from work. One day, I was walking from his house to mine when I ran into Charmaine and Lydia. Lydia purposely bumped into me, knocking my books out of my hand onto the ground. I scrambled to pick them up when Charmaine grabbed my sketch pad.

They made fun of my sketches, saying how cute it was I wanted to design clothes for farm animals. Then they stumbled onto something I wasn't planning on anyone seeing. My little heart-shaped sketch where I wrote Future Mrs. Myers inside of it. Lydia cackled while the icy glare that came from Charmaine sent chills down my spine.

*"Oh, sweetie. How silly of you to think Dylan will ever find you attractive with all your rolls and belly flap. You think he could see himself married to*

*someone who looks like you?" Lydia sneered. "He needs someone to balance his charm, someone more his type. Like Charmaine."*

*"How would you know what his type is?" Not sure where the bravado came from, but dang, it felt good to stick up to those two finally.*

*"Because a hottie like Dylan would never downgrade to an ugly," Lydia said. "Besides, he's already taken."*

*"What? By who?" Dylan had never mentioned he had a girlfriend, and the thought of him dating someone sent an ache to my chest.*

*"Awe. He never told you?" Charmaine cooed as if I were a baby. "By me. Duh! I was just coming to see him so we can make plans for our first date."*

*"Whatever you say, Charmin." It was the only mean thing I could think of, with the jealousy and anger clouding my thinking. I snatched my sketch pad from her hands and darted to my house, blocking out their taunting.*

"God, I don't get what he sees in her," Josie says, bringing me back to the present.

"Who knows," I say, gathering my things to head inside.

The beep of my car locking distracts the couple, and Dylan's face morphs from annoyed to one of happiness when he sees me, but Charmaine gives off her typical death glare. Dylan goes to wave at us, but Charmaine grabs his face and pulls him in, giving him a deep kiss.

"Fucking skank," Josie mutters under her breath.

"That's not nice, little sis," I say, giving her a small fist bump because, well? She's not one to hold back her mind, and I love her for it. I'm just glad she's on my side.

We make our way into the house. Josie heads upstairs to clean up while I get to work on making us lunch. I don't see Mom, which means she must be at pilates. The woman never misses a class. I am certain she takes one every single day.

"Hey, Mase," Josie calls as she makes her way to the dining table to eat her lunch. "Do you think you can drop me off at Sabrina's for a sleepover later?"

"Sure thing, but shouldn't you run this by Mom first?"

"Like she's even going to be here." Josie rolls her eyes. "It's easier just to ask you."

"When did you want to go?"

"Her parents need to run a few errands first, so probably five thirty."

"Sure thing, but I'd still like to run it by Mom first." Whenever she gets home, of course.

Josie and I spent the afternoon lounging on the couch watching our favorite TV series, with Jinxy snuggled in a ball between us. Mom got home sometime around three to clean up for her night out.

"You think Mom's going clubbing or has a date?" I ask my sister once I hear Mom's bedroom door close.

"Mmm ... judging by the pep in her step? Date."

"Okay, not everybody is 'giddy' or 'peppy' if they have a suitor."

"We'll see when she comes downstairs." She smirks.

An hour and half later, Mom descends the stairs all dressed up in a black dress that shows off her figure.

"You look stunning, Mom. Got special plans tonight?" Josie asks.

"As a matter of fact, I do. I'm going to dinner with a total hottie. He'll be here soon to pick me up, so don't wait for me. Do you girls have any plans for the evening?"

*Told you*, my little sister mouths to me, and I gently shove her.

"Josie wants to go to Sabrina's house for a sleepover. Is that okay?"

"Yeah, yeah. Fine with me. Just make sure to check in with your sister. What about you, MJ?"

"Oh, I don't—"

"Maisie's going on a date too," Josie interjects. I scowl at her for blabbing that to our mother. Especially since I haven't even made that decision.

"Oohh, a date. That's wonderful!" My mom perks up. "Anyone I know?"

"Well, actually ... I have to message him when he gets off work. But I don't know ..." I'm not sure why this is so awkward for me. A lack of dating experience will do that, I guess.

"Maisie, if a guy reaches out to you, clearly you have his attention. Don't pass that opportunity up. Who knows when you'll get that chance again?"

What is that supposed to mean?

"Are you forreal?!" Josie jumps up, her temper taking charge. I grab my sister's arm and pull her back on the couch, smothering her mouth with my hand.

"Please don't," I whisper in her ear.

A knock at the door breaks up the tension in the room. "Oh, there's Richard now. I'll see you girls later. Jojo, have fun at your sleepover. Maisie"—she pauses at the door—"wear something flattering, something dark. It will make you appear smaller."

Josie squirms in my arms, trying to break my hold on her. Mom is out the door before I release my little sister, and she springs off the couch.

"How the hell are you just going to sit there and let Mom berate you like that? Don't you think what she said is fucked up?"

"Because I don't see the point in sparring when I refuse to let her words affect me." Josie paces back and forth in front of me, her nostrils flaring and mouth firm. "Why are you so upset over this?"

"You are a beautiful woman, Mase, and it grates me that Mom doesn't see you like that. It's bad enough Charmaine and all her bitchy friends bully you at school, but to come home to Mom doing it too? She's never going to stop complaining about your weight if you don't put her in her place."

"Jojo ... I love you, and I love how much you care about me. Trust me when I say this. I'm good. I don't need Mom's approval."

She stares at me, and I watch as the anger slowly leaves her tense body. "You deserve better, big sister. You deserve to have at least one supportive parent."

She gathers up her blanket and picks up the trash from our snacks.

"Why don't you get your stuff ready for Sabrina's. I'll clean up in here."

She nods, gathering her things, and hurries upstairs. I place the popcorn bowl in the sink and toss our soda cans in the recycling bin before heading back into the living room to wipe down the coffee table and fold my blanket.

Thinking about how I'll be home alone, I wonder if it would be so bad to reach out to Brock and make plans. I mean, could my mother be right? Would this opportunity ever happen again? Brock is pretty cute, and it couldn't hurt to see how things play out.

I search the couch for my cell phone, checking all the crevices and underneath the cushions.

"Where the heck is it?"

Moments later, Josie thunders down the stairs.

"Hey, Jojo. Do you know where my phone is? I can't find it."

"Yeah, I have it," she says, her sneakered feet appearing in my peripheral.

"You're an angel!" I say as I get off the floor and adjust my skirt.

"Well ... I hope you will still think so, because I stole your phone and put Brock's number in it before I sent a text telling him you're looking forward to your date tonight."

"You did what!?" I stare at my sister, with a mischievous smile on her face, looking so proud of herself. "Why would you do that?"

"You weren't going to do it. Knowing you, you would have festered around the idea before talking yourself out of it, then spent the evening alone in your room either reading or sketching. So I took the liberty of removing the doubts, and did it for you." She places her hands on my arms, her brown eyes staring into my blue-gray ones. "You need to start living for yourself and take some gosh darn risks. Go out with the guy. Give him a chance to make you happy."

Damn her for knowing me so well. "You're a pain in my ass, you know that?"

"You love me. Now, do me a solid? Go upstairs and fix yourself up. Brock's going to meet you at the carnival by the ferris wheel around six."

"But—"

"No buts! Get to stepping!" My sister shoves me toward the stairs, ushering me to my room.

"Okay, okay. I'm going!"

I dash into the bathroom to reapply deodorant and spritz on my apple blossom body spray before hurrying into my room. After cleaning up my eyeliner, reapplying lip gloss, and running a brush through my waves, I stare back at my reflection.

Taking a deep breath, I close my eyes and exhale all the nervous energy. "You can do this. You can do this. You can do this."

The chime of a text alert makes me jump. Picking my phone up off my bed, I see a message from Dylan.

DYLAN

You look nervous. Everything okay?

My brows furrow before another message comes through.

DYLAN

I can see you in your window.

I look out my bedroom window, and there he is, staring back at me through his window, waving his phone.

MAISIE

I am nervous. Have a date tonight and I'm hoping it goes well.

Bubbles appear before his reply comes through.

DYLAN

If you're nervous, go somewhere public. It will put you at ease, especially if it's your first date.

MAISIE

We're meeting up at the carnival after he gets off work, so it's pretty public.

DYLAN

Good. Then you can play some games, go on some rides. You'll forget about being nervous because you'll be too busy having fun.

MAISIE

That's true, when you put it that way.

Thanks for the pep talk, D. I'm starting to feel a little better about this.

DYLAN

Anytime, Freckles.

Dylan makes a valid point. I can't be nervous if we have fun, and I can have fun. I can do this, right? I do another once-over when another chime goes off.

BROCK

Looking forward to it. See you at 6, beautiful. ;)

No getting out of this now.

# Chapter 4

**Dylan**

Maisie disappears from view, taking her vibrant beauty with her. Is she leaving to meet him now? It's not even five thirty yet. The carnival doesn't open until six.

I reread our texts, a feeling similar to jealousy hitting me like it did the moment I read about the date. Who could she be seeing? And why do I feel like I want to find out who he is so I can punch him in his face?

I shoot off a text to my friend Zion.

What? You know if you don't show up to Davenport's party, Charmaine's going to have a bitch fit.



Let her bitch. Maybe I'll get lucky and someone can get actual proof of her cheating so I can finally break things off.

Charmaine's another reason I want to avoid the party. Rumors have been swirling about her making out with someone who isn't me, but there has been no proof of it. Things between us have been rocky, especially since her cousin got knocked up by Brady. It's like Charmaine morphed into a super mean girl, and honestly, if you have to put others down to feed your ego, it's a complete turnoff.



Just dump her ass already.



Would love to, but I need proof so I have validation to end things.



And just breaking up isn't good enough?



Charmaine doesn't like being called out and every time I try to break things off, it doesn't get through to her. Calling her out feels like the only way.

Every year, farmer Higgins allows a portion of his property to be used for the town carnival. Profits made from the carnival go directly back into Bellwood to help with any expenses, like equipment for the fire or police department, road fixtures, building repairs, and so on. It's been four years since I've been to the carnival, right before Carver left for the Army.

Pushing the thought aside, I find a parking spot and make my way toward the entrance where I spot Zion.

"About time you showed up," Zion says as he grabs my arm and pulls me in for one of those one-armed hugs.

"Dude, they just opened. I know your ass wasn't waiting for long."

"True. So ..." He claps his hands together and rubs them. "What do you want to do first?"

"I don't know. It's been a minute. Want to walk around?" Walking around would allow me to find Maisie and whoever the hell this mystery guy is.

"Sure, as long as we stop so I can get a funnel cake. It's been on my mind since you mentioned coming here."

"Sure thing, buddy," I say, and pat his back. We walk to the nearest funnel cake stand, and I stay off to the side, glancing around as people pass us by, and search for any sight of coppery tresses as Zion orders his fried treat.

"Looking for somebody in particular? Or just people watching?" My friend appears, shoving a big ass chunk of funnel cake in his mouth.

"Just watching." He doesn't need to know my true intentions for skipping the party.

Zion scarfs down his funnel cake in minutes, then releases the loudest burp I've ever heard and tosses his plate into the nearest trash can.

"Dude! Did you even taste it?" I ask.

"Oh, yeah," he says, patting his belly. "Alright, what first?"

"Let's play some games and hold off on the rides for a bit. I don't feel like getting puked on."

"Fair enough. Want to do that hammer game and see which of us has the better strike?" He points over to the game in reference.

"I'm pretty sure I can beat you." I smirk at him.

"Oh, you think so? Let's go find out. Right now!"

"You're on!"

We make our way over to the small line that's formed, and while awaiting our turn, someone says my name.

"Dylan?"

Zion and I turn around to Maisie, a vision to see, standing next to some tall blond-haired guy wearing a black tank top and some dark jeans. He's got to be about six foot three, give or take, just slightly taller than my six foot one.

Finally, I can put a face to the guy. Now I need his name, so I divert my eyes back to the red-haired siren before me.

"Hey, Freckles." Pulling her in for a prolonged hug, I make direct eye contact with the fucker she's with and give him my best devilish smile.

Yeah, take a good look, buddy. You won't be around for long.

The returned smug look from wannabe Ken doesn't sit right with me. Does he think he actually has a chance?

"What are you doing here?" Maisie asks, pulling away from me. "Alora mentioned Anthony and the guys were going to a party. Aren't you, like, mandated to go?"

"Wasn't in a party kind of mood. Plus, Zion here had a craving for funnel cake." Out of the corner of my eye, I see Zion about to protest, so I elbow him in his side, warning him not to say anything. The last thing I need is for Maisie to find out I'm only here because of her and the guy who doesn't look right standing next to her.

*He doesn't look right because you know you should be there.*

Fucking inner thoughts.

"Who's this?" I ask.

"Oh, my gosh. So sorry! This is Brock. Brock, this is my best friend Dylan and his friend."

"Nice to meet you," Brock says, extending his hand out to shake Zion's first, then mine. I give an extra squeeze, a subtle warning. If he so much as thinks about hurting her—

"Are you going to do this?" Maisie's beautiful voice breaks through my inner monologue, and she points toward the hammer game.

"Yeah. Dylan and I are going to see which one of us has the better strength. Fairly certain I'm going to beat him."

"In your dreams, Z," I retort.

By that time, we are at the front of the line. "You fellas next?" the person in charge of the high striker asks.

I look at Maisie and smile. "Ladies first," I say, gesturing for her to go ahead of us.

"Oh … no. Definitely not my style. We didn't mean to intrude," Maisie says before turning to Brock. "Hey, why don't we go walk around and find another game. Maybe get on the ferris wheel?"

"Anything you want, beautiful." The smile he gives her makes me want to gouge the asshat's eyes out of his skull.

"Later, guys!" Maisie says, reaching for his hand and dragging him along behind her, like he's some lost puppy.

*Bet you want to be that puppy.*

"Fellas? Are you taking a turn or not?"

Zion goes first, grabbing the hammer, or mallet, whatever the hell it's called, and raises it above his head. He slams it down onto the block, his strike going just past the eight mark.

"Your turn, bro." Zion hands me the mallet.

I stand before the game, irritation and annoyance at Brock coursing through me. I raise the hammer and slam it down, watching as the lights go up, marking me close to the nine.

"Impressive. You want to go again?" the gentleman manning the game asks, but I just hand him the hammer and walk away.

"Uh … so sorry. Here," I hear Zion tell the guy, probably paying for our rounds before he chases after me. "Bro, you want to tell me what the hell that was back there?"

"I'll cover the next game," I state.

"I'm not worried about the money. I'm talking about the way you were acting toward that guy. What's his name?"

"Brock," I growl out.

"Do you know him or something? Is he bad news?"

"No, I don't know him," I grit out.

Zion stops walking, forcing some carnival goers to yell at him for stopping in their path. "No. Fucking. Way. You're jealous that Maisie is here with that guy."

"Ha. No," I say, but even I know that was nowhere near convincing enough.

"This is why you changed our plans, isn't it? You found out she was going to be here, and you wanted to spy on your girl."

"Shut up!"

"Ladies and gentleman, I don't believe it. Could it be my best friend is finally admitting—"

I rush Zion, slamming my hand over his mouth to shut him up. "Not. Another. Word."

Bellwood's a small town, and word would travel so fast the last thing I need is for Zion's words to get twisted and back to Maisie. Or Charmaine.

I spot a vacant spot and nod toward the fairly empty picnic area. The fewer ears close by, the better.

"Look. Maisie mentioned she was nervous about going on this date. I stated a public place would help her be less nervous, and she mentioned coming here, but never mentioned the guy. I just wanted to make sure she was safe."

"Because you're finally admitting you have feelings for her?"

"What!? No! She's my best friend. I don't want anything bad to happen to her," I state.

Zion's eyes narrow. "You sure about that? Because from where I stood, it looked like you were trying to piss all over her when she introduced him to us."

"Whatever, man." I glance around, hoping I can get a glimpse of Maisie with that doofus. "Let's just go play a few rounds of games, hit up some rides before calling it night. Sound good?"

"Sure bro. I'll play along, for now." He shakes his head. "Let's go have some fun."

Zion and I played all the classic carnival games—ring toss, throwing darts at balloons, the hoops contest—and rode several rides. I might have ensured that wherever we were, Maisie was within viewing distance so I could keep my eyes on her without making it obvious to Zion.

It was close to nine thirty when Zion and I decided to call it a night. The carnival will be closing soon, and I want to make sure I get back before Maisie.

"Hey, man. Thanks for hanging out with me tonight. It was honestly nice skipping that party to come here."

"Yeah, I got to admit. Felt like the good ol' days ... being young and just living life. Crazy that this time next year, we will be parting ways to face the real world. You heading to Harvard and me heading to LSU hopefully."

"LSU would be stupid not to take you. Just keep the faith." We give each other another bro hug. "See you Monday to help Payson with the girls combine event?"

"Oh, you know it!"

Zion and I part ways in the parking lot. Once I make it back home, I take a seat on my front steps and wait for Maisie since her car isn't in sight.

A million thoughts run through my head. Did they meet up somewhere? What if he takes advantage of her? Would he physically harm her? Is she okay?

The sound of a car draws me back to the now, and relief rushes through me at seeing Maisie's green car pulling up. I speed walk across the front yard, meeting her on the sidewalk in front of her house.

"Hey, Freckles."

Maisie's head pops up, her brows furrow a tad, and her adorable nose slightly scrunches.

"You know I hate it when you call me that," she says, though there's no real bite in her voice. "Where's Zion? You guys aren't hanging out?"

"Uh, no. He went home after the rides made him nauseous. Weak stomach." I smile at her. "Where's, uh … what's his name?"

"Brock?"

"Yeeaaah … him. Shouldn't he be dropping you off and walking you to your door?"

"Jeez, what are you, my dad?" She laughs, gently shoving me. "My mom is out on a date, so I had to drop Josie off at her friend's house for a sleepover. Brock didn't get off his shift until five and said he wanted to freshen up before Josie told him to meet at the carnival."

"What do you mean Josie told him?"

"My deviant little sister thought she would steal my phone along with the note that had his number and message him for me without my knowledge. She basically set it up so I wouldn't think about declining him. The nerve of her. If I had it my way? I would have been snuggled up with Jinxy reading a book or watching a movie."

So she didn't want to go out with him?

"Did you have a nice time?" *Please say no.*

"It was ... nice." She smiles one of her more radiant smiles, and it's like a punch to my chest. "But—"

Wait. Did she say but?

"But? But what? He didn't do anything to make you uncomfortable, did he?" I nearly growl that last part out.

"No, no, no!" She grabs my hands, soothing me to keep me from flying off the rail. Which, I would've if he had hurt her. "He was a complete gentleman the whole time. We had fun, I won't deny that, but there just wasn't any ... chemistry between us."

A wave of relief washes over me. "So, I don't need to hunt down a giant blond and beat his ass?"

She lets out the sweetest chuckle. "I love knowing that you would defend my honor, to be a knight in shining armor, but I'm no damsel in distress, Dylan."

"Still doesn't hurt to have someone looking out for you, Freckles." I gently brush a stray hair from her face and tuck it behind her ear, not missing the small gasp she lets out, and damn if that sweet sound doesn't go straight to my dick. "May I walk you to the door?"

"Sure. If it will help you sleep tonight." She places her hand in the crook of my arm, and I escort her the short distance to her front door. Once she gets inside the door, I shoot an arm out to prevent her from closing it.

"Before you close this, I need you to do something for me."

Her eyes bounce back and forth with mine, her brows slightly creasing. "Anything," she replies.

"Lock the door as soon as you close it. I won't move until I hear the clicking sound. I need to know that you're safe. Can you do that for me?"

"Of course," she whispers. "Thank you for walking me to my door, Mr. Myers. I hope you enjoy the rest of your evening." I remove my arm, allowing her to close the door.

"Good night, Freckles," I whisper into the night. The moment I hear the door lock, I release a long breath and make my way to my house, in need of another cold shower.

# Chapter 5

## Maisie

As soon as I close the door, I press my forehead against it, letting the chill calm me from being within close proximity to Dylan.

"Good night, Freckles," he whispers from the other side of the door, and I have to fight the urge to rip it open and confess my whole heart to the only guy I wish I had been spending the evening with.

Brock was sweet and nice and easy on the eyes, I can admit to that, but he isn't Dylan.

*Am I going to be hung up on my neighbor for the rest of my life?!*

After getting a drink of water from the kitchen, I head upstairs, ready to shower away the summer heat and perspiration from the humid evening. Not to mention the sweat I've accumulated in my bra. What's the term for when it feels like swamp ass but instead of your butt, it's between your boobs? Swamp bags? Muggy titties? This is the downside of being a busty woman.

Once I'm in the bathroom, I strip out of my clothes and get everything ready for my postshower skincare routine while I wait for the water to warm up. Taking a glance in the mirror, I note the redness of my skin and mentally smack myself for forgetting to apply sunscreen today. Now I'm going to look like a lobster for the next three-to-four business days. It's a struggle having fair skin; I wish I tanned like Alora, instead of turning into a tomato.

As I cleanse my body, my thoughts drift back to the carnival, to certain moments where it felt like Dylan was everywhere Brock and I were. Was it my imagination or was he following us around?

*Chill, Maisie. It's not that big of a carnival.*

True, but what was with him when I introduced him and Zion to Brock? He almost seemed ... jealous?

*It's in your head. You're projecting your personal feelings into assuming Dylan feels some sort of way toward you.*

Maybe ...

Freshly showered, with clean silky jammies and my skin feeling reinvigorated, I pad my way to my bedroom, tossing my sweaty clothes into the hamper. After grabbing my sketch pad from my side table, I plop belly-down onto my full-size bed and flip through the pages to my latest sketch—a beautiful gown I plan to have Alora's grandmother help me make for homecoming.

As I work out the detailing on the bodice, Jinxy's bell on her collar jingles as she jumps onto my bed, then she brushes against me before making a few circles and plopping her fluffy body down onto my sketchbook.

"Uh, excuse me, miss. I'm kind of working on something." Jinxy doesn't care though. She drops back so she's lying on her side, expecting me to rub her belly. "Fine, I'll rub your belly for a minute, but then I have to get back to my sketch."

After rubbing her belly long enough to satisfy her highness, I push her across my bed, but Jinxy isn't having it and plops right back down on top of my sketchbook.

"You little brat!" We do this a few times before I relent and move to the bench seat in front of my bay window. It's my second favorite place to sketch. When the sun shines through on a sunny day, I enjoy basking in the warmth of the rays. Or when I can look up and see the stars and the moon on a clear dark night.

Moments later, Jinxy scurries off my bed and hops onto the windowsill, where she settles beside me.

"Let me guess. This is retaliation because we didn't cuddle today, isn't it?" She stretches her neck, giving me eskimo kisses with her little pink nose. "I'm sorry for that. Alright? I just had so many things to ... do ..."

My eyes catch onto lights beaming from across the yard coming from Dylan's bedroom. I can see perfectly inside, and oh ... my ... lanta. He's standing in his room, browsing through his dresser with only a towel wrapped around his waist. His gorgeous, toned torso is on full display, with the v peeking out the top of his towel, and damn, if that isn't enough to make a girl drool.

Wait ... I am drooling.

I quickly swipe the saliva that escaped my mouth as I ogle the one guy I wish I had the guts to admit my feelings for. If only he wasn't with Charmaine and I wasn't worried he didn't feel the same way. Girl code says you should never go for your friend's ex, but does that still count if she's your ex-best friend? The exes should cancel out, or does that only apply to math?

"Jinxy, what do you think I should do? Text him, letting him know his curtains are open and I can see him? Or is that creepy?" She doesn't respond. Her eyes are closed, content in her own little world, purring away now that she's by my side. "What good are you?" I rub her soft head, my gaze returning to the window, only this time, Dylan's staring back at me.

Oh, shit! I've been caught!

I raise my hand and do one of those finger waves, my cheeks warming from embarrassment, unknowing how he will react. The sexiest smirk one man could ever give appears on his face, that one dimple popping on the side. Damn, could he be any more handsome?

As if in slow motion, his hand releases the towel just as he pulls the curtain closed, giving me a flash of skin before disappearing from sight.

Holy hell. What just happened? Did ... he ... just ...

Seconds later, my phone starts going off, alert after alert, and a tinge of panic sets in. Crap! What if it's Dylan?

I creep from my window to my bed, eyes tightly shut as my hand wraps around the rectangular device, not ready to read whatever messages are displayed on the screen. My phone chimes again with another alert. Taking a deep breath, I slowly open one eye. Relief washes over me when the several messages are coming from the group chat with Alora and Mirko.

ALORA

[image attached: Charmaine making out with some random guy]

[image attached: Charmaine straddling same random guy]

OMG!!! Mase!

Can you believe this skank???

MIRKO

Damn, bitch is tongue deep in his throat. Ain't she?

She trying to taste what he ate for dinner?

ALORA

LMAO

Charmaine's cheating on Dylan? So the rumors are true? I don't understand why she would do that? She has Dylan, the most amazing guy a girl could have. Who is better than him?

MIRKO

Real question. Where was Dylan at? I overheard some of the football players saying he wasn't at the party.

MAISIE

He wasn't at the party because he was at the carnival.

ALORA

Seriously??

MIRKO

Who goes to the carnival when there's a party?

Wait, better question. How do you know this?

ALORA

OMG!! Were you and Dylan hanging out!???

MAISIE

No! I was at the carnival with Brock. Dylan and Zion just happened to be there too.

Is Brock the cutie from the coffee place??



You texted him!!!??? Hold on. I'm calling you right NOW!

I'm about to respond when Alora's FaceTime comes through.

"Why does this conversation need to be over the phone when I can just text?" I whine.

"So I can hear you and see your face when you tell me everything! So spill it. I want all the deets!"

"Where are you?" I squint at my screen, trying to make out the background.

"I believe it's Mrs. Davenport's walk-in closet. Or a small department store. I'm not entirely sure." Alora flips the screen around so I can see, and damn, talk about impressive. Everything appears to be designer—Chanel, Dolce & Gabbana, Burberry, Valentino—oh, my fashionista heart would be in heaven standing in that closet.

"Wait. Why are you in the closet?" Seems like an odd place to be during a party. "And where's Mirko?"

Alora's face returns to my screen. "For starters, it was one of the few places that was quiet and away from the noise. Also, I'm sort of in hiding. My brother almost caught me making out with a guy, and you know how he gets."

She gives an overly dramatic eye roll, and I laugh. Anthony has become overbearingly protective of his twin sister, especially since their older brother, Dominic, graduated.

"Mirko is somewhere, probably making out with his boyfriend. Now, stop deflecting and get back to your date with the coffee-shop guy!"

I sigh. "Okay, first off, I didn't text him. Josie did. She snuck my phone while I was cleaning up our snacks and messaged the guy and told him to meet me at the carnival."

Alora chuckles. "Oh my God. I adore your sister. I may have to get her a thank you gift."

"Please don't encourage her."

"Girlie, if I want to encourage her to push you out of your comfort zone, I will, because clearly, Mirko and I are not doing enough," she states. "So ... was he a gentleman? Did he kiss you?" She waggles her brows for added effect.

"He was very polite. Paid for our tickets and food. We did the bumper cars and the scrambler. Then we got on the ferris wheel and just as it stopped at the top, he kissed me. And ... well ..."

It sounds romantic when I tell her, but in actuality, it caught me off guard. Knowing this was a chance to see if I could move past these harbored feelings for Dylan, I kissed Brock back, waiting for the butterflies or something magical to happen, but I ended up with nothing.

"Well what?" Alora's voice breaks the memory. "Was he a bad kisser? Did his breath smell? I know that can totally ruin the moment."

"I don't know if he's a bad kisser. I pulled away the moment he tried to shove his tongue down my throat."

Alora's face twists, her nose scrunching as though she inhaled something foul. "Oh no, honey."

"It just didn't feel right, Lor. I feel like I'm cursed or something. Am I constantly going to compare every single guy to how I feel about Dylan? That I'll never be able to feel things for someone else the way I feel for him?" I lean back against my throw pillows. "Am I broken? Or just pathetic?"

"Neither, and I stand on that! But ... I wouldn't stress it, though. It's our final year, and you've got better things to focus on, like fashion school and graduation. We shouldn't let boys get in the way of our future."

I give her my best pointed stare. "Says the girl still hung up on her basketball playing ex-boyfriend."

"Girl, screw Trey."

"You want to be," I tease, and wait for her catty response, but when she says nothing ... "Oh. My. God! Trey is the guy you were making out with. Wasn't he?"

"Guilty," she says, looking down. "Also, I may or may not be waiting for him to come to me."

"Are you sure you should be messing around with Trey after everything he did?" If I come off concerned, I have every right to be. Things between them got really ugly, and I'm worried my friend could be putting herself into a toxic situation again.

"I'm fairly certain I can differentiate sex and love, Mase." The sound of someone knocking on a door can be heard in the background. "Oh, I think that's Trey!"

"Wait! I didn't get a chance to tell you about Dylan's behavior tonight." This causes my friend to pause. Good. Maybe I can get her talking to me and she'll avoid making a mistake with Trey.

"Dylan was acting weird? How so?" Another knock echoes in the background, and I can see the internal conflict playing out on her face.

"I think he was following Brock and I around the carnival. I swear everywhere I turned, Dylan and Zion were a few feet away from us."

"It's not that big of a carnival. I'm sure it was a mere coincidence."

Fair point.

More knocking can be heard, along with some mumbling I can't discern.

"Girl, hold on." There's some movement on Alora's end followed by a door opening and a mumbled "Shit."

"Shit is right. Why is this punk ass up here, sis?"

"That's none of your business, Anthony! Let him go!"

"Nah. That's where you're wrong. Anytime this fucker is near you, I make it my business."

"Fuck you, Anthony!" comes from someone else in the background; someone who isn't Anthony.

A smack sounds in the background, followed by more voices and chaos before the FaceTime ends and I'm left with a black screen.

What the hell? I attempt to call Alora back, but it doesn't go through, so I decide to try a text.

MAISIE

What is happening!???

Lor, you okay?

Minutes pass, and I grow more impatient by the second, hoping Mirko or Alora answer me. After what feels like an eternity, I finally get a reply.

MIRKO

Damn. Did shit go down? Andrew wanted to leave a little earlier. He was feeling a type of way.

(¬‿¬)

ALORA

Sry. Anthony and two of his friends found Trey knocking on the door. Someone tipped him off. They saw me go upstairs and saw Trey follow me shortly after. Anthony punched Trey, which was unfair because Anthony's friends were holding Trey and that was before Anthony hauled my ass out the house.

MIRKO

First, you leave me out of the conversation with Maisie and then shit went down? Whoa is me.

MAISIE

Don't be a drama queen, Mir. You were with your lover boy.

Lor … are you okay?

ALORA

I'll be fine. Just extremely pissed off with my brother at the moment. But I'll yell at him later. Right now, he's really worried about Colton. They put him in the back seat, and he's black-out wasted. Zealand thinks he may have alcohol poisoning, and the guys are freaking out over what to do. Anthony's dropping me off at home before he takes Colton to Zealand's.

MAISIE

I hope Colt's okay. I thought he wasn't into drinking?

ALORA

The guys said the same, but Anthony mentioned Colt has been "off" the past few weeks and the guys are worried about him.

BTW Maisie, I'm coming over tomorrow. I need you to explain to me what you said before my brother ruined my night.

MIRKO

Why am I being left out again?

ALORA

You're not. You have a family reunion tomorrow at the lake. Remember?

MIRKO

Yay me

(¬_¬)

You bitches better fill me in

MAISIE

Don't worry. You'll get the tea.

I wonder if I should tell Alora about what happened moments ago with Dylan in his window and how I nearly saw him in all his naked glory.

A shame I didn't get a full-frontal view—

A new message comes through, and when I see the name, I nearly chuck my phone.

DYLAN

Did you enjoy the peep show, Freckles?

Oh, I definitely did, but I won't be admitting it to him. I plead the fifth.

# Chapter 6

**Maisie**

"Get on your knees for me, Freckles," Dylan growls, and I instantly drop to my knees, my gray-blue eyes peering into his. His blue eyes deepen, shifting with an intensity that speaks of unspoken desire. "Good girl. You listen so well."

I clinch my thighs, his praise a fire that spreads through me, igniting every nerve, every part of me that aches for him.

"Now, take me out and open those perfectly plump lips for me."

Wanting to be his good girl, I do as he commands. My hands glide up the front of his slacks, undoing the button and zipper before releasing his cock from his pants. It springs forward, nearly smacking me in the face. I lean over, swiping his tip with my tongue, and relishing the noise that comes from this man's lips.

Using my hand, I guide him inside my mouth, taking him as far back as I can before my gag reflex kicks in. I pull back slowly, my tongue swirling around until I pop off him. Taking in a breath, I hollow my cheeks and draw Dylan back in my mouth, going a little farther. Bobbing my head, I start out slow, then gradually pick up my pace.

"Fuck, baby. That mouth feels so good."

I whimper around him, his words making me wet, my clit swelling with need. I move my free hand to my center, needing to touch myself to give me relief from the pressure.

Just as my fingers brush the little bud, Dylan yanks himself free and pulls me up.

"You think you can touch yourself? Pleasure yourself as you pleasure me?"

I nod in response.

"Baby, your pleasure belongs to me. Only I get to give that to you. If you need a release, all you have to do is ask nicely."

My eyes bounce between his. "Please, Dylan. I want you to make me cum."

"I should make you beg for it, but damn I'm not that patient of a man."

He guides me back to the bed, slowly lowering me onto the mattress. His toned, warm body crawls over me, his erection sliding between my legs where I need him most. He grabs my hands, pushing my arms over my head and locking me in place.

"Are you ready for this, Freckles? Because there's no going back from this."

"Yes, Dylan. I've been ready for this, for you. You're the only one I want."

He leans down, pressing his lips with mine, tasting me. The two of us moan, wanting and needing to be close to each other.

"I'm going to make you mine, Freckles. So when you cum all over my cock, make sure you scream my name."

His tip presses into me, his hardened length slowly inching inside of me. My clit swells, and my pussy gets wetter as he slowly presses inside.

Just as he's almost completely seated inside of me, a noise blares from somewhere in the room, and the feeling of Dylan is gone.

I wake slowly, reluctant to leave the warmth left behind after my dream. A lingering heat curls in the pit of my stomach, my skin still humming with the phantom touch of a dream that felt too real. My breath catches in my throat, and I'm not sure if the aching desire is from the dream itself or from something more.

I guess when you come close to seeing a guy almost naked, you end up having sex dreams about him.

How am I going to look him in the face now?

I make my way to the bathroom sink and splash cold water on my face, needing to shock myself awake so I stop thinking about the way Dylan's body hovered over mine, with his erection pulsing between my thighs.

"Pull yourself together, Mase!" I tell my reflection. "It's a sex dream, and that's as close as it will get between the two of you. It's never going to happen in real life!"

After brushing my teeth and using the bathroom, I go downstairs to tend to Jinxy's needs before making myself a bagel, egg, and cheese sandwich.

I get to work gathering my favorites: mashed avocado, a slice of provolone cheese, and everything but the bagel seasoning, because nothing starts my day better than the simple comfort of my favorite breakfast food.

Once I've assembled my delicious sandwich and set it on a plate, I reach into the refrigerator for the orange juice. As soon as the fridge door closes, I let out a scream.

A strange man I've never seen before stands a few inches away, perusing me from head to toe, like a wolf sizing up its prey.

"Who the hell are you?" I yell, my heart racing, feeling unsettled by his very presence.

"I'm Richard. And who might you be, pretty girl?" He extends an arm, his hand open, inviting me to touch him.

"No one you need to concern yourself with," I snip back. This guy is giving me major predatory vibes, and I have never been more grateful that Josie spent the night elsewhere.

"Mmm ... you've got some bite to you," he says with an interested undertone. "I like them feisty—"

"There you are!" My mom appears in her fuzzy pink bathrobe. She wraps her arms around this guy's middle before placing a kiss on his cheek. Her eyes, all bright and sparkly, glance from the perverted man at her side to me, as if she just realized I'm standing here. "Oh, Maisie. You're here?"

My brows furrow. "Yeah. I live here, remember?"

My mom lets out a fake laugh. "Of course. I just meant, I assumed you would be out? You know, staying with friends?"

Rolling my eyes, I grab my plate and make my way to the dining room, putting some much-needed distance between the woman who birthed me and her creepy one-night stand.

"I'm so sorry. I truly thought we had the house to ourselves. I promise to make it up to you. Can I make you something to eat? Coffee?" my mom rambles in the kitchen.

"I appreciate the offer, but I really should be going," the pervy man tells her right before they walk past me to the front door. "I'll call you later, gorgeous."

Pervy man leans in and kisses my mother, but just as he pulls away from her, he glances in my direction, a darkness in his brown eyes that makes my skin crawl.

And there goes my appetite.

Once the front door closes, my mom joins me at the dining table. "So ... that was Richard."

"Yeah, I got that much info out of him," I retort, annoyance laced with disgust. "Why was he here? It's not like you to bring the guys home."

"I invited him over. We had a really great time last night. We ate at this nice Italian restaurant, Sapori d'Italia. The food was delicious! Then we drove all the way to Thornridge to dance at this nightclub and we danced until our feet were numb. Oh, I hadn't had that much fun in years! Absolutely one of the best dates of my life. I just wasn't ready for the night to end."

I love the happiness radiating from my mother. She deserves it, honestly, especially since she's been raising Josie and me on her own for the past twelve years. I just wish she hadn't brought him here after their first date.

"So you brought him home to have sex with him?"

My mom's eyes widen, her jaw dropping. "Excuse me?"

"Please, don't act like I am not familiar with what grown adults do when they go to someone's house late at night."

"He still had another thirty minutes until he made it home. I wasn't comfortable letting him drive since he had a few drinks and as late as it was, so I told him he could stay here and leave in the morning."

How late was she out? I don't recall hearing her come in, but I did pass out shortly after my conversation with Alora, which had to be at least eleven.

I cross my arms over my chest. "So, where did he sleep? I don't recall him being on the couch when I came down this morning."

"What is this? An interrogation?" she asks, massaging her forehead. "Who I bring home and where they sleep isn't something you need to concern yourself with."

"It does when you have children in the house, Mom," I grit out. Does the safety of her daughters not matter?

"Josie wasn't here, and I had assumed you were out."

"Well, you assumed wrong. Did you bother to do a background check on this guy before you went on a date with him? Or are you that desperate for male affection?"

"Don't you dare judge me, Maisie Janine!" She points a manicured finger in my direction. "You have no idea what it's like to be a single mother raising two daughters while working a full-time job."

"I never said I did, but I'm old enough to understand your choices. I just wish you would put more focus on us rather than finding a man."

"I've put my focus on you girls since the day your father walked out on us! Everything I do is for you and your sister, but it doesn't help the fact I'm lonely and just want some companionship. Now, I will not tolerate any more of your outbursts. I'm still your mother and will not hesitate to punish you, regardless of whether you're almost eighteen!"

"Then you can punish me after I say this." Pushing back from the table, I slowly rise from my seat, staring at my mother. "Next time you want to consider bringing someone of the male species home, why don't you background check them first to make sure they aren't on the sex offender registry!"

I storm out of the dining room, tossing my sandwich into the trash before rinsing my plate, my mother hot on my heels.

"Now wait a damn minute. What are you implying?"

"Not implying anything. I would think that as a woman with two young daughters, you would take more precautions. Don't you ever check social media? Or the news?" How does she not know how unhinged people are these days? "What bothers me is how easily you can trust this guy without fully knowing him and allow him into this house after spending a few hours with him."

My mom rests her hands on top of the island. "And how does that tie in with sex offenders?"

After I place the dish into the dishwasher, I turn to face my mother. "It was the way he looked at me before you showed up. Like I was some piece of meat he wanted to devour."

She scoffs at my response. "I'm sure you're exaggerating. Richard isn't like that. He's a complete gentleman."

"A gentleman doesn't ogle his date's teenage daughter," I retort. "You didn't see the way he was looking at me."

"Richard is harmless," she insists, but I can tell by the slight uncertainty in her eyes that my words have planted a seed of doubt. "No way could he ever find you attractive."

"What's that supposed to mean?"

"Men don't go for unfit, plumpy women. Sure, they love curves, but they only love them here"—she points to her chest, then her ass—"and here. Anywhere else repulses them. They prefer women who take care of their bodies. You know ... eating right and exercising. I mean, just take your father, for example—"

"Don't you dare bring Dad into this. He does not represent the vast majority of men."

Raising her hands in surrender, my mom takes a deep breath before she speaks. "Fine. Maybe you're right, but Maisie, I just want you to understand that in this day, appearances matter to the world. I'm not just referring to men, but the fashion world too. I respect your dreams, but if you're truly going to make this a career, you need to start getting on board with what society wants. What they've always wanted."

She walks over and presses a gentle kiss to my head. "I'm going to shower and then check to see if Josie needs to be picked up. Just keep what I said in mind. Okay?"

The front doorbell rings, breaking the tension. "I'll go get that. It's probably Alora."

My mother nods. "And as for Richard, I will look into him and decide from there."

"Thank you," I mutter.

My mom heads for the stairs as I open the door, grateful to see my gorgeous friend. Alora stands on my porch in denim shorts and a cropped tank top, her hair pulled into a high ponytail.

"You look like crap," she announces. "What happened?"

"Mom and I just got into it. She brought home some creepy guy last night," I say, pulling her inside. "And he was giving me major predator vibes this morning."

Alora's eyes widen. "Ew! Are you okay?"

"Yeah, just grossed out." I lead her upstairs to my room, eager to put this morning behind me. "How about you? How's Colton doing after last night?"

"Anthony texted me this morning. Said Colton's extremely hungover and most likely feels like shit. They're hoping some breakfast food at Munson's Diner will help."

"Oh, they have the best breakfast!" I groan. Maybe we should go there for brunch? "What about you?"

"I'll be fine. Trey hasn't bothered to check in with me, and I'm still pissed at my brother. Probably more so than last night."

"What did he do now?" These twins argue so much that I wonder how their mother tolerates it.

"Overheard my mother on the phone with someone talking about a girls football combine for tomorrow. So I messaged Anthony about it, and he said he wasn't sure if it was true and if it was, he would forbid me from going. The fucking audacity of him."

"Why the hell would he do that?"

"To fuck with my life more than he already does. God, I don't understand why he's so damn overbearing. Just because our dad walked out on us and Dom's off to college, he acts like he's the new man of the house."

"It's how he shows he cares," I assure her. Not that I would know what it's like, considering I'm the older sibling in my home.

"He cares way too much." She rolls her eyes, pulling out her cell phone. "I'm going to find out about this football thing, and if it's true, I'm doing it."

"Really? You would play football?"

Alora's eyes narrow in my direction. "What are you trying to say?"

"I'm not saying you can't. It's just ... you've played soccer since you were in middle school. You'd really give it up to play football?"

"Hell yeah. Did you not see how Payson owned the field last year? The girl was such a freaking badass, it made me want to put on a uniform myself."

She paces between my bed and window, lost in thought. "What if joining the football team allows Anthony to see me differently? He's never really watched my games because our schedules always clashed, but what if I can get him to see me more like a teammate than his sister, more than someone he feels the need to protect?"

"So there's an ulterior motive to your madness." I chuckle, but I understand her thought process. Maybe joining the team will be good for them, help them to bond rather than be at each other's throats. "I say you should go for it."

"Really?" She pauses in her circular pace. "If I do this, you have to do it too."

"What!? Are you crazy?" She can't be serious. "I don't have an athletic bone in my body. What makes you think I would willingly join the football team?"

"One, you say your mom gripes about your size, right? Well, the football team gets free rein of the workout room before and after school, which leads me to number two. It'll help you get into shape, which will make your mom happy."

"I don't need to get back into shape. I've never been 'in shape' according to my mother." I flop on my bed, running my hands through my hair, trying not to think about my mother's words from earlier. "Besides, this isn't about her happiness. It's about mine."

"Exactly my point. You need to do things that make you happy, not her. And maybe football isn't your thing, but trying something new might be. And who knows? Maybe you will end up liking it."

I stare at my friend, contemplating whether I should just agree or continue to fight with her on this. Alora's always been able to convince me to do things I wouldn't normally do, like sneaking into the old abandoned house on Whispering Hills that everyone claims is haunted. Or getting on the roller coaster at Palmetto Peaks when I am terrified of heights. So far, everything she's pushed me to do has worked out for the better.

"You're still not convinced? Okay. Numero tres. You'd get to see Dylan in those tight football pants."

My face flushes at the thought. "I see him almost every day."

"Not in those tight pants that hug his ass and that bulge—"

"Alora!" I throw a pillow at her, my face burning even hotter. "Stop it!"

"What? It's true. I've seen him in those pants, and girl, let me tell you, I'd climb him like a tree if he wasn't practically your man."

"He's not my man," I mutter, suddenly feeling the weight of those words. "He's Charmaine's, even if she doesn't deserve him."

"Speaking of which." Alora pulls out her phone, showing me the photos from last night again. "I wonder if Dylan's seen these yet."

The images of Charmaine wrapped around some random guy make me sick. How could she do that to Dylan? He deserves so much better.

"I don't know," I say honestly. "And it's not my place to tell him."

"Well, someone should. He deserves to know what her extracurricular activities are when he isn't around."

I nod, knowing she's right. "So, about this football thing … you're seriously considering it?"

"Absolutely. And you should too. What's the worst that could happen?"

"How about I could trip and face plant right into the turf in front of the entire school, as if putting my fat ass on the football field isn't asking to be ridiculed or bullied already."

"Dramatic much?" She gently shoves me. "You do realize there are like a hundred practices before the first game, right? Plenty of time for you to learn the ins and outs of the sport. And who knows, maybe you'll discover a hidden talent."

"I guess when you put it like that …" Would it really be so bad to try this?

"Come on, just think about it. For me?" She bats her lashes and pouts her lips, her hands clasped together.

"Fine, I'll think about it." I sigh, knowing full well I'll probably end up doing it just to make her happy. "But if I die, I'm haunting you for eternity."

"Deal." She grins, flopping down beside me on the bed. "Now, tell me more about what happened with Dylan at the carnival. You said he was acting weird?"

I fill her in on how Dylan seemed to pop up everywhere Brock and I went and how he seemed to hug me longer than usual after I introduced him to Brock.

"Oh, and get this. Dylan walked me to my door last night."

"Wait, what?" Alora's eyes widen, her brows shooting up to her hairline. "How did that happen?"

"When I got home from the carnival, he was sitting on his porch, like he was waiting for me. Said he wanted to make sure I got home safe." I try to hide my smile but do a terrible job at it. "Is that something a guy does for his female friend? Or do you think he sees me as more?"

"I don't know. It could go either way." Alora's expression hardens, her gaze intense. "But, Maisie, I don't want to give you false hope only to have it shattered."

I exhale slowly, a tightness in my voice. "Yeah ... I don't want that either."

It's why I can't let myself feel anything more for him. If there's one person capable of breaking me—really breaking me—it's him. And if that happened, I'm not sure I'd know how to put the pieces back together.

# *Chapter 7*

## Maisie

"I can't believe I let you talk me into doing this."

"Oh, come on. It's going to be fun!" Alora singsongs, her presence palpable from the passenger seat of my car. "And don't forget the best part. Hot. Football. Players."

"Oh yeah. So many hotties, Anthony included," I tease.

"Please do not put hotties and my brother's name in the same sentence." She makes a gagging noise, as if she's about to throw up. "By the way, thanks for letting me stay over last night. If Anthony found out I was going to the combine, he would have locked me in my bedroom, ensuring I never made it out of the house."

I wouldn't put it past her brother to do something like that. "Do you think he's going to be there?"

"Payson's the one who put this thing together. If Payson asked Colton, knowing how tight those two are, I have no doubt Anthony will be helping out. Colton's one of his best friends."

It makes me wonder if Dylan will be there, too. I'm not sure if he is super close to Colton, but I'm sure he would want to help out. Question is, am I ready to come face-to-face with him after I never responded to his text Saturday night?

Moments later, I pull into the parking lot closest to the football stadium. Alora and I grab our water bottles and head for the field. We've just stepped onto the track when a shout echoes across the field.

"Absolutely not! You've got to be out of your mind, Alora Saige Lewis!" Anthony storms toward us from the far end of the field, his pace as furious as his tone.

"Shit!" Alora says under her breath. "I didn't think he would already be here. He's never on time for anything."

"You want me to stay with you?"

"No, no. You go ahead. This is my shit show to deal with." She sighs. "Hey, little bro."

"That's not going to piss him off even more," I say with a smirk, veering off toward the field where a few girls are standing around. Anthony's taller and broader than Alora, but she was born about ten minutes earlier, so calling him "little bro" is one of her favorite ways to get under his skin.

"He deserves it," she mutters through clenched teeth just as Anthony reaches her.

"Let's go!" is all he says before latching onto her arm and dragging her toward the parking lot, Alora going off on him in the process.

Standing on the field, I'm genuinely surprised by the turnout. Girls of various shapes and sizes mill about, some stretching, others chatting excitedly. There must be at least twenty of us here, each with our own reasons for showing up today.

Glancing around, I notice several guys from the football team setting up different stations around the field. My heart skips when I spot Dylan among them helping Zion set up some orange cones. He's wearing a cutoff Eagles shirt that shows off his toned arms, and the memory of Saturday evening flashes in my mind, forcing me to look away.

I glance toward the stadium entrance and spot Alora marching back onto the field, her face flushed with anger. Anthony trails behind her, looking slightly defeated, deep in conversation with Colton Reynolds. The moment Alora spots me, she makes a beeline in my direction.

"I'm staying," she announces as soon as she reaches me. "And if my idiot brother tries to stop me again, I'll break his arm."

"What happened?" I ask, glancing at Anthony, who's now conferring with some of his teammates by the sidelines.

"I told him I'm almost eighteen and he can shove his overprotective bullshit up his ass." She grins, fixing her ponytail. "Then Colton showed up and attempted to defuse our argument, but you know how my brother and I are. He just doesn't want to accept that he's worried I'll show him up in front of all his football buddies."

"And let me guess, you are going to do just that, aren't you?"

"Oh, you best believe I am," she says, a mischievous grin crossing her face.

The girls start talking, some discussing their summer, and others, obviously checking out the football players setting up. As we stand around waiting for the coaches to call this event to order, I notice a short blonde standing off by herself.

Is she new? I've never seen her before.

As someone who hates to see people being left out, I approach the girl with pink in her hair, hoping to help her feel more welcomed.

"Are you as nervous about this as I am?" I ask. A simple question I'm sure will help break the ice.

The girl shrugs but says nothing and looks around. Is she looking for someone?

"I'm Maisie, incoming senior. This is my first time trying football. What about you?"

Still no response. Okay. Maybe she's not much of a talker. Or maybe she doesn't speak and uses sign language to talk? I'm about to ask when a voice shrieks through the quiet morning air.

"Porkenstein! What are you doing here? Did old farmer Higgins let you out of the pig pen today?"

I grit my teeth as I turn to face the girl I once called my best friend. "I think the real question, Charmin, is what are you doing here? Aren't you afraid you might break a nail?"

The girl beside me lets out a scoff, and I inwardly smile.

"It's Charmaine! And don't be ridiculous! You could never catch me breaking a sweat or putting on that gaudy uniform." She rolls her eyes and tosses her hair over her shoulder. "For your information, I'm here to drop off my sister, Corrine."

I glance behind her and spot sweet, quiet Corrine. They've always looked similar, but the two are polar opposites, especially since Charmaine grew into the mean girl she is today.

"Now, if you'll kindly move your lard ass, I need to speak to whoever is in charge of this thing."

"Oh, this big ol' thang?" I turn to the side, emphasizing my ass. "Yeah, I'm surprised it took you so long to notice, considering your boyfriend hasn't stopped staring at it since I got here." I'm not sure if Dylan has once noticed my presence, but she doesn't need to know that.

"Dylan's here!?" Charmaine shrieks, searching the field until her eyes land on him standing with the guys. "Dylan! Dylan!" she yells, storming off, and her sister follows close behind.

Once the two of them are out of earshot, I turn to the new girl. "He hasn't been looking. I just knew it would piss her off."

To my surprise, we laugh together, and she raises her hand for a fist bump, which I eagerly return.

"Respect. Got to say, Red, that has to be the highlight of my Monday."

"Well, when you're the victim of Charmaine's constant bullying for as long as I have been, you tend to get tired of all the fat jokes and just have to fight back."

"Fair point," blondie states. "So, what's the deal with those two?"

Thankful the new girl is actually conversing with me, I give her all the tea on everything about Charmaine Summers. How she is the typical "mean girl" at school, obsessed with her looks, designer clothes, and being the center of attention. Spoiled by her wealthy parents, she's developed an inflated ego, especially after her cousin's pregnancy forced her out of the spotlight and made Charmaine the new queen bee at Bellwood High. Her younger sister, Corrine, is often overshadowed by her, and though Charmaine tries to make people think they're twins, they're actually about thirteen months apart. Corrine tends to stay in Charmaine's shadow, either out of loyalty or because others avoid her to escape Charmaine's wrath.

The sound of a whistle blows, effectively ending our conversation. The group of coaches, along with Payson, gather the small group of girls at the fifty-yard line.

"Huddle up, ladies," the rounded-belly old guy shouts. "I'm Coach Watson, Bellwood's head football coach. The gentleman next to me is Coach Harbaugh." He points to the guy beside him, a tall gentleman with salt-and-pepper hair and a matching beard and mustache. Thank God my mother isn't here, or she would be all over him. Then again, it would get rid of Richard.

I shake the thought from my mind as Coach Watson continues to introduce the coaching staff. "The other two gentlemen are my offensive and defensive coaches, Coach Freeman and Coach Wells." The two darker-complexion coaches are equally as handsome as the silver fox. The one looks like Dwayne Johnson's doppelgänger, whereas the other is slightly shorter and not nearly as bulky but still extremely good-looking.

Where did they find such smoking-hot coaches? Amazon?

"Depending on if you decide to continue with football and what position you are strongly suited for, you will be working with one of them. We are going to get started on some drills, but I want to take a moment to introduce you to the young woman behind today's camp, Miss Payson Moore."

Everyone claps and cheers, and some football players whistle as Payson stands in front of the coaching staff. Her long brown hair is pulled up in a ponytail, with a baseball cap in place to help shield her eyes from the blazing sun. Rocking a black sports bra that shows off her flat stomach and athletic shorts that hit just above her knees, she looks every bit the toned athlete.

Damn, she looks good. Like, really good. And it's fine—I can think another girl looks hot, right? It doesn't mean anything. Just a normal, harmless observation. People notice attractive people all the time. Still... this isn't exactly the first time I've had this thought. Maybe I'm a little bit bi? Who knows. I'm not making a big deal out of it. Just... noticing.

Payson introduces herself and shares her story. How her military family moved back to Bellwood after her father retired from the Army. She goes into how she went from being well-respected with her previous school to having to fight and earn the respect of the coaches and her new teammates here, which she gained even more when she made the team state champs.

The guys start chanting "State champs" over and over, their voices growing louder until Payson steps in and tells them to calm down. All of them quiet—except for Dylan, who seems caught in a heated conversation with the pompous evil queen standing by the bleachers.

"I'd like to think that what I did for Bellwood High opened their eyes in more ways than one. Are there still people who feel some type of way about me? Absolutely. Are there people who don't think girls should play in a sport dominated by boys? Without a doubt. I would like to think that when I took on the quarterback position and led this team to its rightful victory, each win garnering more support, I opened this small town up to see the beauty that not everything is blue and pink. Which leads me to today. I wanted girls who never thought they could be a part of a physical and aggressive sport like football simply because they are female to have the opportunity. I want other girls to see that they can do anything they want, be a part of a male-dominated team, and show them that we are just as equally capable as they are. Today is about empowerment and depleting gender stereotypes."

Wow, those are some motivational words. For the first time today, playing football might not be such a bad idea.

"In case you didn't notice, I brought some of my former teammates along to help out today. It is their job to be an extra set of eyes, to see what position is best suited for you as you go through the different drills. If at any point you don't feel like this is something meant for you, that's okay. There is no shame in that. You came out and gave it your best, and that in itself means more to me than you could possibly know. With that said, how about we get started?"

Payson leads us to the first station. Two orange cones sit on the goal line, with another pair down the field.

"Alright, ladies. This station we are going to see how fast you can run."

"Did she say run?" I squeak, turning to Alora. "My fat ass does not run!"

Alora places her hands on my shoulder. "Relax. You've got this! It's a quick little run, so it'll be over before you know it."

"What if I fall on my face in front of everyone?"

"You won't."

"How can you be so sure?"

"Anyone here want to go first?" Payson asks the group.

For a moment, it seems no one wants to step up, then Alora steps forward. "Alright, I'll go first. Alora Lewis."

Payson appears to be amused. "Lewis? Any relation to Dom and Anthony?"

"Yeah. I'm the older twin to the one who's pouting on the side over there." She nods in Anthony's direction.

"I heard that!" Anthony yells out, unamused. Alora takes her position, awaiting the whistle, then guns her way down to the finish line.

Wow, she's fast! Those years of soccer really paid off.

"Four-point-six-two!" Kai Nguyen calls out. "Anthony, I believe your sister just destroyed your run time, dawg."

"Shut up, Kai!" Anthony yells.

"Don't be such a sour puss, little bro. You just hate that I'm showing you up and proving I'm going to be better than you on the field." Alora taunts her brother, which leads to the two of them going off on each other.

The rest of the girls go through with their runs as I wait anxiously for my turn. I close my eyes, taking in deep breaths. *Don't trip and fall. Don't trip and fall. Don't trip and fall*, I repeat like a mantra.

"Hey. It's your turn. Are you ready?"

Opening my eyes, I'm met with a pair of pretty green ones staring back at me.

"I'm not sure I'm any good at this stuff. Running isn't my strong suit," I murmur.

"Hey, it's okay. It's not about being good or perfect. It's about stepping outside your comfort zone and giving it your best." Payson's eyes look off to the side before returning to mine. "And not allowing anyone to diminish your light. Show them, but more importantly, show yourself, you can do anything."

"Has anyone told you that you would make a great motivational speaker?"

Payson laughs. "Only my girlfriend and a handful of family. Now, are you ready to run this thing ..."

"Oh. I'm Maisie."

"Let's go, then, Maisie! C'mon!" The way she is so pumped for me, the belief she has in me, lights a fire within, and I stand at the starting line, more sure of myself than I was moments ago. The whistle blows, and I charge down the field, my eyes locked where Kai and Zion are standing, ready to clock my time.

"Five-point-eight-three!" Kai shouts as I cross the second pair of cones, and I'm relieved I didn't stumble and faceplant.

"Great job, Maisie!" Zion states, giving me a high five. I return the gesture as I struggle to get air into my lungs.

Maybe I should start going for runs around the neighborhood. Or, you know... speed walking. Power strolls. Aggressive meandering.

"Don't forget to reward her with some chocolate milk, boys," Charmaine sneers as she walks past. "Heard that's what farmers do to reward their little piggies after a race."

"Keep talking, Charmaine, but it's getting hard to hear over the sound of your own desperation for attention." A tall guy, with a buzzed head and biceps that look like they could crack watermelons stands beside me. He looks familiar, but I can't place the name.

Watching Charmaine's sneer fade as she storms down the track toward the exit, it's clear the guy's words hit a sore spot.

"Thank you for speaking up, but you didn't need to defend me. I normally just ignore her."

"Sometimes, it's hard to stay quiet when someone's out of line. You shouldn't have to just ignore it." He gives me a wink before walking off with some of the guys.

"Damn, when did Tristan turn into a man?" Alora says, sidling up next to me.

"Wait. Tristan? Tristan as in Tristan Kelby?"

"The one and only. He must have been hitting the gym extra hard this summer, because d-a-m-n, he's fine." Alora ogles him for a moment before turning back to me. "And I think he sees something he likes in you."

"What? Don't be ridiculous!" I glance to where Tristan stands near the water refill station. Our eyes lock, and he gives a small wave before returning to his conversation with his teammate. "He's just being polite."

"Oh, yeah? If he was just being polite, then why is Dylan Myers looking at Tristan like he's ready to throttle his neck?"

My eyes snap to Dylan, his gaze locked on Tristan. His brows are furrowed, jaw tensed, and his fists clench and unclench with barely contained frustration. Meanwhile, Tristan remains oblivious of the glare piercing him from across the field.

What timeline did I stumble onto?

# Chapter 8

## Dylan

I'm standing with Zion and Chase when someone calls my name.

"Dylan! Dylan!"

"Don't look now, but here comes your girlfriend," Zion mutters, as annoyed by her presence as I am.

"Pookie bear, didn't you hear me calling you?" Charmaine slinks up beside me, wrapping her arm around mine. Zion and Chase snicker at the pet name, and I shoot them a glare that silences them both.

"Hey, we should probably go check if Coach needs help with anything else," Chase says.

"You know, I think I heard someone mention needing help at the watering station," Zion adds. "We'll just ... go."

Zion and Chase speed walk away, leaving me alone with Charmaine and her sister, Corrine.

"What are you doing here?" I grit out. "This isn't exactly your sort of thing."

Pleading to a higher power, I beg to the universe that Charmaine isn't trying out for football.

"Puh-lease. I'm going to tell you the same thing I told chunky Ariel back there, I'm just dropping off Corrine," Charmaine says, her manicured nails digging into my arm. "I didn't know you'd be here though."

Chunky Ariel? My eyes sweep the area, landing on Maisie, the only redhead here, and my frustration with Charmaine's ignorance simmers beneath the surface.

"Payson asked for volunteers, so I said I'd help," I explain, trying to keep my tone neutral. "I didn't realize your sister was interested in football."

I'm genuinely surprised. While Corrine is athletic in her own right, I never imagined this would be the sport for anyone in the Summers family.

"She's not," Charmaine says. "Our parents are making her do more sports so it looks good on her college applications next year. I thought she would go for cheerleading or at least volleyball, something with cute uniforms, but to our surprise, she chose football. So here we are."

Corrine stands a few feet away, staring down at her shoes. I've always felt a little sorry for her—forever the supporting act in the Charmaine Show. When they were younger, Corrine used to talk more, even smile. Now, she barely does either.

"Not everything's about looking cute, right, Corrine?" I say, offering her a small smile. "Football's a great sport. I think you'll enjoy it." I look at my watch to check the time, hoping Coach starts soon so I can get away from Charmaine. "You may want to head over to the group. We should be starting any minute."

She gives me a small nod but doesn't say a word, then walks over to the girls on the field. I turn to Charmaine, expecting her to leave, but she doesn't move.

"If you're planning on sticking around, you're going to have to sit on the bleachers."

"You really expect me to sit on those sun reflectors and risk burning my beautiful skin? Please! You know me better than that."

Has she always been this vain?

"Now that my sister isn't around, I wanted to talk to you about Saturday night. You never showed up to the party."

"Yeah, I wasn't in the party mood," I say, trying to keep my tone neutral.

"Everyone was asking where you were. It looked bad that my boyfriend wasn't there with me."

"I'm sorry if it embarrassed you," I say, not feeling sorry at all. "But I needed a break."

"A break?" Her voice edges up, sharp with disbelief. "What's that supposed to mean?"

"Just what I said. I needed a break from the party scene." *And from you.*

Charmaine's eyes narrow. "This is about those stupid rumors, isn't it? People saying I was with someone else?"

I study her face, looking for any sign of guilt, but her expression remains controlled. "Were you?"

I have no proof she was messing with anyone. No one ever came forward with evidence, so either she was incredibly sneaky, or they were too caught up in having fun to notice.

"Of course not!" she snaps, looking genuinely offended. "How could you even ask me that?"

I shrug, keeping my expression unreadable. "People talk, Charmaine."

"And you'd believe them over me? Your girlfriend?" She steps in closer, her voice dropping to a whisper. "Look, I know things haven't been great between us lately, but I would never cheat on you. I love you."

I hold her gaze, trying to read the truth in her eyes—but it's hard to tell with Charmaine. Words come easy to her. Too easy.

Once upon a time, some part of me might've wanted to believe her. But now? We've been drifting for months, and I've caught her in enough lies to know when she's not being honest. Throw in the mean-girl antics, and yeah—I'm just done. Done with this relationship. Done with her.

Maybe it's finally time to end it.

"Don't you love me back?" Charmaine asks, her voice cracking when I don't return the sentiment.

"We'll talk about this later," I say, noticing Payson waving the volunteers over. "I need to go help."

"No!" she snaps. "This isn't something that can wait. What's going on, Dylan?"

I press my fingers to my forehead and let out a frustrated sigh. "I'm not doing this here, Charmaine. You need to leave so I can focus on what I came here to do. We can talk later."

"No, we're talking now!" She stomps her foot, throwing a tantrum like a toddler. "Are you breaking up with me?"

I glance over at the field when the guys start chanting, but Payson quickly gets them to settle down and picks up where she left off with her speech. I guess it's now or never.

"I think we both know this"—I gesture between us—"hasn't been working for a while. With senior year, football, keeping up with my grades, and trying to get into Harvard, I've got a lot on my plate. Plus, there's some news about Carver that's been occupying my mind, and I can't afford any distractions right now. So, yeah, Charmaine, I'm breaking up with you."

"You don't mean that," Charmaine says, her voice trembling.

"No, I really do. It's time to cut the bullshit and go our separate ways," I say, my tone clipped. "You're free to do whatever you want."

Charmaine's body stiffens, her spine straightening as her trembling fades. Her blue eyes narrow, locking onto mine with a fiery intensity.

"No! You don't get to break up with me, Dylan Myers. I'm not the girl who gets dumped!" Her voice rises, a mix of disbelief and anger lacing her words. She steps forward, her face inches from mine, as if daring me to take it back. "I decide when this ends. Not you. Not ever."

"Hold on." I reach into my pocket and pull out my cell phone, unlock it, and pull up my social media profile. I raise the screen so Charmaine can see, deliberately navigating to my relationship status. With a few taps, I change it from "In a Relationship" to "Single."

I let the silence hang between us, her eyes flickering with disbelief as she processes the change. "I believe that makes it official in your book."

Her jaw tightens, a snarl ripping from her throat as she storms off. I glance over to the starting line, where Maisie stands, her body tense, eyes wide with anxiety. It's clear she's terrified. But then Payson leans in, whispers something to her, and for a split second, I see a shift—like a spark of confidence ignites within her. The whistle blows, and she bolts forward, her red hair whipping behind her like a blazing flame.

"Five-point-eight-three!" Kai shouts as she crosses the finish line.

Pride swells in my chest as Maisie celebrates with Zion. I'm about to call out to her when Charmaine's venomous voice cuts through the air.

"Don't forget to reward her with some chocolate milk, boys. Heard that's what farmers do to reward their little piggies after a race."

My blood boils at her words, her attempt to humiliate Maisie. I'm ready to step in when Tristan beats me to it.

"Keep talking, Charmaine, but it's getting hard to hear over the sound of your own desperation for attention."

Her face contorts with anger before she stomps off toward the exit. *Good riddance.*

But then my eyes snap to Tristan, that goddamn smile on his face as he looks at Maisie, and the way she's gazing up at him with those mesmerizing steel-blue eyes.

What the hell?

When did Tristan start noticing Maisie? And why does that bother me so much?

Three hours later, the combine camp is officially over. I'm drenched in sweat from head to toe, but overall, I'm impressed with the turnout and hope Payson feels the same. The impact she's had in just one year here is incredible. I'm not sure all these girls are here for football, but it's obvious who's taking it seriously and who's just here to flirt.

Maisie was a surprise. I never knew her to show any interest in football, aside from showing up to my games to cheer me on. The few times I caught her in drills, she impressed me. Apparently, the coaches too. I overheard Coach Wells talking to Coach Watson about her being a good fit for the defensive line, either as a defensive tackle or defensive end.

I'm packing up the equipment when I catch sight of Tristan walking toward Maisie. My jaw tightens when he hands her a water bottle, that smug grin plastered on his face. Seeing them together stirs something inside me—an unexpected, unsettling surge of possessiveness. It's like a switch flips, and suddenly, the idea of Maisie with anyone else—especially him—feels unbearable. I didn't expect to feel this way or to care.

"You good, bro?" Zion asks, appearing beside me as we collect the last of the equipment.

"Just peachy," I grunt out.

Zion stares at me in disbelief. "Seriously, man. I'm good."

"Right. And I'm not sweating my ass off in this heat." Zion lets out a laugh. "Dude, I've known you since we were in diapers. I know when something's bothering you."

"Nothing's bothering me."

"So you're not jealous that Tristan's over there flirting with your girl?"

"She's not my girl," I snap, my words sharper than I meant. Immediately, regret hits me, but I can't shake the irritation gnawing at my chest. "Sorry. I just... I don't know what you're talking about."

Zion lifts an eyebrow, a smirk tugging at his lips. "Sure you don't." He picks up another cone and tosses it in the air like he's got all the time in the world. "But just so you know, Tristan was asking around about her earlier."

My stomach drops. "What?" I whirl around to face him, every nerve on edge. "What did he want to know?"

"If she was single, if anyone knew anything about her. The usual stuff a guy would ask when one is interested in a girl." Zion watches me carefully. "I told him I didn't know much, but that you two are pretty close."

"Why would you tell him that?"

"Because it's true?" Zion raises an eyebrow. "And I figured maybe it would light a fire under your ass to finally make a move."

"Why?"

"I heard you finally broke up with Charmaine. About damn time, man."

That went around fast. Not surprised in this town. "Yeah, well, it was long overdue."

"No shit. So now that you're single ..." Zion nods in Maisie's direction.

"Don't start," I warn him.

"Fine. All I'm saying is, if you don't make a move soon, someone else will. Like Tristan over there."

I glance back at Maisie and Tristan, now joined by Alora. They're laughing about something, and Maisie's laugh rings out across the field, light and effortless. It's a sound I could listen to for hours. The sight of her smile hits me like it always does, a little jolt to my chest. She's had that effect on me for as long as I can remember, even when we were kids.

"It's complicated," I state.

"Only because you make it that way." Zion shakes his head. "Look, I get it. You've known each other forever, you're neighbors, best friends, blah, blah, blah. But man, I see the way you look at her. And I'm pretty sure she looks at you the same way when you're not watching."

"You don't know that." The thought lingers, making me wonder—have I never really paid attention? Is it possible she feels the same way too?

"I just broke up with Charmaine. I'm not looking to jump into anything right away."

"Sure, man. Whatever you say." Zion claps me on the shoulder. "Just don't wait too long. Girls like Maisie don't stay single forever."

While carrying the equipment bag toward the storage shed, Zion's words echo in my mind. He makes a valid point. Maisie is stunning—how could any guy not notice her?

The thought of her with someone else—especially Tristan—stirs an unfamiliar pang of unease in me. I remind myself how I handled her date with what's his face. What did she say again? That they didn't connect? Maybe the same will happen with Tristan and any guy who dares to pursue the most incredible woman on the planet.

For now, though, I have to push these feelings aside. Why get worked up over someone I *might* have feelings for after ending a four-year relationship with someone else? It's not like Maisie would jump into a relationship with someone, especially given what I've heard about her mom's dating habits.

Maisie might test the waters, but she'd never dive into something new so quickly.

Besides, even if I wanted to jump straight into a relationship with the curvaceous redhead who's been occupying my thoughts lately, I wouldn't put it past Charmaine to twist it into something it's not. She would be a nightmare, stopping at nothing to tear us apart, driven by her bitter jealousy, and that's a mess I'm not willing to get caught up in.

# Chapter 9

## Maisie

"Josie, c'mon! You don't want to be late for your first day of freshman year!" I exclaim, pounding on my sister's bedroom door.

I'm still trying to wrap my head around it being the first day of school, the start of senior year. It feels like summer break was over before it even started. I guess that's what happens when you land the defensive tackle position on the football team.

Mom's reaction was exactly what I expected when I got the email saying I made the team. Flabbergasted, she went on a whole spiel, unable to understand why I'd want to play a "man's sport." It wasn't until I mentioned the gym access and how it would help me get in shape that she finally relented. *Go figure.*

Three weeks of conditioning drills, learning the game, and how to properly tackle to avoid serious injury have occupied a few hours of my days. Despite the late-July, into early-August summer heat, it wasn't as bad as I had anticipated, especially being surrounded by so many hot, shirtless football players, or in my instance, the only one worthy enough to captivate me truly. At seeing Dylan up close and in his element, biceps flexing as he throws a pass, he became the star of many, many spicy dreams.

Josie's bedroom door swings open, and I'm met with my scowling little sister still dressed in her pajamas, with her hair disheveled.

"Don't rush me, Mase! You have no idea how hard it is to find the perfect first-day fit for high school."

*Dramatic much?*

"Really? I don't know anything about that?" I raise an eyebrow, like I wasn't once a freshman.

"You know what I mean." She scoffs. "You're the one with the fashion sense. Help me, please?"

My baby sister is asking me for fashion advice? Awe. How can I say no?

"Let's see what we can come up with."

We rummage through her closet, pulling out different items until we nail down the perfect look: a mint-green lace baby doll top that will bring out the red in her hair, paired with distressed cutoff shorts, and finished with white Converse sneakers. I help pull Josie's strawberry-blonde waves into a half-up style, securing it with a white flower claw clip. Then Josie adds some chunky gold hoop earrings and a few gold bracelets to complete the outfit.

After putting the finishing touches to our makeup, we grab our backpacks and the breakfast sandwiches I prepped the night before on our way out the door, not wanting to be late for our first day.

"Are you going to be okay finding your classes?" I ask. "Or do you need me to help?"

"I'll be fine. I've already printed a copy of the school blueprint and mapped out all my classes so you don't have to escort me around." She glances at me. "Wouldn't want to embarrass you."

"Why on earth would you ever think that? I'm not one of those older siblings who is going to shut you out the moment we walk through the front doors. It's not who I am."

She shrugs and leans back in her seat. "Okay, then let me put it this way. I don't want to give Charmaine any more fuel to bully you with." Josie sinks lower into the passenger seat. "That she-devil will use anything to make your life miserable, and I don't want to add to that."

I'm surprised by how much my sister seems to care about my issues with Charmaine. "Listen, Jojo. You don't need to worry about that. Alright? I can handle Charmaine. I just have to deal with her until graduation. What's another couple of months?"

Once we've made it to Bellwood High and I've parked in my assigned spot, Josie and I part ways as soon as she sees her best friend, Sabrina. The girls instantly fall in step with each other, already in full conversation, taking me back to my first day of high school. It's hard to believe that was only a few years ago.

As I stop at my locker to drop off my backpack and a few supplies, I hear "It's Charmaine!" over the students bustling toward classes. When I glance down the hall to see who is upsetting her royal pettiness, I spot Hollis Whitlock. I'd recognize her small stature and blonde hair, only instead of pink, she's changed it to blue.

I'd been trying to have conversations with her at practices over the summer, to break the ice and be welcoming since she would be new to Bellwood, but she's like a wall made of titanium. There's clearly a story there. No one is that shut off from people unless they have been through something.

The moment Hollis snaps one of Charmaine's nails and that witch lets out an ear-piercing scream, the entire hallway goes dead silent. It's clear things are about to get ugly—and I'm not about to let that happen. As soon as Coach Harbaugh steps into the hall, I jump in to back Hollis up. The last thing we need is her getting in trouble with the coaches.

"Ms. Summers, is everything all right?" Coach Harbaugh asks.

Charmaine points to Hollis, then shows him her disfigured manicure. "That heathen broke my nail!"

"No idea what she's talking about. I'm just trying to find my first class when she bumped into me," Hollis says, raising her map as evidence.

"Oh no. Charmin! I told you the sketchy nail salon you go to is a fraud. You need to go to a higher-end one," I say, with a condescending tone. Words don't describe the internal joy of watching Charmaine's face turn even more red than it was a second ago.

"I ... you ... gahh!" Charmaine screams before storming off to who knows where.

"Alright. Scene's over. Everyone, let's get to class!" Coach Harbaugh says as he ushers some students away, their conversations returning and the squeaks of new sneakers hitting the tile flooring as they shuffle along to their first class.

"That ... was ... awesome!" I exclaim. "I've never seen anyone lay a finger on Charmaine. She's one of those girls who likes to use her father's name to get away with just about anything."

"Great," Hollis mutters, glancing from the doors to her school map.

"You need help?" I ask, even though she doesn't seem like the type who'd ever admit it. "What do you have?"

She checks her school schedule. "Chemistry with Mr. Feeser."

"Oh, that's in the hall where all the science classes are. My first class is on the way there. I'll walk with you."

"Thanks" is all Hollis says before following me through the crowded hallways.

"No problem," I say, giving her a warm, friendly smile. "Us football girls have to stick together, right?"

Hollis simply nods, not saying another word. Okay, she's definitely going to be a hard one to crack.

We head toward the science hall, me doing most of the talking while Hollis stays completely silent. As soon as we turn the corner to the science hall, we nearly collide with a group of guys all wearing letterman jackets.

"Whoa, ladies. Our bad. We weren't paying attention. Please excuse us," Anthony says. "Wait ... diner girl?"

"It's Hollis," she snaps, her tone sharp enough to cut. Yeah, *diner girl* was definitely the wrong thing to say. "You might want to remember that next time you come in and get seated in my section. I'll be sure to remember this moment and, I don't know, mess with your order." A smile curls at the corner of her lips, sharp and predatory, and her eyes glint with mischief.

Note to self: do not get on Hollis Whitlock's bad side.

"I'm sorry. I didn't mean for it to come off like that. It's just ... I was used to the pink hair, and it took me by surprise seeing that you changed it up. Digging the blue, though," he says with a corny grin, giving her two thumbs-up.

"You'll have to ignore Anthony. His brain doesn't know how to function on the first day of school," Dylan says before looking my way. There's something different in how he's looking at me in this moment, a sparkle in his beautiful eyes, and I feel my cheeks warm.

"Whatever. I need to get to class," Hollis states. She thanks me for helping her before walking into her classroom.

"I should probably get to class too. I don't want to be late! See you guys around," I say, and make my way to French class.

After school, Alora catches a ride home with Josie and me. We stop by my place so Josie can change into her dance gear and grab a quick snack before we drop her off at the studio on the way to the mall.

I find a good spot near the food court entrance and head inside, the smell of different foods hitting me instantly.

"You know what? A pretzel sounds really good right now. How about you?" Alora asks.

Right on cue, my stomach growls. "A pretzel sounds perfect."

With pretzels and sweet tea in hand, we snag a table near the fountain—perfect for people-watching—and dive into our first-day recaps before the conversation drifts into the usual girl gossip.

"Do you think there is something going on between Hollis and Colton?"

Alora raises a finger, finishing her bite before she speaks. "You think there is?"

"I'm not sure. Just ... when I walked Hollis to her first class, we almost ran into some of the guys. Colton was with your brother and Dylan, and there was this very subtle moment between them. Then, at lunch, I thought I saw them have a stare-off."

"I haven't noticed, but I think they would be cute together. Have you noticed anything at practice?"

"Well ... um ... not really. My focus has been ... elsewhere."

"And would this *elsewhere* happen to be a six-foot something football-playing hottie?" Of course she'd go there. My best friend knows me too well.

The chair next to mine gets pulled out, and someone sits down in it while another person takes the seat next to Alora.

"Did someone say football-playing hottie? Because my ears were ringing."

Tristan Kelby is tall, with short dark-brown hair styled in a clean, neat way and a touch of stubble across his chin. When he smiles, it's a mix of charm and mischief—something that could make any girl weak in the knees.

I almost didn't recognize him at the football camp when he defended me against Charmaine.

He's always been tall, well over six feet, but where he used to be scrawny, now he's built—muscular and athletic, with a frame that clearly shows off his strength and agility. His broad shoulders and powerful arms are a testament to the dedication he put in at the gym over the summer.

All that hard work didn't just pay off physically—it's done wonders for his confidence too. No longer the shy, timid guy, Tristan now exudes a presence that's undeniably commanding.

"It could be anybody," Alora teases. "Didn't your mama teach you not to eavesdrop on girl talk, Kelby?"

"Sorry. We didn't mean to disrupt. I just had to come say hi." Tristan turns to face me, his light-brown eyes taking me in. "And tell you that you look absolutely stunning today, Red. When are you going to give me those digits?"

I have no doubt I'm blushing under the heat of his stare. Tristan has been flirtatious at practices, constantly making small talk during our water breaks. He's very handsome and seems like a nice guy, but I can't shake the underlying cockiness of him. Cocky guys are a turnoff for me. Maybe that's why I can't bring myself to give him my phone number.

"Why do you want it so bad?" I ask, a teasing smile tugging at my lips.

"How else am I going to invite you to the bonfire party down at Lake Seraphine this Friday night?"

"Oh, I don't know. There's this thing called social media?"

Tristan laughs, shaking his head. "I like the challenge, Red. But seriously, I'd really like it if you came to the party. Most of the team will be there, and it's a great way to celebrate the end of the first week of school."

I glance over at Alora, who gives me a small, encouraging nod. "I'll think about it."

"That's all I'm asking for." Tristan's smile widens, and I can't help but notice how his eyes crinkle at the corners. "But if you do decide to come, wouldn't it be nice to have my number, just in case?"

I roll my eyes playfully. "Fine, persistent one." I hold out my hand for his phone.

He places it in my palm, our fingers brushing briefly. I quickly type in my number and pass it back to him.

"There. Happy now?"

"Ecstatic." He winks before standing up. "Parker and I should get going. Don't want to steal any more of your girl time. Good evening, ladies," he says with a slight bow. "See you at practice tomorrow, Red."

Shortly after they leave, Alora leans forward, her eyes wide with excitement. "Oh. My. God. Tristan Kelby is totally into you!"

"He's just being friendly," I say, trying to downplay it.

"Friendly? The guy's been flirting with you for weeks! And did you see the way he was looking at you? Like you're the last slice of pizza and he's starving."

I laugh at her analogy. "You're insane."

"No, I'm not! I'm pretty sure I also saw Dylan glaring daggers at Tristan the other day at practice when he was helping you with your stance."

My heart skips a beat at the mention of Dylan. "Now you're just making stuff up."

"Am I? Because ever since you two had that little window peep-show moment—"

"It wasn't a peep show!" I hiss, looking around to make sure no one heard. "He just happened to be changing with his curtains open."

"And you just happened to be watching," Alora teases. "Look, all I'm saying is that something's changed between you two. I can *sense* it, even if you're not ready to admit it yet."

I sigh, taking a long sip of my sweet tea. "Even if something has changed, it doesn't matter. Dylan ended his long-term relationship with Charmaine weeks ago and is no doubt enjoying the single life for a while. No way is he going to jump into something new, even with me."

"You mean with someone who actually cares about him and would never cheat?" Alora raises an eyebrow. "Yeah, sounds terrible."

"You know what I mean," I mutter, rolling my eyes. "Besides, I'm not even sure if he sees me as anything more than just his childhood friend."

"Well, there's only one way to find out." Alora grins mischievously. "Go to that bonfire party, wear something that shows off those *irresistible* curves, and see how he reacts when Tristan inevitably flirts with you."

"You're such an instigator!" I toss my straw paper ball at her.

"Guilty!" she grins, clearly enjoying herself. "Look, my instincts are rarely wrong, okay? You and Dylan? The two of you are endgame. I'm calling it! Soulmates are supposed to be your best friend, and the two of you have had that for ages. Now it's the matter of getting you from the friend zone to the love zone."

"Love zone? Really?" I laugh.

"Hey! Do not come for my football analogies, okay?"

"Whatever you say, bestie."

Alora glances at her watch. "Ooh! Do you mind if we stop by the sports shop? I need to grab my first paycheck."

"Yeah, no problem." We gather up our trash and clean up our area before Alora and I link arms and head toward SportsXtreme, where she recently started working.

"Afterward, we should definitely go find you the perfect outfit for the bonfire party—something that'll have all the guys swooning and Dylan realizing what he's been missing right in front of him."

"I wish I were as optimistic as she is. If Dylan and I are meant to be, the universe will make it happen. The right things come to us when they're meant to, at the right time. Wouldn't interfering just disrupt fate?"

# Chapter 10

## Dylan

We're only halfway through the first week of school, and adjusting to the new schedule has been tough. Waking up an hour earlier to fit in my run before school, then classes from eight thirty in the morning to three thirty in the afternoon, followed by two hours of football practice. After that, it's home for dinner and homework, and by nine o'clock, I'm ready to crash.

As soon as I get home from practice, I head straight upstairs, my muscles aching from Coach Watson's brutal conditioning drills. The hot water from the shower helps ease some of the tension, but I know I'll feel it in the morning. After toweling off, I pull on some sweatpants and a T-shirt, then collapse onto my bed, staring at the ceiling.

My phone buzzes with a notification. It's a group text from Tristan to the football team about the bonfire at Lake Seraphine on Friday. I roll my eyes at his excessive use of fire emojis, but my attention catches on one particular line: "Really hoping you'll bless us with your appearance, Red!"

*Red.* As in Maisie?

Something in my chest tightens at the thought of Tristan and Maisie together. I've noticed him hovering around her at practice, always ready with a water bottle or a joke to make her laugh. And she laughs—that infectious giggle that makes her nose scrunch up in the most adorable way.

My phone buzzes again with another text, this one from Zion.

ZION

Yo. You going to this bonfire thing?

DYLAN

Probably. You?

ZION

Yeah. Chase and Kai want to go.

DYLAN

Cool. You guys riding with me or taking your own car?

ZION

We'll ride with you. Less designated drivers needed that way if we're drinking.

DYLAN

Smart thinking. Pick you guys up at 8?

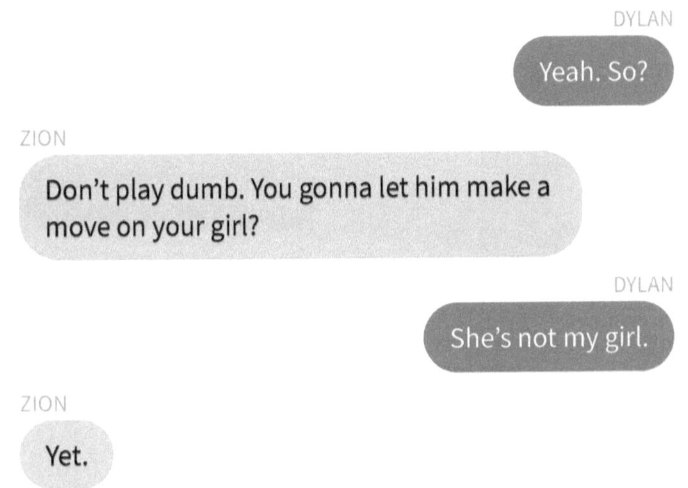


I stare at his text for a long moment before responding.

I toss my phone aside, not wanting to continue this conversation. It's not that simple. Maisie and I have been friends forever. Sure, she knows me better than anyone. The question is, would I be willing to risk all of that for something more?

I glance out my window toward Maisie's house. Her light is on, and she is sitting in her window hunched over what I assume is homework. Or a new clothing design sketch. Her red hair falls in waves around her face, and every few seconds, she tucks a strand behind her ear.

The memory of her catching me nearly naked a few weeks ago flashes through my mind. I remember the sweetest blush spread across her cheeks, the way her eyes widened before she quickly looked away. I'd been bold enough to give her a little show, dropping my towel just as I pulled the curtain closed.

Thinking back, I'm not sure what came over me. Maybe it was the rush of knowing she was watching, or maybe it was something deeper—something I'm not ready to acknowledge yet.

I should text her, see if she's going to Tristan's bonfire on Friday. The thought of her with him doesn't sit well with me, but I've been trying to ignore the feeling. She deserves to be happy, even if it's with someone else.

Before I can overthink it, I grab my phone.

DYLAN

Hey Freckles. You up?

I watch through the window as she reaches for her phone, a small smile forming on her lips as she reads my text.

MAISIE

No, I'm sleep texting.

DYLAN

It doesn't look like you're sleeping to me.

She looks in my direction, a pearly white smile on display as she waves at me.

DYLAN

What are you working on?

MAISIE

AP Lit assignment. You?

There's a pause as she types, then stops, then types again. I watch as her teeth catch her lower lip, like she's holding something back, weighing every word.



Why am I encouraging this? The thought of her at the bonfire with Tristan—or any guy—makes my stomach twist. Jealousy coils in my chest before I can stop it. But what right do I even have to feel this way? I've never said anything. Never told her how I feel. Maybe because deep down, I don't know if I can. I don't know if I *should*. Crossing that line could change everything, and once it does, there's no going back.

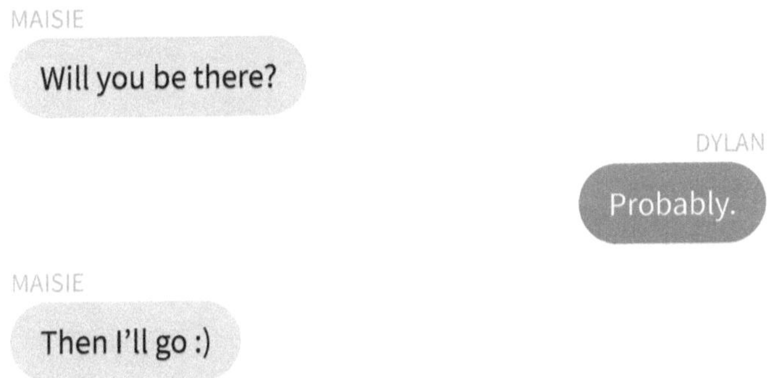

Walking into the school library, I feel a sense of relief wash over me. The quiet atmosphere is a welcome reprieve from the loud chaos of the halls. The noise always overstimulates me, so being in a calm space like this makes all the difference. I take a seat at a table by the window, the farthest one from the library doors. After dropping my binder onto the table, I pull out my notebook, ready to get some work done, though my mind keeps drifting elsewhere.

Coach Watson has been on my ass the past two practices, telling me I need to step up my game, especially since we are scrimmaging against the Winfield Commanders tomorrow. If I don't, he may bench me and put in Parker Malone as the starting quarterback. Parker is decent, but I need to be the starter to get myself out there and have something to show Harvard on my application.

On top of football, Carver sent a text this morning letting me know he got confirmation on his next deployment. The Night Stalkers will deploy next week, and we won't have contact until they return.

*If they return.*

Closing my eyes tightly, my heart rate quickens, so I take a few long, slow, deep breaths to bring it back down.

In for five, out for five. Repeat.

"Are you okay?" a soft whisper asks from close by.

Slowly opening my eyes, I'm greeted with steel-blue eyes surrounded by an array of freckles framed with copper tresses.

"Uh, yeah," I quickly say, but Maisie doesn't buy it. She takes the seat right next to me, brushing against me as she sits, and I'm instantly hit with her scent of sweet florals and the faint tang of green apples.

She faces me, taking my hand into her soft ones. "Dylan Beckett, I don't buy that for one second. You know I'm here for you, always have been and always will be. You can tell me anything, and I'll listen."

I stare into her eyes, how striking the blue and gray blend and shift with the lighting. Gorgeous. Breathtakingly beautiful. Mesmerizing.

"Dylan?"

Fuck. Being this close to her, able to smell and touch her, I got lost in her beauty, a sailor being drawn by a siren.

"I'm sorry. I … uh … I zoned out." God, I hope she bought that excuse. "Just a little overwhelmed, I guess. Coach has been on me to do better, and I'm trying. I really am. But taking over after Brady and Payson?" I let out a breath. "It's like this constant voice in my head, telling me I'm not good enough. I already feel like I'm letting everyone down before I've even had the chance to prove myself."

"That sounds like you're putting too much pressure on yourself when you shouldn't. Brady and Payson were great in their own unique ways. You just need to give yourself credit with a dash of grace. You are an incredible quarterback, D, and I have no doubt you're going to make Coach swallow his words. You just got to believe in yourself like I do."

"Damn, Freckles. You really know how to boost a guy's ego." I chuckle, earning a smile from those pouty lips. "It's not just that, though. Carver is leaving next week for another mission, and this one is pretty dangerous. I'm trying not to dwell on it too much, but … it's hard. What if—" I clear my throat, my voice wanting to crack with emotion. "What if he doesn't come back this time?"

Tears well in my eyes, blurring Maisie's face, and I'm instantly pulled into her, my body pressing against hers as she squeezes me in a comforting hug. Her hands move up and down my spine, attempting to soothe away my fear.

"Your brother is a fucking badass soldier. He's done hundreds of these missions, all of them dangerous in their own way, yet he's made it back home every time. This time will be no different."

We pull apart, and Maisie's hands move from my back to cup my face. Our faces are inches apart, our noses so close to touching that anyone walking by would think we were having an intimate moment.

"Your brother is going to come home. We just have to put it out in the universe."

"And how do we do that?" I whisper, a tear descending my face.

Maisie brushes the wetness away with her thumb. "We just have to believe he's coming home safe and alive. No negative thoughts, no fears. We simply just need to believe he is one hundred percent coming home."

"Okay," I whisper. There's a moment of silence between us, our eyes locked. The world seems to have disappeared, with the two of us in some sort of bubble. "Do you have any idea how incredibly lucky I am to have you, Freckles?"

Slowly, I lean in, hyperaware of the space between us—how small it is, and how impossible it feels to cross. Our lips are so close now, I can feel the warmth of her breath against mine, but it still isn't enough. The tension clings to the air, thick and suffocating, and I wonder if this is all we'll ever be—just an aching, unspoken almost. My heart hammers in my chest, but part of me hesitates, terrified to close that final gap ... to give in and risk everything.

Because once we cross that line, there is no turning back—everything will be different.

Just as I'm about to seal my lips with hers, the bell rings, shattering our bubble and pulling us back into reality.

Maisie jumps out of her seat. "Okay! Wow. Uh ... so ... I hope I helped you feel somewhat better. But I got to get to AP Lit, so ... I'll see you at practice yeah?" She gathers her books quickly and speed walks out of the library, as if she can't get away from me fast enough.

*What the hell was I thinking!?*

My heart's still pounding, fast and uneven, a blur of confusion and regret clouding everything.

The thought of losing her, of ruining the one constant in my life, the one person who's always been there, no matter what, settles like a weight in my chest. Did I really just risk our friendship over a single, impulsive moment?

I stand there, barely breathing, wondering if there's any way to make it right—or if I've already gone too far, ruining everything beyond repair.

This has been one of my best practices since football season started. I'm nailing my passes to my wide receivers, handing the ball off to my running backs without fumbling, not to mention, I've avoided five sacks, one almost made by Maisie herself.

"Alright, team. Last play of practice, then ya'll can go home. Let's make this count," Coach Watson shouts before blowing his whistle.

Everyone gets into their positions, waiting for me to make the play call. I call out "Crimson Option Left, Set, Hike," and Chase Lambert, my center, snaps the ball. I glance around for a running back, but Corrine and Armando are covered by defenders, so I tuck the ball under my arm and make a run to the left side of the field to gain as many yards as possible.

Maisie is quick to notice the change and guns right for me until we are mere inches apart. Her arms go to wrap around my legs, but I quickly step out of bounds to avoid getting tackled.

"Damn it!" Maisie slams a fist into the ground, clearly unhappy she didn't take me down.

"You almost had me there, Freckles." I hold out my hand to help her off the ground and am relieved when she accepts the offer. "Nice job!"

"Thanks." She smiles, but it's not the vibrant one she usually gives me.

Shit. I must have fucked this up.

"Hey, can we talk—"

Coach blows his whistle.

"Bring it in, ladies and gents," Coach Watson calls us to gather around him. "That was one of the best practices you guys have had to date. I want to see more of that from here on out. You keep practicing like that, we are going to have one kick ass season, maybe another championship. Tomorrow, we scrimmage against the Winfield Commanders, here on this very field at four o'clock. Make sure you leave as soon as the dismissal bell rings and get to the lockers. I want you dressed and out on the field to stretch and warm up before they arrive. Hands in. Eagles on three. One, two, three!"

"Eagles!" we shout in unison before departing to the locker rooms.

I'm about to go after Maisie to talk about what happened in the library earlier, when the last person I want to see blocks my path.

"Not now, Charmaine!" I say, irritation slipping into my tone. "I don't have the time for you."

I go to pass her, but she blocks me again. "Dylan, please. Just hear me out," she pleads, her voice softer than I've heard it in a long time. "I miss you. I miss us."

I sigh, running a hand through my sweaty hair. "There is no 'us' anymore, Charmaine. I broke up with you, remember?"

Her eyes soften, but she steps closer, placing her hand on my chest, her voice trembling slightly. "But we don't have to stay broken up," she says, the desperation creeping into her words. "We were together for four years. That has to mean something."

"It did mean something," I admit. "But people change. We've changed. And I think we both know this relationship ran its course a long time ago."

Her blue eyes fill with tears, and for a moment, I see a glimpse of the girl I once cared about. "Is there someone else? Is that why you won't give us another chance?"

My gaze automatically shifts to Maisie, heading toward the girls' locker room with Alora, Corrine, and Hollis. Charmaine follows my line of sight, her expression hardening when she realizes who I'm looking at.

"Her?" Charmaine scoffs, the vulnerability in her voice disappearing in an instant. "You'd rather be with that fat cow over me?"

And just like that, any sympathy I might've felt for her evaporates. "Don't talk about her like that."

"Why not? It's true! She's nothing but a pathetic, frumpy little—"

"Enough!" I snap, my voice low but laced with frustration. "This conversation is over, Charmaine. We're done. Get over it and move on."

I brush past her, not bothering to wait for a response. As I make my way toward the locker room, I hear her call after me.

"Dylan! Wait! Just—I can help you get into Harvard!"

After stopping in my tracks, I slowly turn to face my ex-girlfriend. "What are you talking about?"

"I know how important getting into Harvard is for you. I also know that you need at least two letters of recommendation from people who know you, and I'm betting your father isn't going to give you one because you're blood. However ... Daddy knows you very well." She steps closer, pressing her body against mine. Her dainty fingers travel up my arm as she continues. "I can make sure he writes that letter for you. All you have to do is ask—and I can guarantee it'll happen."

"What's in it for you?"

A villainous smile slowly spreads across her face. "We get back together."

"Hard pass," I state, turning around to go to the locker room.

"Oh, there's one more thing I forgot to mention. What was it?" She taps her finger against her chin, pretending to think. "Oh, right! Daddy's best friends with the admissions guy at Harvard—like, they're so close, they're practically family. It's a done deal, Dylan Beckett. We get back together, and you'll be walking right into the college of your dreams."

"And what if I refuse?"

She shrugs, all faux innocence. "Then I guess you can kiss Harvard goodbye."

*Fucking hell.* She can't be serious.

"What's *really* in it for you?" I ask, my voice low, eyes narrowed. There's got to be a reason she's so desperate to get us back together.

"To have the love of my life back with me," she says, batting her fake lashes with a smile that's almost convincing. "I mean, come on—it's senior year. Prom, parties, everyone expecting us to be *us*. We were *the* couple, remember?" She leans in slightly, voice softening. "I just want to end things right. No drama, no mess. We finish the year together, like we're supposed to ... and then after graduation, we walk away clean. I'm heading to Miami, you'll go up north. It's easier if we leave it on our terms. So ... do we have a deal or not?"

"I need to think it over."

"Don't take too long. I'm not a very patient person." Charmaine presses up on her toes in an attempt to kiss me.

I ignore her completely, not even sparing a glance as I walk away. I push through the boys' locker room door, where most of my teammates are already changing, leaving her behind—frozen in place, like she never meant a damn thing.

"Ex-girlfriend drama?" Zion asks, eyebrow raised as he pulls his pads over his head.

"Something like that," I mutter, opening my locker. "She doesn't know how to take no for an answer."

"Charmaine Summers? Accept rejection? That'll be the day," Tristan chimes in from across the room. "The girl's got an ego the size of Texas."

"Speaking of egos," Kai says with a smirk. "How's it going with Maisie? You manage to get into her good graces?"

"We've been talking since I got her number at the mall. Think we are officially friends ... for now." Tristan winks. "I'm working on changing that status, hopefully tomorrow night."

"Good luck with that," I say, trying to keep my tone neutral despite the jealousy burning in my gut. "Maisie's pretty selective about who she dates."

"Oh, I'm aware," Tristan smirks. "I'm not someone who backs down from a challenge, though."

I glance at Tristan, his smug expression making me want to say something—anything—that will shut him down. But what good would it do? Maisie's her own person, and she's capable of making her own decisions. Still, the way he talks about her like she's just some prize to claim doesn't sit right with me.

I want to warn her, to tell her exactly how he's playing this game, but I know better than to get involved. It's not my place, and the last thing I need is to make things more awkward between us. So I swallow my thoughts, forcing a tight smile, and turn away before Tristan can say anything else.

Tomorrow night will tell me everything I need to know.

And somehow, I can't shake the feeling I won't like what I find out.

# Chapter 11

## Maisie

Dylan leans in closer, the air between us crackling with energy. His lips are barely a breath away from mine.

"Do you have any idea how long I've wanted this?" he murmurs, his voice thick with hunger. "How long I've imagined the taste of your mouth, dreamed about those soft, pouty lips melting into mine? The way your body would feel pressed up against me—every soft curve, every inch—while I finally take my time savoring you?"

"Not nearly as long as I've been waiting for you to make the first move," I whisper. "Please don't make me wait another second longer."

As our lips finally meet, a rush of excitement and longing sweeps over me, giving in to temptation at last, and being claimed by the one guy who's truly held my heart. But then a sound in the distance cuts through the moment, growing louder, closer, until I finally recognize it for what it is.

The jarring ring of a cell phone shatters the moment, making Dylan vanish before my very eyes.

"What the hell? Dylan? Where'd you go?" I shout into an empty void.

I blink, disoriented, and the sound drags me back to reality. My eyes snap open, my room coming into focus. Looking over at my side table, my phone's screen lights up, and I groan inwardly as I reach for it.

"Hello?" I answer, my voice still full of sleep.

"Biotch! Have you checked social media?"

I pull the phone away from my face to check the time. "Mirko, it's five thirty in the morning." I groan for emphasis. "My alarm isn't set to go off for another thirty minutes, and I was dead asleep, having an amazingly wonderful dream before you disrupted it. Now, why the hell would I be on social media this early in the morning? Wait, why are you on social media this early in the morning?"

"Girl, don't worry about the why. And side note, we *will* be discussing the details of said dream in French class. So you haven't seen it?"

Being woken up before I'm supposed to get up makes for a very cranky Maisie.

"Mirko. If you don't just freaking spill it alread—"

"Dylan and Charmaine are back together!"

The words sting like a slap. I jolt upright, my heart pounding. "Wait—*what*? What do you mean they're back together?"

"Hang on. I'm sending you the screenshot from Dylan's page now."

A moment later, the text notification pops up. I quickly tap on the white box, bringing up the screenshot. Sure enough, Dylan's handsome profile picture appears—his smile wide, showing off his pearly white teeth and the cutest dimple. As my eyes slowly move down the picture, my heart starts to beat a little faster, afraid to see the truth for myself.

There it is, posted only hours ago, his profile picture right next to hers.

In a Relationship with Charmaine Summers.

"That can't be right, Mirko." I rub the sleep from my eyes and blink to ensure I'm not seeing things.

"The proof is in the pudding, sweetie."

"You don't understand. Dylan's been avoiding Charmaine ever since their breakup, and that was before he nearly kissed me yester—oop." Shit. I didn't mean to let that slip. I hadn't brought it up to anyone—not even Mirko or Alora—because I was still trying to process what happened.

"*Wait. Hold on*—" Mirko's voice jumps a full octave. "*He nearly kissed you?* Yesterday? And you're just now telling me this?!"

"I wasn't going to say anything, but since I basically let it slip." I sigh. "He was in the library when I saw him, and he looked a bit stressed, so I sat with him. I gave him one of my best pep talks to cheer him up before we hugged. But as we parted, there was this moment between us, and he leaned forward like he was going to kiss me when the bell rang. Then I ... sorta ... quickly took off."

"Girl! What is wrong with you? You have been pining for that boy for years, and the moment he reciprocates something more than a friendship, you take off?"

Crap! Is this why he's back with Charmaine? Did I make him think I didn't like him like that, and he decided he would go back to her?

"How do we know it's legit? I mean, it could be Charmaine's doing. What if she had someone hack into his account and change it?"

"Listen, the girl can be a bit excessive, but I doubt she'd go to those extremes. I mean, probably. But... some people said they saw the two of them after practice yesterday—standing way too close, her hands all over him. It didn't exactly look *intimate*, but it definitely didn't look innocent either."

"Psh. It's all just some rumors." At least my heart hopes they are.

"Mm, you mean like the ones about her cheating?" *Dammit, Mirko! You're not helping.*

"I refuse to accept that they're back together. Dylan has been very happy since he dumped her sorry ass, and until I see it with my own two eyes, I don't believe he would go back to her."

"You believe it now?" Mirko whispers in my ear as we stand in the student parking lot watching Charmaine lace her fingers with Dylan's while they walk into school together—back as a couple. Around us, students murmur in hushed tones, some excited to see their QB back with Miss Popularity.

As for me, I'd rather see her *with someone else*. Maybe a circus clown. At least then, I could pretend this whole thing was some kind of bad joke.

I don't get it. How could he go back to her after what happened yesterday? After nearly kissing me? Does he think everything will just fall back into place, like none of it ever happened? No check-in, no acknowledgment of the tension between us—of what we felt in that moment?

I never had the chance to process it, to sort through the whirlwind of emotions that hit me all at once. One minute, we're talking like usual, and the next, I'm caught in the chaos, everything feeling hazy and uncertain. I didn't know how to react, and by the time I could even gather my thoughts, the moment was already gone.

Worst of all, we never got to sit down and talk to each other about it. Or maybe that was wishful thinking on my end.

For the first time ever, anger pulses through me, sharp and burning. It's unfamiliar, so much so it feels like a foreign presence inside me—rage, but not the kind I usually feel when I think of Dylan. It's not the gentle, fluttering frustration that's always been tangled with affection. This is different—raw, unfiltered, and it has nothing to do with butterflies or heart eyes associated with the boy next door.

By lunch time, I barely touch my food, nauseous from having to witness Charmaine and Dylan's excessive PDA. Can the girl go two seconds without needing her claws attached to him?

I do my best to avoid Dylan and Charmaine for the rest of the day, not wanting their little reunion tour being slapped in my face, and even leave my final class five minutes before the dismissal bell rings so I can drop my books off to my locker and head to the girls' locker room to get ready for the scrimmage game.

A few moments after I enter the locker room, Alora and Corrine walk in.

"Hey. How are you doing?" Alora asks, like I'm some injured puppy. I shake my head no, and tilt toward Corrine, hoping to convey this is not the place to discuss my feelings.

"Oh. Right," she whispers before heading to her locker and grabbing her gear.

A few minutes later, Hollis walks in, looking unusually upbeat—far from her typical "feral cat" vibe.

"Hey, Hollis! Ready for the scrimmage?" I force the words out, my voice bright and enthusiastic, but it feels like a mask. My heart's not in it, but I don't let it show—pretending to be excited when all I want to do is crawl into myself and hide from everything. I can't let my mood affect the team, though. If we're going to play our best, we need to be a unit—and that means pushing my personal feelings aside for the sake of the game.

"As ready as I'll ever be. Are you nervous?"

I shrug, honestly unsure. "A little. But mostly excited. It'll be good to see how we measure up against another team before the actual season starts."

As I'm tying the strings on my shoulder pads, trying to adjust the damn things to fit properly over my full chest, I have to wonder if they make custom ones designed specifically for women with big breasts. A sports bra can only help so much, but it's clear these are not made for the female anatomy.

Alora brings up the bonfire party as she joins us, fitted in her game attire, sans helmet, and hair pulled back in a low ponytail.

"Hard pass for me," Hollis states as she works a French braid. "I've got work early in the morning."

"Ah, that's a bummer." Alora pouts. "I was hoping all of us girls could get dolled up and have some fun together."

"My sister's forcing me to go," Corrine says, adjusting the belt on her pants. "Where there's a party, Charmaine must be in attendance, and where she goes, I go. Honestly, I think she's only going to make sure Dylan doesn't cheat on her."

"Dylan's not the cheating type," I say, keeping my temper in check. "That boy is loyal to a fault."

"You would know, wouldn't you?" Alora asks, wiggling her eyebrows, but I ignore her and finish getting myself together for our game.

The four of us step out of the locker room and head toward the field to line up for warm-ups. The scorching August sun beats down on us relentlessly, its rays intensifying the humidity, while the weight of our football equipment adds to the heaviness of the air.

The opposing team arrives moments after we start warm-ups, and I can't help but take in their sizes. They're massive—towering figures in their pads, shoulders broad enough to block out the sun. I look over at Hollis and Corrine, our smallest players, and dread consumes me at how they'll fare against these giants.

"Jesus," Alora whispers behind me as we wait our turn. "Being on the field versus sitting in the stands brings on a whole new perspective."

"Yeah, I'll say. But we can still take them on ... right?" My nerves start to settle in, and for the first time, I catch myself wondering—why am I even doing this?

To prove a point to yourself and your mother that curvy girls can do anything. *Right.*

After we get through warm-ups, Coach calls us together to give us a pregame pep talk before we break on "Eagles!" Since we are scrimmaging, we skip the kickoff, and the Commanders allow our offense to go first.

The whistle blows, signaling the start of the game. Dylan makes a pass, and Hollis manages to break her defender, catching the ball to secure a first down.

"Yes!" Alora and I shout, high-fiving each other.

On the next play, Dylan hands the ball off to Corrine, who slips through a gap in the offensive line, sprinting twenty yards before stepping out of bounds in time to avoid a massive Commander defender closing in on her, who clearly held back when he was too close. Something their coach notices as well, as he yells at the defender to make the tackle, regardless of if the offensive player is a girl or not.

As the offense lines up again, I notice Hollis is verbally sparring with their opposing team's cornerback and have no doubt she's giving him hell too. The ball gets snapped, and Dylan launches it down the field. As it flies in the air, Hollis keeps track of it. The cornerback is right on her heels and nearly comes close to intercepting it as Hollis gets her hands on it and takes off down the field to score the first touchdown! Alora and I squeal, jumping up and down while everyone on our sideline erupts in cheers and whistles.

I don't think I've ever been so pumped up like this in my life.

"Alright, defense, let's go!" Coach Wells shouts. I pull my helmet on and jog out to the twenty-five-yard line.

"Maisie, be sure to cover number eighty-nine," Jeremiah informs me. I nod and line myself directly across from the tight end.

"If it isn't my lucky day. I get covered by a pretty girl," the titan of a football player says, giving me a wink.

"Too bad she's fat," his teammate beside him snarks, grinning like he just dropped the best line of the century.

"Dude!" Mr. Eighty-Nine says, offended on my behalf.

I wave him off. "Don't sweat it," I reply, throwing a smirk their way. "I'll just use my 'fat ass' to knock your buddy flat on his—don't worry, I've got plenty of cushion for the pushin'."

The whistle blows, and the Commander's quarterback shouts, "Red forty-two! Red forty-two! Hike!"

The center snaps the ball, and I immediately charge forward, eyes locked on the quarterback. He drops back, scanning the field for an open receiver. Number eighty-nine tries to block me, but I use my weight to my advantage, pushing him back a few steps before breaking through.

Just as the quarterback is about to throw, I burst through the offensive line. He sees me coming and tries to scramble away, but I'm faster than I look. With all my strength, I drive my shoulder into his midsection, taking him down hard for a sack.

The whistle blows, and I hear my teammates cheering from the sidelines. As I rise, I offer my hand to the quarterback, who takes it with a mix of surprise and begrudging respect.

"Nice hit," he admits, his tone laced with a hint of respect he clearly didn't expect to give.

"Thanks," I reply, a surge of pride flooding through me. I take a moment to let the victory settle in, then turn my gaze to the guy who made the fat comment earlier. He's standing there, still looking smug, but I don't let him off the hook. "How's that for fat?"

For the next hour, we continue to scrimmage, trading possessions back and forth. Our offense scores two more touchdowns and two field goals. The Commanders fought hard as hell, almost making a comeback, but we held our own.

By the time Coach Watson blows the final whistle, we've won the game twenty-seven to twenty-four. I'm exhausted but exhilarated. If this is what it feels like to be part of something bigger than yourself, to contribute to a team's success, then I understand why Dylan loves this sport so much.

As we head back to the locker room, I can't help but feel a sense of accomplishment. Not just for proving to myself that I could do this, but for showing everyone else too. My size doesn't define what I'm capable of—if anything, it's become an advantage.

"You were incredible out there, Maisie!" Alora exclaims, bumping her shoulder against mine. "That sack in the first quarter? Chef's kiss!"

"Thanks." I laugh, pulling off my helmet and shaking out my sweat-soaked hair. "You weren't so bad yourself. That interception was sick."

"The look on that quarterback's face when he realized a girl picked him off?" Hollis grins. "Priceless."

After we hit the showers and change back into our regular clothes, I can't help but notice how good it feels to be celebrated for my physical abilities rather than criticized for my appearance. If only my mom could have been here to witness it.

"So, are you still coming to the bonfire tonight?" Alora asks as we gather our things.

I hesitate, thinking about seeing Dylan and Charmaine, but to hell with them. I deserve to have some fun and celebrate today's victory with my teammates.

"You can count me in." I loop my arm through hers, and we head out to meet Josie in the parking lot. "Let's go get ourselves all dolled up for tonight."

And make Dylan Myers eat his heart out while we're at it.

# Chapter 12

## Dylan

Winning our game against Winfield today was the confident boost I needed. Not only did our team work like a well-oiled machine, but I proved to my coaches they could trust me to get the job done.

With Maisie's faith in me and her words replaying in my mind, I pushed through the anxiety and performed with the confidence of a quarterback determined to win and take us to the state championship game for a second year.

Maisie did amazing in her first football game, even if it was just practice. She, along with all the girls on the team, came to play, and it showed on the field. Corrine racking up the yards, Hollis scoring a touchdown, Alora with that interception that led to the winning score—then seeing my girl make tackles and even get a sack on her very first play? The energy was unreal.

Yesterday's almost-kiss flashes in my mind for the thousandth time since it happened, and I'm overcome with guilt once again. I'm not sure if I crossed a line, but I feel like the biggest jackass for not reaching out to her so we could talk about it after practice ended. I meant to, but then Charmaine bullied me into being her boyfriend again.

She wants me to be her man? Fine. I'll play along—as long as she keeps her promise to get me that letter of recommendation from her dad. But until then, I need to find something on her, anything that gives me leverage to keep her from messing with my chances at Harvard. The moment I have that letter in hand, I'm done with her. No way in hell am I sticking around, faking this until graduation.

"Dylan! Your friends are here!" my mother shouts from downstairs.

"Coming!"

My eyes are drawn to look out at *her* window, hoping to get a glimpse of her, but I'm disappointed to find her curtains closed. I know she's in there; I can see her bedroom light peeking through. I'm tempted to text her and ask if she's still planning to go, but I don't know what good that will do. If she was avoiding me today, I clearly upset her, and that's the last thing I ever want to do.

Ensuring I have my wallet and keys, I head downstairs to greet the guys.

"Well, it's about time!" Zion exclaims. "You don't need to make yourself any prettier."

"Whatever, dude." I chuckle. "You guys ready?"

"Yes. And starving! Please tell me we're getting food first," Chase whines.

"Don't worry, buddy. We're feeding you first," Kai reassures him.

I give my mom a tight hug. "Bye, Mom. I'll be back later," I say, planting a kiss on her cheek.

My friends "Aww" in unison, but I don't care. If there's one thing having a brother in the military has taught me, it's to never take time with your loved ones for granted.

"You boys behave, ya hear? Don't do anything that'll have Mr. Myers billing your parents for legal services!" my mom calls out with a grin, half-teasing, half-serious.

"We promise to be on our bestest behavior." Zion bats his eyes, as if he is so angelic.

We pile into my car and head out for the night. The weather is warm, the moon is bright, and I can't wait to let loose and have some fun.

We finally roll into Lake Seraphine two hours later, and it's exactly the kind of fun we needed. The bonfire pits are crackling, the bass from the hip-hop blaring is vibrating through the air, and Bellwood juniors and seniors are scattered all over the beach, laughing and chatting, making the whole place feel alive.

The guys and I weave through the crowd, searching for a spot to claim as our own and kick back.

"Yo! Myers!" someone shouts, and I turn to see Brandon Wallace, our left tackle, sitting on his truck bed. "You're welcome to chill here."

"Thanks, man."

"No problem. I've got a cooler filled with water and soda, and another one with snacks. If you want to drink, your best bet is hitting up Ronnie and Tristan. Think one of them managed to get a keg."

"Ronnie's probably got the keg. His older brother's known for getting his hands on a couple. Who wants to go?" Chase asks.

"Not me, man. I'm the designated driver tonight," I state. No way am I risking my car, my friends' lives, or anyone else's. The last thing I need is a DUI on my record and Harvard finding out. There's no room for mistakes when it comes to my future.

"I'll go with you, bro," Kai says, following Chase to hunt down the keg while Zion stays behind with me.

Zion grabs a Pepsi from the cooler and takes a seat on the truck bed. "So ... you went back to Charmaine?"

"Here we go," I mutter.

I knew this question was coming. The moment Zion saw the post, he started blowing up my phone. But my head's been buried in the scrimmage, and truthfully...I've been avoiding him. Not because I don't owe him an explanation—I do. I just didn't know how to give it. Between that and Charmaine glued to my side at lunch, I haven't had a second to face the conversation I've been dreading with my friend.

"Yeah, here we go. Because what the fuck, man?"

"Listen, Z. I know, okay? But the truth is..." I lower my voice, glancing around to make sure no one's close enough to overhear. "It wasn't exactly my choice."

Zion leans back like I've just spoken a different language. "Da fuck are you talking about?" His brows knit together, disbelief etched across his face. "You *chose* to take her back, Dylan. You *chose* to update your relationship status. And you sure as hell *chose* to let her hang all over you at school like it meant something. So forgive me if I'm struggling to see how any of that wasn't your decision."

"Because I didn't *want* to!" The words come out harder than I mean them to, frustration bleeding through. "I'm being blackmailed into this relationship."

Zion blinks. "What?" His voice drops, more stunned than angry now. "How the hell are you being blackmailed? By *Charmaine*? What could she possibly have on you?"

I take a step closer, my voice barely above a whisper. "It's not what she has *on* me—it's what she can *do* for me." I pause, jaw clenched, swallowing the knot of shame in my throat. "Her dad's tight with Harvard's admissions guy—like, inner circle close. She promised he'd write me a glowing recommendation and pull strings to get me in." I look away for a second, hating how the words taste coming out. "But only if I agreed to play along. Date her. Publicly. Until graduation."

Zion stares at me like I've just confessed to selling my soul. "So she's holding your future hostage."

I nod once, the weight of it settling heavy in my chest. "And if I don't play nice? She pulls the offer, tanks any chance I have of getting in. She knows exactly what she's doing."

"Are you fucking for real?" he says, eyes wide. "So you're telling me that you basically sold your soul to the she-devil on the premise of being guaranteed entry to the college you're set on attending?"

"Precisely what I'm saying." I drag my hands down my face. "You want to hear something else that's gonna make your head spin?"

"Sweet baby Jesus. Tell me you didn't knock her up?"

"What? God, no!" A cold shiver runs down my spine. Charmaine made several attempts in our relationship to have sex with me, but I could never go through with it, thanks to my anxiety.

*Or could there have been another reason why you couldn't go through with it?*

"I almost kissed Maisie yesterday," I blurt out, hoping like hell no one heard me. Zion does some little robotic dance as he faces me.

"I beg your pardon. Did I just hear you say you almost kissed Maisie?"

I simply nod.

"The Maisie... with the red hair, eyes that shift colors, lives next door to you, with that delectable, curvaceous figure that could make any grown man weep?"

"Watch how you talk about her," I snarl, stepping into Zion's space. Who the hell does he think he is, speaking about her like that?

Zion raises his hands in mock surrender. "Hey, I'm not trying to claim her like that. But that reaction? That's exactly what I was hoping for." His grin spreads across his face. "You just proved it, man. You care about her as more than a friend, and you can't deny it. Just accept it."

Damn it. He's right. Hearing him talk about my Freckles like that—like she's up for grabs—has me seeing red. The jealousy that flared when Tristan was talking to her, making her laugh? Guess I'm no longer in the "just friends" zone. Somewhere along the way, I crossed that invisible line, and it stings more than I expected.

"So why didn't it happen?"

"What?"

"With, you know …" He looks around before whispering, "The kiss."

"Oh. The bell rang just as we were about to. But I don't know if she feels the same way about me. As soon as the bell broke the bubble we were in, she kind of freaked out and left rather quickly. What if this is all one-sided?"

"Oh, it's been one-sided. On her side."

"How can you be so sure?"

"I'm not blind, dude. I've seen the way that girl looks at you from across the cafeteria when she thinks no one notices."

"Let's say you're right."

"But I am right."

"Hypothetically speaking—"

"There is no hypothetically, theoretically, hyperbole … whatever. I am without a shadow of a doubt certain that girl wants you!"

"Then how come she's never told me?"

Zion gives me his "are you stupid" face. "Could it be, oh, I don't know, for the same reasons you won't admit your feelings for her?"

Could Maisie be harboring feelings far stronger than friendship, afraid to explore where things could go, scared that it might not work out and risk ruining what we already have? Does she, too, feel like she'd be lost in a world where we couldn't be around each other anymore?

"Holy. Fucking. Smoke. Show." Zion lets out a low whistle, repeatedly smacking my shoulder.

"Dude, what?" He grabs my shoulders and turns me around, moving my face to show me what, and fucking smoke show is right.

Maisie arrives with Alora and Mirko by her side, radiating confidence in an outfit that turns heads. She's wearing a white lace top that complements her figure, the tops of her breasts on display, making me want to bury my face between them. She's paired the top with light-colored frayed denim shorts, her legs exposed to the evening summer air. Her fiery-red hair is styled in a half updo, the waves cascading down her back. She looks effortlessly stunning, and all eyes are naturally drawn to her.

Including Tristan's.

As soon as he spots her, he makes his way toward her, eyeing her like she's some tasty meal and he's a starved man who can't wait to devour her.

"Like fucking hell, Kelby," I growl out. I'm about to go to her when arms snake their way around my midsection.

"There you are, Pookie Bear. Did you miss me?"

Not in the slightest. Every fiber of my being is screaming to walk away, but I don't.

"Well ... this night just got a whole lot more interesting," Zion says from somewhere behind me, his voice laced with amusement but edged with something else.

Indeed, it fucking has.

# Maisie

"You sure it's not too much?" I study my reflection in my mirror, taking in my outfit. I absolutely love it, but I'm worried my boobs may pop out of the top. The top makes them look extra ... voluptuous.

Mirko walks around me, inspecting me for any imperfections. "You look so fucking hot, every single guy is going to be salivating when they see you. Dylan included."

"I still can't believe he got back with her," Alora sneers.

"Listen, can we not make tonight about Dylan? For whatever reasons we don't know, clearly Charmaine's the girl he can't let go, and it's just something I got to accept." Just wish my heart would get on board with it. "Tonight is about having some fun and savoring every moment we have together before graduation."

"Couldn't agree more. Now, can we please go? Andrew has already texted me like a hundred times asking where we're at."

"Yeah, yeah. Tell him we're coming. We just got to drop Josie off to her friend's house on the way."

It's a Friday night, which means my mother is going out again. I'm not sure if it's with that Richard creep or someone new, but since I decided to go to the bonfire party, I needed to ensure Josie had somewhere to go, just in case. She begged to come with us, and I told her sure, but she would be wearing one of those children's leashes because no way in hell was I letting her out of my sight. She relented and packed an overnight bag for McKenzie's. I don't trust these upper-class boys, and no way in hell would they be getting within five feet of her.

Once we arrived at Lake Seraphine, we made our way to the beach. Alora brought a beach bag packed with a blanket for us to sit on and a few mini liquor bottles she swiped from her older cousin. She's been trying to get me to take a shot since I usually avoid the party scene. Mostly because I knew Dylan and Charmaine would be there, and honestly, my heart can only handle seeing the two of them together during school hours.

Mirko went off to search for his boyfriend while Alora and I found a spot on the beach close to an unoccupied fire pit to set up our spot. Some classmates are mingling, deep in conversations, and others are snuggled up with somebody, making out.

"We should find you someone to make out with," Alora says, bringing my attention back to her. "You know what? We should make a list for you to check off!" Her eyes go wide with excitement.

"I don't know, Lor. This is a first for me, and I think I just want to keep it chill."

"C'mon! You need to have some fun for once in your life." She reaches in her bag and pulls out two mini bottles with a red cap and a demon breathing fire. "Here. Take a shot with me."

"Fireball? Does that mean it's spicy?"

"More like that cinnamon gum we had when we were kids." She raises her bottle to mine for a toast. "To trying new things!"

We clink our bottles together, then guzzle them down in seconds. The bold, spicy flavor with a sweet cinnamon kick burns on the way down, and I cough slightly, wincing. It doesn't go down smoothly—probably because of my little experience with alcohol.

"Gah," I manage, wiping my mouth with the back of my hand. "I'm not sure I'm cut out for drinking."

"Liquor's better when it's mixed with something. Maybe we can find someone who brought mixers," Alora says, rising to her feet and scanning the crowd for... something. Then her tone shifts, playful and alert."Oh, Maisie. It seems you've caught the attention of Tristan; he's heading right in our direction."

"Evening ladies," he says, with his charming smile on full display. "I'm so happy you could join us tonight." He peruses my body, the weight of his gaze making me shift uncomfortably, a slight knot tightening in my stomach.

Alora must sense my discomfort. "Tristan! Where might we be able to find something to mix with our liquor shots? Maisie, here, is in need of a cocktail."

"Brandon brought a cooler with sodas. I can take you both to him." He reaches his hand out to me, offering to help me up, and I accept it, only Tristan doesn't let go. With his fingers interlocked with mine, he leads us to a black truck, its tailgate down, with a few people hanging around.

I nearly stop in my tracks when I see Dylan sitting on the truck bed with his arm wrapped around Charmaine, and her claws clinging to his skin.

Charmaine's eyes light up when she sees Tristan approaching, but the moment she notices me standing beside him, they darken into a scowl.

Huh. That is ... interesting.

Her scowl deepens, and her lips curl into a devilish grin, a wicked thought clearly crossing her mind. The harshness of her expression shifts into something more mischievous, almost as if she were savoring the chance to cause trouble.

Charmaine shifts, turning to face Dylan as he talks with Zion. Without warning, she grabs his face, pulls him in, and kisses him—slow, deep, and possessive. A statement.

For one breathless second, I expect him to pull away. To flinch. To do *something*.

But he doesn't.

He lets her kiss him.

The air leaves my lungs. My chest tightens, heavy and hollow all at once.

He's not fighting it. He's letting it happen.

And somehow, that hurts more than I thought it would.

Maybe they were always meant for each other.

I need to accept that and move on—to focus on *my* life and make the most of it.

And that starts now.

# Chapter 13

## Dylan

I'm caught off guard when Charmaine yanks me toward her and starts kissing me. I try to pull away, but her nails dig into my skin with such force I wonder if she might actually break the surface.

When I'm finally free, I glare down at her, ready to go off on her for pulling that stunt, but her eyes keep darting to the side. I follow her gaze and see Alora, Tristan, and Maisie—her hand in Tristan's.

Does this mean they're together?

Maisie's brows furrow slightly, her eyes wide but clouded with confusion, as if she can't quite make sense of what's happening, and the hurt in her eyes cuts through me like a knife. I want to push Charmaine away and explain everything—that this isn't what it looks like, that I'm being blackmailed, but I can't risk everything I've worked for, not when Harvard is within my grasp.

"Hey, Brandon," Tristan calls out, breaking the tense silence. "The ladies were hoping to mix some drinks. You still have that cooler of soda?"

"Yeah, man. Help yourselves," Brandon says, gesturing to the blue cooler at his feet.

Maisie looks away from me, putting all her attention on Tristan as he leads her toward the cooler. She laughs at something he says, and the sound twists in my gut like barbed wire.

"What was that about?" I hiss at Charmaine once they're out of earshot.

"What?" she asks, batting her eyelashes. "Can't I kiss my boyfriend?"

"Not like that, no." I push her hands away from my chest. "We had an agreement."

"An agreement that you'd be my boyfriend," she states, her voice sickeningly sweet. "And boyfriends kiss their girlfriends, Dylan. If you want that letter from Daddy, you'd better start acting more convincing."

I glance over at Maisie again, my gaze lingering as Tristan mixes her a drink. His hand brushes against hers—and she doesn't pull away.

Something twists in my chest. She's smiling, relaxed, and letting him touch her like it's nothing. Like I didn't almost kiss her yesterday. Like none of it meant anything.

"Fine," I mutter, defeated. "But next time, give me some warning."

Charmaine's smile is victorious as she leans against me. "Of course, Pookie Bear. Anything for you."

"There you are!" Tessa approaches, slightly out of breath. "We need another person for the juniors versus seniors volleyball game. You in?"

"And miss out whipping their asses? Of course I'm in!" She turns to me, placing a kiss on my cheek, and I'm grateful it wasn't my lips. "Don't miss me too much."

"Not likely," I mutter under my breath.

Since I'm stuck playing the role of the doting boyfriend, I make sure to keep my eyes off Maisie throughout the night, but it's becoming more and more difficult.

I thought I'd caught a break when Tristan was called away by one of his friends, but that relief was short-lived. It felt like the green light went on for anyone who was single.

Every time a guy talked to her, I couldn't help but notice the way their eyes would drop, staring at her chest instead of appreciating the beauty in her eyes.

Watching her dance around the fire, carefree and full of energy, was intoxicating—until some guy with half a brain thought it was his turn to move in. The way she placed her hands on him and the way they moved together, had me wanting to march over there and knock his lights out.

"Dude, you need to chill," Zion whispers, noticing my death grip on my water bottle. "Your girl's just having fun."

"She's not my girl," I remind him, and myself, the words bitter on my tongue.

"Not with that attitude, she's not," he counters. "Look, I get you're in a tough spot with Charmaine, but the truth? You can't expect Maisie to wait around while you figure your shit out."

He's right, and I hate that he is. I have no claim on Maisie, no reason to feel jealous. But that doesn't stop the fiery knot forming in my chest when Tristan comes back.

I can't tear my eyes away as they take a seat by the fire pit, watching them like a predator eyeing his prey.

Maisie's on her second, maybe third drink now. Her cheeks are flushed, her hair glowing like fire in the light of the flames. She's laughing more freely, and I hate that I'm not the one making her laugh. Then again, maybe it's the alcohol talking, because Tristan isn't that funny. A small smile tugs at my lips.

The evening wears on, and I'm caught in my own personal hell, forced to watch Maisie and Tristan grow closer by the minute while playing the part of Charmaine's boyfriend. When Charmaine returns from her volleyball game, she makes sure to put on a show in front of others, draping herself over me, planting kisses on my cheek, whispering things in my ear that make me want to recoil.

I'm about to make an excuse to leave when I see Tristan lean in toward Maisie, his intention clear. My heart stops as his lips meet hers, and for one excruciating moment, I think she's going to kiss him back, but then she pulls away, shaking her head and saying something I can't hear from where I'm standing.

Relief floods through me, but it's brief. Tristan doesn't seem deterred, his hand coming up to cup her face as he tries again. This time, Maisie places her palm firmly on his chest, pushing him back.

"I think she said no," I mutter under my breath, my fists clenching at my sides.

"What was that?" Charmaine asks. She follows my gaze to where Maisie stands, clearly trying to create some distance between herself and Tristan.

"Nothing," I say, tearing my eyes away. "How was volleyball?"

"We won, obviously," she preens, already shifting her attention elsewhere. "Is that Tristan making a move on Porkenstein? God, you'd think he would set better standards since he's turned into a hottie." She laughs, joined by her snobbish friends.

"That's enough!" I snap, my voice sharp with fury.

Charmaine's eyes narrow. "Excuse me?"

"I can't stand you talking about Maisie like that. You have no right to tear her down just because you think it makes you feel better about yourself."

"Whatever." Charmaine scoffs, but I can see the edge in her eyes. "I'm going to get a drink. Want anything?"

"I'm fine," I state, my gaze drifting back to Maisie. She's walking away from Tristan, her steps a little unsteady as she makes her way toward the water's edge.

The moment Charmaine is out of sight, I slip away from the group, following Maisie at a distance. I shouldn't, but I can't help myself. I need to make sure she's okay.

She stops at the shoreline, her arms wrapped around herself as she stares out at the dark water. In the moonlight, her fiery hair loses its burn, dimming to something softer as it dances around her in a cascade of quiet flame. Her freckles seem to glow, like constellations mapped across her skin. My breath catches in my throat, captivated by the sight of her.

"You all right, Freckles?"

"Mm-hm." It's a quiet response, barely audible.

That wasn't quite an answer.

"You're staring at the water like it holds all the answers to life's greatest mysteries," I murmur, stepping closer to stand beside her.

"Maybe it does." She shrugs, her voice distant.

"A penny for your thoughts?" I ask, just wanting her to be open with me.

We stand in silence, the laughter and music from the bonfire fading away, being replaced by the soft rhythm of waves lapping against the shore. The night air is warm, but a gentle breeze carries a coolness that offers a welcome relief from the heat.

"Why did you do it?" she asks, her voice quiet but steady.

"Do what, Freckles?"

"Get back with Charmaine." Her gaze locks with mine, searching, unblinking. "I thought you were completely done with her."

I swallow hard, the truth choking me. How do I explain this without sounding pathetic? Without exposing how desperate I am for that Harvard acceptance?

"It's complicated," I say, fully aware it's a cop-out.

"That's not an answer, Dylan."

"I know, Freckles. But it's the only one I've got." I shove my hands into my pockets, resisting the urge to reach for her, to tell her everything.

Her tongue darts out, wetting her lips. "So after twelve years of friendship, of being open with each other, you can't be honest with me about this?"

Before I can even respond, Zion rushes over, followed by a few guys from the team, cutting through the moment.

"Sorry to interrupt," he says, trying to catch his breath. "But we need you two." He slaps a hand on my shoulder, still trying to steady his breathing.

"What's the problem?" Maisie asks, her voice sharp with worry.

"Trey ... and some guy ... are fighting over Anthony's sister," he explains, struggling to catch his breath.

"Lead the way," I state, Maisie and I following close behind. "Is Anthony here?"

"I'm not sure," says Kai. "I haven't seen him."

We follow Zion up the beach, toward the break in the tree line. A narrow path leads to a cluster of cabins people can rent out if they want to escape the noise.

No sooner do we cross the tree line than we spot the two guys rolling on the ground, fists flying. Alora is trying to pull Trey off the other guy, but Trey smacks her, sending her crashing to the ground. That's when my teammates completely lose it.

Kai charges straight at Trey, tackling him to the ground. Zion's right there, helping hold him down while Chase grabs Trey by the shirt and locks his arms behind his back. Trey's not going anywhere with Chase in control—Chase is a stocky country boy, and there's no breaking that grip. Brandon manages to take down the other guy.

Maisie rushes to Alora's side, her voice full of concern. "Alora, are you okay?" She checks her over quickly, looking for any sign of injury.

"Yeah, yeah. I'm fine," Alora groans, wincing as she gets to her feet.

As Brandon helps the unfamiliar guy to his feet, he suddenly charges at Trey. "I oughta rip your fucking arms off!" he growls, his voice low and threatening.

"Whoa, easy there, killer!" Zion holds his hands out, doing his best to block Trey from his sight. "We have some questions that need answering. For starters, who the hell are you?"

"I'm—"

"LJ McAlister," Anthony snarls, stepping out of a cabin with a girl on his arm, his eyes burning with hatred.

Alora rushes over, quickly positioning herself between her brother and LJ. "Anthony! Anthony, stop. You need to listen to me."

"You need to leave. Right. Now," he snaps at his twin, but Alora stands her ground.

"No! Not until you hear me out!"

"I'd listen to your sister, Lewis," LJ says, but his words seem to set Anthony off even more.

"How about I come over there and whoop your motherfucking ass!" He makes a move, but Maisie steps right in front of him, one hand firmly gripping his face while the other jabs a finger toward him, warning him to back off.

"You need to calm the hell down so we can figure out what happened here. I am not above embarrassing you in front of your boys. I will sit my entire ass right on top of you—and trust me, it won't be fun. Do I make myself clear?"

That shuts Anthony up real quick.

"Yes, ma'am."

She gives the side of his face a light tap. "Good boy."

The way she whispers it—low and smug—paired with the mental image of her straddling me? Yeah, let's just say my body has a mind of its own.

Fuck. Now's not the time or the place for this.

Trying to shake off the thought, I remind myself I need to handle this situation the right way before things get out of hand. The last thing we need is for the cops to get involved.

"Alora, can you tell us what happened?" I ask, keeping my voice even and composed—trying to steady the moment, like a captain pulling his team back in line.

"Trey and I were talking. Things got out of hand, and he got in my face before pushing me," she says, her voice trembling for a moment before she steadies it. "LJ saw it happen and stepped in. He wasn't trying to start a fight—he was just defending me."

She turns to her brother, her eyes blazing with frustration. "You don't get to be angry at him for protecting me when you weren't even here."

Anthony's expression hardens, and for a split second, his shoulders slump in a way that betrays his guilt.

"This true, Trey?" I ask, my voice calm but sharp, watching him closely for any sign of hesitation or lies. He refuses to answer, his silence speaking volumes.

"With his record and history with my sister, I'd believe it," Anthony growls, clearly fuming. "What I don't get is why McAlister is out here. You're a long way from your gated community, rich boy."

"Not something you need to worry about, Lewis," LJ shoots back, his tone biting as he straightens. "Just be thankful I stopped things from getting worse." With that, he turns and strides off toward one of the cabins, leaving behind a trail of tension thick enough to cut through.

"What should we do about Trey?" Brandon asks, his eyes flicking between me and the rest of the group.

I take a deep breath, looking over at the chaotic scene before me. The air feels heavy, and I know it's up to us to handle it.

"See to it that he leaves this party. I don't care how, just make it happen." My voice is firm with no room for debate.

Without a word, Kai and Chase exchange a look, both understanding what needs to be done. Brandon's face hardens with determination, and he steps toward Trey, his long strides purposeful. Chase follows suit, moving quickly to make sure no one else tries to escalate things.

The rest of the team huddles together, ready to back each other up, the unspoken agreement clear: no one messes with the team, and no one threatens Maisie or her friends.

As Brandon reaches Trey, I see the tension in the air—no words spoken, just the heavy expectation that Trey knows exactly why he's being escorted out. The team moves like a well-oiled machine, making sure Trey leaves without further incident, the night's drama slowly being quelled by the collective power of the group.

Exhaling, I feel the weight lift just a little. For now, the situation's under control.

I walk over to where Maisie is comforting Alora. "Are you sure you're okay? Do you want me to talk to my dad about a restraining order?"

"No! Please don't," Alora replies quickly. "Things just got a little out of hand. Honestly, I'm just ready to call it a night."

Maisie wraps a protective arm around her friend. "Okay. Let's get your stuff, and I'll take us home."

"Whoa! Hold on, Freckles. I need you to hand me your keys."

"What? Why?" she asks, brow furrowed, a hint of annoyance and confusion in her voice.

"You've had a few drinks, and I don't feel comfortable with you driving."

"Oh. Right," she says, confirming my suspicion that she's not in any condition to drive back to Bellwood.

"Do you have a designated driver?"

"Well—"

"Actually, forget that I asked. I'm taking you both home."

"But what about your car?"

"Z!" I shout.

Turning from his conversation with Anthony, I toss Zion my car keys. "Can you drive my car back to my place? I'm driving Maisie and Alora home."

"I've gotchu."

I follow the girls back to the beach to grab their belongings, relieved when we don't run into Tristan. As for Charmaine, she's the least of my concerns right now. My only priority is getting Maisie and Alora home safely and without any more drama.

# Chapter 14

**Dylan**

The drive back to Bellwood is heavy with silence, the kind that wraps around you like fog and refuses to let go. Only the low hum of the engine and the occasional, muffled sniffle from Alora break the stillness.

Maisie sits beside me, her arms folded tightly across her chest, eyes locked on the dark stretch of road ahead. She's been quiet since we left, but the tension in her jaw speaks volumes. In the back seat, Alora is curled up against the door, knees tucked to her chest, her face turned toward the window. She hasn't said much either, but the way her body trembles tells me she's still reeling from her ordeal.

"You okay back there?" I ask gently, catching Alora's reflection in the rearview mirror.

"Yeah," she whispers, her voice brittle and uncertain "Just... ready to be home."

I nod, understanding completely. "We'll be there soon."

It's not long before the familiar landmarks of Bellwood come into view. I keep glancing at Maisie, worry gnawing at me, but she just stares out into the night like she's trying to outrun her thoughts.

Finally, we pull up in front of Alora and Anthony's house. She unbuckles slowly, her movements sluggish.

"Thanks for everything, you guys," she says, her voice a little stronger now, but her eyes still glassy with unshed tears.

"No problem," I reply, offering her a slight nod.

"Text me, okay?" Maisie adds, her voice softer than usual.

We both watch as Alora walks up to the door, fumbling with her keys. I don't put the car in drive until I see her safely inside, the porch light casting a warm glow over the front steps as the door finally shuts behind her.

Only then do I exhale, the tension in my shoulders still far from gone. "Text her to lock her door."

"Was already ahead of you, Mr. Knight in shining armor." There's a hint of a smile. "Who knew you had such a hero complex."

"A what?" I ask, pulling away to take us home.

"In simple terms? It's a person's desire or need to help others, to solve their problems or rescue them at the expense of their own needs or boundaries."

"And you think that's me?" I ask, eyebrows lifting in surprise.

"Kind of," she mutters, that hint of a smile playing on her lips again.

It doesn't take long to reach our street, and the familiar sight of our neighborhood brings a sense of home. I shift the car into park, turn off the engine, and quickly make my way to Maisie's side. I help her out of the car, her steps a little unsteady, but she leans on me for support as we make our way toward her house.

Jinxy, Maisie's cat, greets us at the door, brushing her body against our legs before flipping on her back and exposing her soft belly.

I crouch down and give her some of the attention she's begging for when Maisie stumbles over the first step.

"You okay?"

"Yeah, yeah. Just a misstep," she assures me.

"Why don't I go with you and ensure you don't hurt yourself." I chuckle, following close behind her.

When we reach the landing, Maisie freezes, putting me on alert.

"What's wro—" I ask before I look past her to see an older gentleman standing in the hallway. Is that her dad? I've never really seen Mr. Jorgensen. Not even a picture. I remember asking her once when I was seven what he looked like, and she said her mom doesn't keep pictures of him anymore in the house.

When I catch him perusing Maisie like she's some heavenly dessert, I clear my throat, ensuring I'm loud enough to have his attention on me.

I step in front of Maisie, reaching my right hand behind me to find hers. Giving her fingers a reassuring squeeze, I guide her gently behind my back and to my left, wrapping my arm around her waist as I shift her to the other side.

I move us close to the other side of the hall, Maisie farthest from him as we head to her bedroom.

"You kids have fun" is all the pervert says before disappearing behind what I can only hope is Ms. Jorgensen's bedroom door.

As soon as we cross the threshold, I shut and lock the door, adding a sense of security to the quiet room. My eyes immediately go to Maisie sitting on the edge of her bed, her shoulders hunched as if she's trying to make herself smaller.

Instinctively, I go to her, kneeling before her, and force her to put those beautiful eyes on me. "I need you to look me in my eyes and be up front with me, Freckles. Can you do that?"

She nods, and I brace myself for the question I'm about to ask. "Has that man touched you, in any manner, that was inappropriate and made you uncomfortable?"

"No." A firm, strong no. A no I've never been more grateful to hear.

"Thank fuck," I let out, relieved to know I won't be catching a murder charge tonight. Harvard would never accept a murderer, but going to jail for killing a man who thought he could touch what's not his, for touching her, I'd do in a heartbeat and smile proudly for that mugshot.

"If he hasn't touched you, why did you freeze up like that? Do you know him?"

Maisie releases a shaky breath, clearly rattled by this man's presence.

"All I know is his name's Richard. He and my mom went on a date around the time of the carnival. Last time I saw him, I had no idea she'd brought him back here—she doesn't usually bring her dates home, at least not that I know of. But that morning in the kitchen... something felt off. The second he looked me up and down, like I was some lingerie model in a *Playboy* spread, every alarm in my body went off."

I clench and unclench my fists, two seconds from calling my father to alert the police and arrest this child predator, considering Maisie is still seventeen for another four days and there's another teenage girl who lives here who could also be in danger.

"Where's your sister?" My heart starts to race as a sinking feeling settles in my chest. Richard was in the hall, and I highly doubt he was using the bathroom in the hallway when there's one attached to her mother's bedroom. I move to stand up, intent on checking on her sister, but Maisie grabs me, pulling me back.

I fall on top of her, using my hands to brace myself to keep my weight off her.

"Sorry," Maisie whispers. "Josie is at a friend's house for the night. Dropped her off myself before we went to the lake. My mom always goes out on the weekend for dates, so I had to make sure Josie wasn't home alone."

Her eyes go wide, and her mouth begins to tremble. "Oh my God. What if I had let her stay home by herself? What if Mom didn't know and that sicko had—"

"Shh ... Deep breaths for me, Freckles," I whisper, and stroke her cheeks, alternating sides. "Deep breath in .... Good. Now out. Just like that ... you're doing so good."

## Maisie

If he calls me his good girl, Lord, you can come and take me.

Something must be wrong with me if I'm thinking about praise kinks while this man is soothing me down from a panic attack.

I'm grateful Dylan wanted to make sure I made it to my room okay. Had he not been with me, I'd hate to think what would have transpired, considering my mom can sleep like the dead.

"Thank you," I whisper, my voice barely audible as I glance up at him again, the sincerity in my words clear.

"For what?" Dylan's voice is soft. His face is so close to mine I can feel his warm breath against my skin.

"For being here. For looking out for me." I swallow, suddenly aware of our position—him hovering above me, my back against the mattress. "For always being my hero, even when you didn't need to be."

His eyes search mine, a storm of emotions swimming in those blue depths. "I'd do anything for you, Freckles."

The moment feels heavy, charged, and I wonder if he means more than just tonight, more than just this situation.

Before I can say anything, his hand slides from my cheek to the side of my neck, his thumb brushing against my skin. My pulse spikes, and I feel the weight of his presence in a way I didn't earlier. My body tenses slightly under his touch, but I can't look away.

"Will you stay with me?" I ask, my voice barely above a whisper, the words slipping out before I can stop them. As soon as I say them, I feel the heat rush to my face, and I shut my eyes, wishing I can take it back.

God, that must've sounded desperate. "I mean … with Richard still here, I'd feel safer if you were with me, you know, just in case. If that's okay?"

There's a pause, and I feel the weight of his eyes on me. Dylan seems to think it over for a moment, the silence stretching between us. My heart thunders as I await his response, unsure of what to expect.

"We should probably get some sleep," Dylan says, his voice a little quieter than before. He pushes himself up and away from me, and the absence of his warmth creates a hollow feeling in my chest.

He glances toward my door, his jaw tightening. "Had you not asked, I probably would have suggested it. I didn't like the idea of leaving you here with that guy still in the house."

A wave of relief washes over me at the weight of his words. Whether he really cares about me or he's just being protective, it feels like a lifeline.

He pulls his phone, wallet, and my keys from his pockets and places them on my bedside table with quiet precision. His eyes stay locked on mine, his gaze steady as he casually removes his shirt, revealing his sculpted abs, each muscle defined and hard under the soft glow of the room's light. My breath hitches, my eyes lingering for a moment longer than I intended.

I quickly avert my gaze, trying to focus on anything else in the room. The tension between us is palpable, electric in a way I've never experienced before.

His fingers gently grab my chin, pulling my face to look at him. "Are you sure you want me to stay?"

I nod, unable to find my voice for a moment. "I'm sure."

He moves to the other side of the bed, sitting down on the edge. The mattress dips under his weight, and I feel myself sliding slightly toward him. My heart races as I realize we're about to share a bed—something we haven't done since we were kids building pillow forts in his living room.

"I should probably …" I gesture to my outfit, suddenly aware I'm still in my clothes.

"Right," Dylan says, quickly turning his back to give me privacy. "Let me know when you're done."

I slip off the bed and move to my dresser, pulling out an oversized T-shirt and sleep shorts. With shaky hands, I change as quickly as possible, hyperaware of Dylan's presence in my room.

"Okay," I whisper when I'm finished.

He turns back around, his eyes softening when he sees me in my sleep clothes. For a moment, we just look at each other, the air between us charged with something I can't quite name.

"Which side do you prefer?" he asks, breaking the silence.

"I usually sleep on the right."

Dylan nods and moves to the left side of the bed. He lies on top of the covers, maintaining a respectful distance. I slip under the blankets, my body tense with nervous energy.

The sound of his phone buzzing on my nightstand breaks the silence, the noise sharp in the quiet of the room. He reaches over to quiet it, his movements slow and deliberate. But before he can pull his hand back, I catch a glimpse of the screen, and Charmaine's name flashes in bold letters. My stomach twists, a knot forming in my chest.

"You should probably get that," I whisper, my voice barely audible.

"Nah. It's not that important."

My heart flips at him blowing Charmaine off. He turns on his side so he's facing me, his eyes soft but intense. "Maisie ..."

"Yes?"

"About what happened in the library yesterday ..."

My heart skips a beat. "What about it?"

"I ..." He stops, shaking his head slightly, as if the words are caught in his throat. "We never got the chance to talk about it, and I think we should. Actually, I know we should, but not tonight. Not after everything that happened." His voice softens at the end, like he's trying to reassure me, but the weight of his words lingers in the air.

I nod, trying to ignore the ache in my chest. "Sure. Another time." I force a smile, but it feels more like a mask than anything real.

Are we going to get to talk about it? Is he going to admit to nearly kissing me, or will he try to brush it off as a momentary lapse in judgment? The latter would hurt even more, and I'm not sure I'd be able to handle that pain.

I turn on my side, facing away from him, trying to calm my racing thoughts.

Just as I'm about to close my eyes, his hand touches my hair, smoothing it away from my face in a gesture so tender it makes my breath catch.

"Good night, Freckles," he murmurs, his voice low and gentle in the darkness.

"Good night, Dylan."

I close my eyes, listening to the sound of his breathing beside me. Despite everything—the party, Tristan's unwanted advances, Richard's creepy presence in my house—I feel safe with Dylan here. Protected.

As sleep begins to claim me, one thought spins relentlessly in my mind: How can I possibly be falling for someone who's chosen someone else?

# Chapter 15

## Maisie

I wake to the warmth of sunlight streaming through my window and the comforting weight of an arm draped across my waist. For a moment, I'm disoriented, my mind foggy with sleep. Then everything comes rushing back—the bonfire, Tristan's attempted kiss, Dylan bringing me home, Richard in the hallway ...

Dylan.

It takes me a moment to realize we've shifted during the night. No longer are we on opposite sides of the bed with space between us. Now we're wrapped up with my back pressed against his chest.

I should move, carefully extract myself from his embrace and pretend this never happened. It would be the smart decision to put some distance between us before this gets any more complicated. But a selfish part of me—the part that's crazy enough to want to move us past being friends into something more—can't bear to break this moment. I can't bring myself to shatter the illusion that, just for now, he's mine.

Closing my eyes, I allow myself to savor this—the feeling of being held by him, protected and cherished. For a few minutes, I can pretend this is what it would be like to wake up every morning, and when he opens his eyes, he'll smile at me like I'm his everything.

His arm holds me close while his steady breathing tickles the back of my neck, sending shivers down my spine. He nuzzles into my hair, my heart nearly stopping. Is he awake? Does he know he's holding me? Or is he dreaming of Charmaine?

The thought hits like ice water being dumped on me. I attempt to shift away, but his arm tenses, keeping me in place.

"Where are you going, Freckles?" His voice, rough with sleep, sends a shiver through me and directly to my core.

"Nowhere," I whisper, barely trusting my own voice. "Just … adjusting."

He makes a sound, something between a hum and a groan, and I feel the vibration of it against my back, along with something else. "You keep adjusting like that, we're going to have a problem."

The said problem is currently poking me in my ass, and suddenly, images of how I'd like to handle it sift through my mind.

"What time is it?" he mumbles, my mind coming back to the present.

I glance at the clock on my nightstand. "It's almost eight."

"It's too early on a Saturday," he mumbles again, his breath warm against my neck. "Go back to sleep."

"Aren't you the one who gets up at the butt crack of dawn to go running on the weekends?"

"During summer break, but since school's started, I allow myself to sleep in until nine on the weekends since I'm running before school starts."

"What time do you get up—"

"Ssshhh, Freckles. Back to sleep."

As if it were that simple. Like my heart isn't racing, my skin burning everywhere we touch, yet I don't move. I listen as his breathing evens out again, and  soon he's back to sleep.

"Dylan?"

I pause, waiting in the stillness to see if he responds. When he doesn't, I draw in a slow breath, trying to steady the tremble building in my chest.

"There's something I need to tell you—something I've wanted to say for a long time. I've just never had the courage to do it." My voice barely rises above a whisper. "Maybe it makes me a coward, saying this while you're asleep beside me. But I need to get it out, even if I never find the strength to say it to your face."

I roll over, studying his sleeping form, watching for any sign—a twitch, a shift, a change in his breathing—that might betray he's awake and listening.

Because if he is… if he's lying there pretending to sleep just to hear what I'll say, I don't think I could live that down. The embarrassment would swallow me whole.

"Lately, I've been struggling with our friendship dynamic, and I'm not sure if you've noticed. If you have, you're being a complete gentleman for not calling me out on it." I let out a lighthearted laugh before I continue with my confession.

"Over the past few years, I've grown to like you more than just as my friend. I've tried to fight these feelings off because I have no doubts this is all one-sided and you could never look at me as more than just your friend you grew up with. And who am I kidding? I'm no Charmaine. People would take one look at us and say how we don't fit together. I don't care about that, though, and I know you enough that you wouldn't be so vain either. But if you only love me as a friend and nothing more? I'd just have to accept that. Or try to, because the biggest thing I'm scared of most? These feelings will cost me you, and I don't think I can imagine my life where you're not in it. That would be my own personal version of hell."

Dylan murmurs something in his sleep, but I can't make out the words. Gently, I press a soft kiss to his forehead, then roll back over, letting his arm rest across me.

Closing my eyes, I let myself drift, savoring what might be my only chance to know what it feels like to be held by Dylan Myers.

A few hours later, I find the space beside me empty, the sheets cool to the touch. I wonder if I had dreamed the whole thing—Dylan staying over, holding me close—until I see a handwritten note sitting on top of the pillow.

***Hey Freckles. Didn't want to wake you, but I had to get home before my parents worried. I made sure to lock your bedroom door behind me just as a precaution. Text me when you wake up. -Dylan***

Reaching for my phone, I have multiple texts—the majority from Alora and Mirko—and one from Dylan.

Skipping over my friends, I go to reply to Dylan's first.

DYLAN

> Hey. Didn't want you to think I dipped out but I did leave a note. Text me when you wake up.

The fact that he not only took the time to leave a note but also texted reminds me that Dylan always makes an effort to show how much he cares when someone truly matters to him.

God, why do the good ones always get taken by people who don't deserve them?

I send him a quick text, letting him know I am awake, and thank him for staying with me and looking after me. I close out the text thread and open the group chat with Alora and Mirko.

MIRKO

What madness unfolded last night?

People are saying there was a fight by the cabins.

ALORA

Not up to talking about it.

MIRKO

Ok. Can I at least get the cliff notes version?

ALORA

Maisie got tipsy. Tristan was hitting on her. I snuck off with Trey, only to end up with Trey getting his ass kicked by someone my brother probably hates more than Trey. The guys from the team handled them. Dylan took Maisie and me home. That's the end.

MIRKO

Your brother hates someone more than Trey? I find that hard to believe.

ALORA

Yeah, well believe it.

MIRKO

I feel like there's a story to tell, but you're not going to share.

ALORA

You would be correct my friend.

Mase, Nonna wants to know if you can come in today to help with a bridal gown?

Looking at the time stamp, Alora's text message came through about ten minutes ago. It's only ten thirty. If I hurry, I can make it to the shop before eleven, giving me a little over an hour before Josie needs to be picked up from dance class.

I'll have to make sure I thank McKenzie's parents for helping with Josie.

MAISIE

Tell her I have to freshen up real quick and then I'll be on my way!

After unlocking my bedroom door, I peek my head into the hallway, listening for any indication there are others awake in the house. When I'm greeted by silence, I grab my chosen outfit and dart down the hall to the bathroom, locking the door behind me. I'm not taking chances if creepy Richard is still lurking around. I make quick work of brushing my teeth and handling my business, having to skip on my morning skincare routine. Throwing my hair into a messy bun, I'm as put together as I care to be. I rush back to my bedroom to toss my smoky clothes from last night's bonfire into the hamper. Ensuring I have everything I need—cell phone, keys, mini backpack—I haul myself down the stairs and out the door.

I make it to Thread & Thimble, an adorable seamstress shop on Main Street. It has a big front window with some of Nonna's handmade gowns displayed so shoppers can admire her handiwork.

"Nonna Cavalli, I'm here!" I call out, the bell chiming above the door as I enter.

"Ciao, Maisie!" She greets me with a warm hug and a kiss on each cheek. Nonna Cavalli is an elderly Italian woman with exceptional sewing skills, whereas I can't sew to save a life.

She opened this shop a few years ago when Alora and I were eleven-twelve years old. Being here, surrounded by all the fabrics and watching Nonna craft the most beautiful gowns from scratch, made her feel like a real-life Fairy Godmother—minus the magic and the wand. Maybe that's why so many of my sketches end up being dresses.

"I hope I'm not too late," I say.

"Not at all. I just had the bride-to-be put the dress back on so we could take a look together."

I follow her toward the back corner, passing all the beautiful gowns displayed on mannequins in the front of the shop, to the fitting room area. The bride-to-be is already waiting for us, looking incredibly beautiful in her dress. It's a white long-sleeved satin A-line dress. The sleeves have a lovely lace pattern going all the way around to her back, with a zipper hidden underneath a row of buttons along the spine.

"Wow...You look like an actual princess! I'm really loving that dress on you!"

"Really? You don't think it looks too bad?" the bride asks.

"Absolutely not!" I walk slowly around her, taking in every angle and detail of the dress. "However, I do think we can make it even better."

"What are you thinking, Rossa?" Nonna asks. I've come to learn that Rossa is Italian for redhead, befitting for me for obvious reasons, but I couldn't love the nickname more.

"Here's what I'm thinking. What if we keep the sweetheart neckline but remove the sleeves completely, from the neckline and along here." I point to the backside, just above the waistline, where it splits into a v. "We repurpose the lace from the sleeves and back area to sew them onto the sweep train in a teardrop sort of formation. It will give an elegant touch to the train and complement the bodice. Or! We could remove the sleeves and lace, create a leg slit in the front, and sew the lace designs along the slit."

"You think I should show some leg?" The bride seems a little insecure with the idea, which makes me sad to think someone made her feel that way. She may not be a size four or whatever society's appropriate number is, but she's a woman who should feel comfortable in her skin and own it.

"Hell yeah! Your hubby-to-be is marrying you for who you are, and clearly, he loves every single inch of you. Why not show a little leg? It would be like you're teasing him the good stuff, yet he can't do anything about it because you'll be surrounded by your loved ones. He's going to be so worked up and anxious to get you alone." I wiggle my eyebrows for emphasis.

For a moment, I think she's going to give in to the negative voice, the one in the back of your mind putting you down because in reality, bigger bodies are often considered lacking beauty. Mine comes in the voice of my mother.

Then I see the moment she takes back her inner voice, her smile shining big and bright. "Screw it! Let's do the damn slit!"

I squeal with joy. "It makes me so happy to hear you say that! You should never have to dim your light because of the opinions of others."

The bride tilts her head, confusion evident on her face. "You could tell?"

"I was there once, until I took back my power and started loving myself more. You can do it too. You just have to promise yourself to never allow anyone to make you feel less than."

"Thank you, Rossa."

"Oh, my name is actually Maisie. Nonna just likes to call me that."

"Well, then, thank you, Maisie. You have no idea how much I needed to hear those words. And I can't wait to see the dress once the changes are made."

"This is exactly why I needed your services today, Rossa," Nonna leans in to whisper. "Alright, Miss Penelope. Let's get you out of your dress.

We've got three months until the wedding to get all the alterations made and ensure the dress fits you perfectly."

After Penelope leaves the shop a happy and hopefully more confident woman, I sit with Nonna back in her sewing room, my sketch pad opened to the dress I'm designing for homecoming.

"Have you selected what kind of fabric you want? The colors?" Behind Nonna is a wall filled top to bottom with rolls of various fabrics in various colors.

"Not yet. I feel like I've barely had time to come see you with football practices."

"Why don't you go ahead and take a look. I'd like to get started on it soon with it being the middle of August. Homecoming is a little over a month away, and you know how crazy it gets around here."

"Please don't remind me." I chuckle, walking slowly past each roll, my hand dragging along, feeling every soft or smooth material.

Ten minutes later, I've made my selections. I'm going with a beautiful satin emerald-green fabric for the body of the dress. It'll be long, almost floor-length, with a sweetheart neckline and capped sleeves. Dark-green lace that looks like ivy leaves, with hints of glitter throughout, giving it a touch of sparkle, will go perfectly over the midsection and into the neckline. Wanting to add a little pop of color, I settled on gold beading, designed like leaves in a Greek crown. This will go along the waistline, accentuating my waist and giving me an hourglass figure.

Looking at everything laid out on the table, my homecoming dress is giving major Poison Ivy meets Greek goddess vibes—with flowing draped sleeves and, of course, there will be a dramatic front-left slit that will be impossible to ignore.

What can I say? I love a good slit.

# Chapter 16

## Maisie

Despite how it started, the weekend ended on a good note. I went back to Thread & Thimble on Sunday to design a few homecoming dresses with Nonna. Every dress in Thread & Thimble is custom-made, whether it's a bridal gown, homecoming dress, prom dress, or special occasion—you will never find the exact dress anywhere else. This is how Nonna makes her money, and with homecoming season around the corner, she needed some fresh ideas. As an early birthday gift, she said she wants to credit the designs by calling it her Rossa Cavalli line. To know I'll have teens in and around Bellwood wearing a dress I designed is a dream I don't want to wake up from. It's a small taste of how I envision my future when I graduate from design school, and I can't wait.

My alarm clock blares the most agitating sound invented on this planet, waking me from another erotic dream with Dylan. Only this time, it warped our snuggle sesh from Saturday morning into a triple-x-rated porno.

Nothing like being woken up early on your eighteenth birthday horny and annoyed because you have to go to school.

After a hot shower and usual morning routine, I grab the outfit I picked out while shopping with my mom on Saturday—a white off-the-shoulder, flare-sleeved shirt embellished with baby-blue butterflies. I've chosen to pair it with straight-fitted, distressed jeans and complete it with matching blue-and-white Nike Air Forces.

With my hair still damp, I part it down the middle and section off two small pieces at the front. Starting on one side, I take a section and French braid it, working the braid tightly along my scalp. Once I reach the end of the section, I gather the rest of my hair on that side and continue braiding it all the way down into a single, neat plait, securing it with a small elastic. I repeat the process on the other side, making sure both braids are even. Not only does this complete my look, but it will also hold up during football practice following school.

French braids are a football girl's best friend; at least if you ask my female teammates. It keeps your hair off your shoulders while allowing your helmet to fit more securely on your head.

By the time I get to school, I have to turn my cell phone off. My phone won't stop buzzing with notifications from social media posts and text messages from friends, family, and anyone else who knows me. It's unbelievable how many people thought to take a few moments out of their day to do something so kind.

At lunch, Alora brought me a homemade cupcake. She made me pretend the candle sitting on top was lit as she sang me "Happy Birthday." Her attempts to get Hollis to join in was like getting those soldiers at Buckingham Palace to move. I applauded her efforts though.

When the bell rings to dismiss us for the day, I make a quick stop at my locker to drop off my belongings before heading to the girls' locker room to change for practice. Just as I open the door, large hands block my vision as a broad body presses into my back.

"Guess who?" is whispered in my ear.

"Gee, I wonder. Could it be … Tristan?"

"Ding, ding. We have ourselves a winner!" he shouts in the hall, causing students to pause and look at him as if he has two heads.

After depositing my notebooks and folders inside, I turn around. "Winner, huh? Does that mean I get a prize?"

Tristan surprises me when he pulls a small black gift box out of his backpack, holding it in front of my face. "As a matter of fact, you do get a prize. Happy birthday, Red."

"Wait. You got me a birthday present?"

"You sound surprised."

"Well, I mean, yeah. I didn't think you knew my birthday, let alone would get me something." I shrug. "You know, after the bonfire party."

"I was in the wrong for that. I shouldn't have tried to kiss you, even when you said no. It was wrong of me, and I wasn't in the right headspace due to drinking. I'm extremely sorry if I made you uncomfortable, and I hope you can forgive me."

Make that two surprises from Tristan Kelby. "I appreciate you for being man enough to come to me and apologize for your behavior. It takes a real one to admit he was in the wrong." I flash him a sincere smile. "All is forgiven."

"Thank God!" He lets out a deep breath. "I don't want to rush you or come off rude, but do you think you can open your present? Because we do have this thing called practice to get to, or Coach Watson is going to make us do line drills. Not sure that is how you plan on spending your birthday."

God, I hate line drills with a passion. The first time Coach Watson made us do them because a few players were late to conditioning, I threw up in the trash can.

"I definitely do not," I say, shaking my head. Taking the box out of Tristan's hand, I slowly open it and gasp at what is inside.

Two bracelets are nestled in the red satin lining of the box. A gold bracelet with an intricate swirl design wrapping all the way around, dotted with tiny red and orange jewels, sparkles under the school's fluorescent lights.

"Oh, Tristan. Wow! This is absolutely stunning!"

"When I saw it, it made me think of you. Seeing you standing there in front of the flames Friday night, you looked like a fire goddess."

A shy smile tugs at my lips as warmth creeps up my cheeks. "You're being too kind, Mr. Kelby."

The other bracelet is more handmade, like the friendship bracelets Alora and I constantly made in fifth grade. Done in an array of colors of beads and letters, it takes me a moment to realize the bracelet is a message. "Will you be my girlfriend?" Tristan has his hands behind his back, looking adorably timid. "You made this to ask me out?"

"I may have had help from my eight-year-old niece who is a huge Swiftie."

"That's quite adorable—" One of our teammates darts past us, cutting the moment short.

"Fuck. We need to go," Tristan says. "Listen, Red, you don't need to answer me right now. I'd rather you take some time to think it over, to be sure of your answer. Just let me know when you have your answer. Okay?"

I give him a simple nod, grateful he's giving me the opportunity to decide what I want without adding any pressure. It shows he's willing to wait me out, and I have to say, it's an attractive quality.

When I make it to the locker room, I place the gift box on the shelf in my gym locker. I quickly change into my practice gear as fast as one can with football pads, praising myself for my hair choice at minimizing my prep time.

As I make my way toward the field, movement in my peripheral catches my attention, and Charmaine steps out from behind the bleachers, followed by—oh, God!

Dylan?

Ever since his status change on social media, it's been nagging me as to why he would go back to her after weeks of being happier without her.

Then the bonfire party? He mentioned it was complicated when I asked him. But the way he said it... something about it makes me think there's more he's keeping from me.

Charmaine makes quick adjustments to her outfit while Dylan fiddles with his practice pants, like a couple of teens who've just snuck off for a quickie behind the bleachers.

*Doesn't look so complicated to me.*

My heart sinks, bile rising in my throat. Reality hits me all at once, cold and sharp. I'll never be the girl he'll choose. Not like her. Not like the ones who always get picked. The pretty, perfect girl who gets the star player, like some cliché out of a bad teen movie.

Maybe the harsh things my mom always said about men—how they always favored more petite girls—and her constant criticism of my weight and size... perhaps it was just her messed-up way of trying to protect me. Protect my heart.

*Time to get a grip, Maisie, and move on from him.*

A whistle blows right as I make it to my spot on the field, calling practice to order. After warm-ups and drills, the coaches put offense against defense, in a scrimmage-like game. This is the best way to run through all our play calls in preparation for our first game on Friday against the Redland Devils.

I take my position on the field directly across from our offensive lineman Brandon, but my eyes are laser-focused on our quarterback. Memories of the past few weeks flash by—Charmaine and Dylan's kiss at the lake, their affection on display in the halls, then the scene of them emerging from the bleachers together. Each one hits me like a punch, and the sadness that stung in that moment slowly twists into raw anger.

Dylan starts the play.

"Ready?"

*You have no idea.*

Down."

*Oh, you will be.*

"Set."

I'm locked and loaded.

Hike!"

Brandon and I collide, his hands trying to reach up under my shoulder pads to hold me back. He does his best to keep me at the line of scrimmage, but it's no use. With all the anger and mixed emotions running through my veins, I break through and lock on my target. I charge at Dylan, who doesn't see me coming as he's about to make a pass.

I slam into him, taking him to the ground with force.

"Damn, Freckles," he coughs out. "Great hit, but next time, ease back. Will you?"

"I hate that fucking nickname," I snarl, pushing off him and going back to the line of scrimmage as Zion jogs over to give Dylan a hand up.

"Miss Jorgensen," Coach Wells calls, "excellent work getting past the line and making a sack. I want to see more of that come game time, but let's try not to take our quarterback out before the season starts. Okay?"

"Yes, Coach."

We line up again for the next play call. I watch the center's hands closely, waiting for him to snap the ball. As soon as he releases the ball to Dylan, I make my move. I outmaneuver Brandon, weaving past Hollis and Tristan, and tackle Dylan from the side.

He grunts as he's taken down. "Damn, Maisie. That one may have bruised a rib."

"Oh, I'm sorry! Let me try again," I snap, stepping back. "Next time, I'll make sure I bruise your heart instead!" I don't bother helping him up.

He jumps to his feet, closing the space between us. "What's going on with you? Did I do something to upset you, Freckles? Because if I did, just tell me and I'll fix it."

Seeing the desperation in his eyes, along with the worry and confusion, almost makes me sorry I'm taking my aggression out on him.

Almost.

"It's a bit … complicated." I shrug, using his words against him before I shoulder check him and take a seat on the bench for a water break.

Zion jogs over to join me on the bench. "I don't know about you, but that second hit looked a little personal. What did my homeboy do?"

"Correction. Both hits were personal," I inform him, taking another swig from my water bottle.

"Damn. So what you're saying is our boy really fucked up?"

"Your boy. Charmaine's boy." I turn to look Zion dead in his face. "He's no longer mine."

Grabbing my helmet, I jog back to the field, ending our conversation, ready to make some hits.

Two hours and several tackles later, it's time to hit the showers. Normally, I would take one in the locker room and put my street clothes back on, but tonight, the sooner I get home, the better. I quickly change into one of the few workout outfits I keep on hand when it's that time of the month and am out of the locker room before the other girls can finish changing.

As I near my car, fumbling with my fob to unlock it, I freeze when I spot a sparkly birthday gift bag resting on my windshield, accompanied by a small bouquet of pink and white calla lilies tucked into the car handle.

Only one person knows they are my favorite flowers, and if I had to guess, the gift bag is from him too.

I grab the gifts, set them on the passenger seat, and head home. The anger that consumed me during practice was left on the field, leaving behind a feeling of quiet numbness. After taking care of Jinxy, I place the bouquet in a clear vase and set it in the center of the dining room table before heading upstairs to shower off the sweat and weight of today.

Afterward, I grab my cell phone and favorite fuzzy blanket and snuggle up on my window seat. As soon as I power my phone on, notification after notification floods my feed.

"Maisie?" Josie calls me from my bedroom door. "Dylan's at the front door asking for you."

"Can you tell him I'm sleeping?" Josie's brows furrow, and I don't have the heart to explain why I'm avoiding him.

"Please?" I plead, hoping she'll do me this solid.

"Sure thing." She nods before disappearing down the hall.

I lean back, eyes to the ceiling as exhaustion slowly creeps in. Just as I close my eyes, my lap buzzes with an incoming alert … from Dylan.

Pressing the little white box, the text opens, and I read back through all his messages from today.

DYLAN

Happy Birthday, Freckles! *cake emoji*

You look so beautiful today.

I've left you a surprise. You'll see after practice ends. I hope you like it.

My body's sore. If I'm feeling it now, I can't imagine how I'll feel tomorrow. I may not be able to go for my early morning run. Lol

C'mon, Freckles. Please don't do this to me. I'm racking my brains at what I could have done for you to be upset with me.

What did Z mean when he talked to you? I'm no longer your boy? What does that even mean?

Talk to me. Plllleeeeassseee

Im leaving school now and when I get home, I'm coming over and we are going to talk.

Come to the door.

Maisie, please come to the door.

Just as I read the last text, a new message appears.

Doesn't look like you're sleeping to me.

Looking out my window and across the yard, I see Dylan standing in his, pointing to his phone. I watch his fingers tap away before I receive another notification.



I'm going to call and I want you to pick up.

Please :(

No sooner than the second text comes through does my phone start to ring. With a deep breath, I answer and brace myself for the confrontation.

"Hey birthday girl."

"Hey."

"Did you like your gifts?"

"The flowers are gorgeous."

"And what about the other one?"

"I haven't opened it yet."

"Oh ..."

Awkward silence fills the call, and I hate that this is where we are. Hate that I couldn't just simply be his friend and had to fall in love with the amazing guy he is. Dylan's always been the one to keep our friendship from tipping over into something else, something more. If I can't do the same, separate my love for him from our friendship, then I'm left with no choice but to do the only thing that might save me from this endless misery.

"What's on your mind, Freckles? I can tell you're in your head."

My throat tightens at his nickname for me, a nickname that had I been honest with him, do not detest. At first, I didn't care for it, but over the years, it grew on me until I found it endearing, his special name solely for me.

I swallow the golf-ball-sized lump in my throat, the weight of it choking me, and force myself to clear my voice. "We can't be friends anymore, Dylan."

"What?" he shouts into the phone. "N-n-no! You don't mean that. I refuse to believe you want to do that."

"I need you to believe it." Emotion tightens in my chest as I fight back the tears. "For me ... I need you to believe this is what's best."

"Best for who?"

I make the mistake of looking over, seeing the pain of what I'm doing to him in his blue eyes.

"I will always care about you, Dylan, but I just can't keep doing this," I whisper, my voice breaking. "Whatever this is between us, I have to let it go. I need to let it go."

His silence is suffocating, and I can almost hear the sound of his heart breaking alongside mine. I close my eyes, taking a shaky breath before adding, "I'm sorry, but this is the only way I can move forward."

And with that, I disconnect the call, the finality settling over me. Over us.

## Dyl

# Chapter 17

**Dylan**

I stare at her window, my phone still to my ear, willing her to open those damn curtains and smile at me. To call me back and tell me this was just some horrible birthday prank.

As seconds drag into minutes and she still doesn't reappear, I realize with a sinking feeling that she's ended our years-long friendship. The question that keeps swirling in my mind is ... why?

I think back to the party at the lake. Was she upset that we didn't hang out more? Charmaine had been suffocating me by being up my ass most of the night, and the last thing I wanted was for her to ruin Maisie's time. So I kept my distance, thinking it was the best for everyone.

Did I fuck up by not waking her up to tell her I was leaving when I snuck out of the house? I just couldn't risk getting caught sneaking back in and having my parents start asking questions about where I'd been all night.

Nothing about this makes sense, especially when I know who she is—my Maisie. My Maisie is understanding, patient, and forgiving. She's never been one to hold a grudge or act out of spite.

Something had to have changed between Friday night and football practice today. There was pain—heartache—in her voice. What happened? What could have made her throw away twelve years of friendship so easily?

My phone chimes, and I quickly check it, hoping it's a text from her, but I'm left disappointed when it's from Zion.

ZION

> Did you talk to her?

Zion agrees with me that something is going on with Maisie. Her behavior at practice was unlike her.

DYLAN

> No. She refused to come to the door. Her sister told me she was sleeping, but I didn't believe her. When I got to my room, I looked out my window and saw her sitting in hers. She's clearly avoiding me. I was able to get her to talk over the phone.

> She told me we couldn't be friends anymore and hung up.

ZION

> Damn, bro. It doesn't make sense. She would never do you like that.

The only other person I could ask is Mirko, but if she didn't say anything to Alora, then she probably didn't tell him either.







I go onto my profile and type Tristan's name in the search bar. As soon as his page loads, it's as if I was punched in the gut. Or sacked by Maisie for the tenth time today.

Tristan Kelby is In a Relationship with Maisie Jorgensen.

It was posted almost five minutes ago. Is he the reason she's cutting me out of her life? Does he know I secretly harbor feelings for her and is so threatened by me, he needed her to cut me out of the picture?

To hell with him. As if I'd let his punk ass believe he can come in and mess with our dynamic. With her. She's mine and has been since the day I first laid eyes on her. I'm the idiot who was too scared to tell her how I truly felt. And in the end, it still cost me her.

Zion and I arrived to school a little early, hoping to catch Tristan and have a nice little chat. Zion found out Reyes saw them together just before practice, aligning with Maisie's changed behavior. Losing Maisie is the result of whatever was said in their interaction, and I will get my answers.

"There he is." Zion taps my chest, pointing toward the black GMC Terrain pulling into a spot a few spaces over—Tristan's.

"Let's go," I snarl, ready to lay his ass out.

As soon as he steps out of his vehicle, I rush him, seeing red as my temper boils.

"Hey! Myers! What's—" I shove him into the side of his car and land two punches before Zion pulls me off of him.

"What the fuck did you say to her, you piece of shit? Huh?" I shout, trying to get to him, but Zion continues to hold me back.

"Man, calm down before the principal or Coach comes out here," Zion mutters. I don't give a shit. The one person who ever got me through Carver's deployments, my panic attacks, and a nasty broken leg injury in sixth grade has been ripped away from me. All because of *him*.

"Man, what the hell are you talking about?" Tristan mumbles, holding his bloody nose.

"Don't play stupid! I'm talking about Maisie!" I shout, not giving a dam if the idiots nearby are eavesdropping, one of them bound to run their mouth to Charmaine.

"What's this really about, Dylan? Is it that I asked her out before you had the balls to admit you like her?" He smirks, all cocky like he's the big dog on campus.

So he *does* know how I feel about her. Maybe it was more obvious to everyone else than I realized. Everyone, except Maisie.

"Or is it because I don't care how she looks? I actually want to be seen with her, to have her by my side and show her off. Because I'm not ashamed to want the girl you keep hiding behind excuses and silence." He steps in closer, his voice low but cutting. "Face it, man. You had your shot. You just didn't take it, and now you're pissed because I'm the one who's gonna find out if the carpet really does match the drapes."

"You know what," Zion says, raising his arms to release me, and thank fuck he did. I land another good punch or two for talking about her like that when Brandon and Chase show up, separating the both of us.

"Oh my God! What the hell, Dylan?" Maisie shoves through the guys, but instead of coming to me, she goes straight to Tristan.

*Can't say that doesn't sting.*

"Oh my gosh, are you okay?" She cradles Tristan's face with her delicate hands, checking his nose before retrieving a tissue from her backpack. Watching her be gentle with him, so nurturing the way she always was with me, hits me in my chest.

After checking Tristan over, ensuring he's okay, she spins on her heel, eyes blazing with fury. She charges at me, grabs me by the arm, and pulls us away from the small crowd so the two of us are out of earshot of everyone.

"What the hell is wrong with you?" Maisie shouts, eyes wide with disbelief. "Why would you punch him? Seriously, Dylan—*what the hell were you thinking?*

"I wasn't thinking—because you cut me out!" I snap. "Because of *him.* I lost you because of *him!*"

Her expression twists, torn between rage and something that looks a lot like heartbreak.

"Are you serious right now?" Her voice rises, sharp, unsteady. "You think this is about Tristan? That I pushed you away because of *some guy?*"

"You and I hadn't had any problems until yesterday at practice. Interestingly enough, Reyes said he passed the two of you on his way there. All of that occurred right before you told me we shouldn't be friends anymore. So, unless I've got something wrong, the math is adding up."

"You really have no idea, do you?" She lets out a bitter laugh, eyes burning. "Tristan wasn't making me do anything. He was just giving me a birthday gift," she says, raising her arm to show me the two bracelets dangling from her wrist. "That was when he asked me to be his girlfriend and told me he'd give me some time to think it over."

"Pft. Didn't take you long to say yes, did it?" The words are out of my mouth before I can stop them, a sharp retort that feels more like a stab than a question. My inner caveman is hurt and jealous, fighting to claim her back as mine.

"Wow. That was a dick ass remark if I've ever heard one." She glances around, hesitant at first, before she steels herself to look at me. "You know what? Let me save you the trouble by just admitting to you what I've been too scared to say to your face."

"You should never be scared to tell me anything, Freckles. You know you can always talk to me about anything. No judgment, remember?"

"Admitting to you that my feelings have grown into love ...," she says, her voice shaky, "it's completely terrifying. I've spent far too much time pretending that I didn't love you, convincing myself that we would be better off as friends. But I can't keep lying to myself."

My chest tightens. Her words hitting harder than I expected. "Freckles—"

"Please stop. I need to get this off my chest while I'm able to."

"Okay," I mumble, motioning for her to continue.

"Truth is, I've been falling for you since the eighth grade. I have had to put my feelings on the back burner when you dated Charmaine. You have no idea how much it killed me to see you falling in love with someone who enjoys tearing others down and tormenting me, all because I'm a big girl. You know, there had been a few moments where I thought maybe you somehow felt something more for me too. Clearly, I was wrong."

The urge I have to pull her into my arms and confess everything—about the blackmail, about Harvard, about how I've been fighting feelings for her too, that go far beyond friendship. But I don't. I can't. At least not yet.

"You know, I couldn't believe you actually went back to Charmaine. I thought there was no way in hell he would be dumb enough to fall for whatever little lies she spewed to slither her way back into your arms. Yet, once again, I was wrong, and I'm tired of being wrong." She takes a deep breath. "Rest assured, you and Charmaine can be truly happy together. I'll be keeping my distance from you because she clearly is insecure when you and I are near each other. And just so we are clear, Tristan and I are dating now. It was high time for me to move on from you, and if dating someone will help me do that, then so be it. Goodbye, Dylan."

She walks away from me, my heart nearly shredding into thousands of pieces. Seeing her step into Tristan's side, the smile she gives him is like a knife twisting deeper into my chest. It's the kind of smile she used to reserve for me, but now, I guess it belongs to him.

I stand there, frozen, feeling the weight of everything I should have said and done.

Watching her slip farther away from me with each step, I can't believe I've lost her, the one who should have been more than just a friend.

# Chapter 18

## Dylan

It's been a month since Maisie told me she loved me and effectively ended our friendship. Thirty agonizing days of watching her and Tristan together, holding hands in the hallway, sitting close at lunch, and him occasionally giving her rides after practice.

Is this what she went through seeing me with Charmaine all those years?

The image of Maisie walking away from me, choosing Tristan over me, replays in my mind like a cruel movie I can't shut off. All this time, she felt the same way I did, only I was too blind to notice the little things—a coward for not speaking my own truth.

My phone buzzes with a text from Charmaine reminding me about some party this weekend, and I'd rather die than attend. I ignore it, like I've ignored most of her texts lately. The only reason I haven't completely ghosted her is because of our Faustian bargain.

"You look like shit," Zion comments as he slides into the seat next to me in AP English.

"Thanks," I mutter, as he drops his backpack on the floor. "How kind of you to say."

"I'm just being honest, bro." He lowers his voice. "Have you tried talking to her?"

"No. Maisie made it pretty clear she doesn't want anything to do with me."

"You know, it's not too late," Zion insists. "She loves you, man. She straight up told you that. You think those feelings just disappear overnight? Feelings she has had since middle school? That doesn't just go away." He snaps his fingers for emphasis. "Like that."

"It doesn't matter. I can't risk Harvard."

"Is Harvard really worth losing the girl you love?" he challenges, his expression serious.

"I'm not getting into this right now," I whisper when the teacher walks in.

Mrs. Peterson starts the class by discussing our essay on *The Great Gatsby*, which is due next week. I try to focus on her words, but my attention keeps drifting to the mess that is my life.

Not only am I missing Maisie and how things were between us, but Carver's been gone on his mission for three weeks now. Not knowing where he is or if he's okay, creating these worst-case scenarios in my mind, has been detrimental to my mental health. Football is going decent. We've been winning our games, but some were too close to being losses. Coach must have faith in me if he hasn't made me the backup. Let me add that I'm failing in physics, which is killing my GPA. Harvard's most successful applicants got in with a GPA range of 3.7 to 4.0. Mine's currently sitting at 3.4. It's not terrible, but I know I need to bring it up if it'll help me.

"Mr. Myers?" Mrs. Peterson's voice cuts through my thoughts. "Perhaps you'd like to share your interpretation of Gatsby's obsession with Daisy?"

Great. Of all the questions the teacher could ask.

"Gatsby's fixation on Daisy represents his inability to let go of an idealized past," I state, the irony not lost on me. "He's built her up in his mind as this perfect woman who will solve all his problems, but the reality can never match his fantasy."

Mrs. Peterson nods, seemingly satisfied with my response. "And do you think his pursuit of her was worth it in the end?"

I can feel Zion glaring at the side of my head. "No," I finally say. "Some dreams should stay dreams. Reality just ruins them."

After class, Zion catches up with me in the hallway. "That was deep, man. You channeling your inner poet now?"

"Shut up," I mumble, but there's no real heat behind it.

"Listen," he says, grabbing my arm to stop me, "I get that you're hurting. But this thing with Charmaine has gone on long enough. You need to come clean about everything and admit your feelings to Maisie."

I shake my head. "I can't. Not yet."

I continue walking, heading inside the cafeteria for lunch.

"Why the hell not? You're miserable; she's clearly not happy with Tristan—"

"She's not?" The question escapes before I can stop it.

My eyes automatically drift across the cafeteria to where Maisie usually sits along with Hollis, Alora, Mirko, and Tristan. She's laughing at something he said, her head thrown back, exposing the delicate line of her throat, and I have to force myself to look away.

"From where I'm standing, she looks pretty damn happy," I snarl at him before going to step in a lunch line. We grab our trays and pick what we want to eat before making our way to our usual spot.

"It's a facade, man! She puts on a front when she's with him, but the moment he's distracted, she's looking in your direction. She lets her mask down for just a few seconds, and it's in those seconds, when she believes no one is paying attention, that she allows herself to be honest with herself. There's a sadness in her eyes, a longing. Deep down, she still wants *you*."

As Zion takes a bite of his lunch, I look over at Maisie. There's a brief second where our eyes lock, and her laughter fades. Her cheeks lightly pinken, and she quickly looks away, as if caught off guard by her own reaction. She's definitely not as carefree as she seems.

Could Zion be right?

"Let me ask you something," Zion says after swallowing a scoop of his spaghetti. "Did you ever notice the way Maisie's eyes seemed to have an extra sparkle to them when you looked at her, the way she just lit up at your acknowledgment of her? Or how quiet she would be whenever you would talk about something Charmaine and you did together?"

Looking back, I guess I never really noticed. I'm about to answer him when Charmaine slips into the seat next to me, her arm wrapping around mine. "There you are, Pookie Bear! I've been looking all over for you."

I resist the urge to pull away, painfully aware that Maisie might be watching. "I've been here. It is lunch time."

"Well, I have the most amazing news." Charmaine continues, either oblivious to or ignoring my lack of enthusiasm. "Daddy just got off the phone with the admissions director at Harvard. He mentioned you specifically, Dylan!"

That gets my attention. "He did? What did he say?"

Charmaine grins, clearly enjoying having my complete focus. "He said he's looking forward to meeting you at the alumni dinner next month. Apparently, Daddy's recommendation has put you on their radar in a big way."

"That's … that's incredible," I say, genuinely stunned. "Thank you."

"Don't you just love the benefits of dating me?" Charmaine brags, leaning over to kiss my cheek.

I stiffen, the touch sending an uncomfortable shiver down my spine. "When exactly is this dinner?" I ask, my voice flat, struggling to focus on the words while fighting the urge to pull away.

"October twelfth. It's in Boston, so we'll be flying out that Friday after the Greystone game and coming back on Sunday. Daddy's already arranged everything." She leans in closer, her voice dropping to a whisper. "And since Daddy prefers having his own space, we'll have our own hotel room—just you and me. Imagine the *fun* we can have."

I feel sick at the implication, my stomach turning, but I force a smile, the edges of it tight and strained. "Sounds...great."

"Oh, and one more thing," she adds, her tone suddenly serious. "Daddy wants to meet with you this weekend. Something about making sure you're the right... investment."

The way she emphasizes "investment" sends a cold shiver down my spine.

"Sure," I reply, my voice flat, knowing full well I have no other choice. "Just let me know when and where."

"Saturday, noon, at the country club by Lake Seraphine." She plants a kiss on my cheek before standing. "Don't be late, and wear something nice."

As she walks away, Zion shoots me a look—equal parts pity and disgust.

"What?"

"Nothing." He shakes his head, his voice tinged with disbelief. "Just wondering if Harvard is still worth all of this."

Yeah, I'm starting to wonder the same, but I don't say that to my best friend.

## Maisie

"So, ladies and gay. What's the plan for this weekend?" I place the last of the snacks on the dining table for us to munch on while we figure out how to spend our bye week. No weekend football game equals more free time for fun!

"Clearly, Hollis is out since she's got her hot date with Colton. Maybe those two will finally cave and deal with all that sexual tension between them." Alora wiggles her eyebrows for emphasis.

"I hope it goes well for them. They're adorable together, and she deserves to be happy," I add. "Mirko. What are you thinking?"

"I was thinking we could Netflix and Girl?"

"What is Netflix and Girl?" Corrine tilts her head, clearly puzzled by Mirko's words.

"It's where we all get together in our comfiest of clothes to watch a chick flick and do girl shit—manis, pedis, face masks, hair, the works!" Mirko explains. "My parents are out of town until Sunday, so we'd have the whole house to ourselves."

"Count me in," Alora says. "I need a break from my brother's constant hovering. Is it possible to have helicopter brothers, or is mine just being excessively annoying?"

"Is he still being weird about LJ?" I ask. Ever since the fight at the lake, things have gotten a little more intense in the Lewis home. I also believe there's something brewing between my friend and the guy she claims means nothing to her.

Alora rolls her eyes. "You have no idea. It's like he thinks I'm going to run off to another country with him or something. Like chill. We're coworkers and nothing more."

"Mm-hm. Bitch please. You know you want to do more," Mirko teases. "I wouldn't blame you, though. He's a total hottie."

"Wait. Who's LJ?" Corrine asks.

"Some guy who attends Greystone Academy," I explain. "Apparently, LJ and Anthony have some kind of history."

"That's putting it mildly." Alora snorts. "They hate each other's guts."

Corrine looks intrigued. "What happened?"

"Well ... Anthony refuses to tell me anything. And don't get me started on LJ."

"What about you, Maisie?" Mirko asks, switching the topic. "Any plans with Tristan?"

I shrug, trying to appear nonchalant. "Nothing is set in stone. He mentioned something about maybe dinner and a movie, but I haven't confirmed yet."

Things with Tristan have been going ... okay. He's sweet, attentive, and genuinely seems to care about me. But there's something missing with us—like a spark, that intensity I felt whenever Dylan was always near. It's not fair to Tristan, and I know it, but I've been hoping that with time, my feelings for Tristan would grow and I could be truly happy with him.

Unfortunately, they haven't.

"You don't sound very excited," Alora states, studying me carefully.

"I'm just tired," I lie. "Trying to keep my grades up while also helping Nonna with homecoming season. She's been teaching me how to sew, which isn't as hard as I had thought, but I'm still learning. Add in everything with football, and it's been way more exhausting than I imagined."

Mirko gives me a look that says he doesn't believe me for a second, but thankfully, he doesn't push it.

"What about you, Corrine?"

"I actually have a family thing tomorrow at the country club," Corrine says. "I wish I didn't have to go, but Mom's making me."

"Sounds boring," Alora says, reaching for the bowl of popcorn. "Watching rich people flaunt their wealth while judging everyone who doesn't fit their standards."

"Not everyone who is rich does that, Lo," she mocks. "She's also pressuring me to bring a date so I'm not alone since Charmaine's invited Dylan."

At the mention of his name, my heart does that annoying little flutter in my chest. I force myself to keep my expression neutral, grabbing a handful of chips to distract myself.

I still can't believe I laid my heart bare to Dylan. Part of me wonders if I made a mistake, but another part of me knows it was the right decision. You'd think that after a month, I'd be making progress in loving him less, but those feelings are still there, buried beneath all the grief. I refuse to admit how much I miss him, miss us, miss our friendship. I had to end it for my own sake, to escape the constant heartache of feeling like I was second best. But then I wonder … Was I even second best?

"Sorry, Maisie," Corrine says, bringing me back to the conversation.

"Sorry?" I ask, unsure what she could be sorry for. These past few weeks, Corrine has had a lot of personal growth. She's slowly opening up, allowing herself to hang out with us outside of school more than usual. I'm surprised Charmaine hasn't lost her shit about it, which makes me wonder if Corrine lies to her about who she's hanging out with.

"I know how much Dylan meant to you. Anyone who isn't blind can tell you cared about him way more than just as a friend, including Charmaine. It's why she's so cruel towards you. If anyone deserves to be with him, it's you, not her." She offers a soft smile. "But I just have to ask—are your feelings for Tristan real? Or is he just a cover-up for losing Dylan?"

The room gets eerily silent, the only noise you can hear is the sound of Jinxy's bell jingling somewhere upstairs. Alora and Mirko lean forward, placing their elbows on the table and resting their heads in their hands, interested in what I have to say.

"Uh, what do you mean?" I say, refusing to look at my friends, finding the hem of my top more amusing.

"You haven't been yourself since you shut him out. You put on a front to hide your pain, and you've distanced yourself in practice. My guess is you don't want to mess with the team's chemistry, which I'm sure the team appreciates."

"Thank you!" Alora praises, raising her hands in the air. "Finally, someone has come out and said it!"

"So, you don't think Tristan and I are the real deal?" I thought I was doing a good job of making it believable that I was happy with someone who wasn't Dylan. Turns out, I'm a shitty actress.

"Oh, honey." Mirko reaches across the table to hold my hand. "We think it's real to an extent. It's you that needs to be real with yourself. Are you dating because you like him? Or is he just a placeholder because you can't be with the one you want?"

"Damn, Mirko. You didn't have to go there." I chuckle. "Starting to feel like this is some kind of intervention."

My phone buzzes with a text from Tristan asking if we're still on for tomorrow night. I stare at the message, and a wave of guilt washes over me. The truth is, I'm not being fair to him. He didn't ask for a girlfriend who is only playing a part to put a Band-Aid on her pain. He deserves someone who can give him their whole heart, not someone who's still hung up on someone else.

<h1 style="text-align:center">Chapter 19</h1>

## Maisie

"That was so much fun. You'll have to tell Mirko we need to do it again!" Josie beams as we walk into the house. It's just after ten o'clock. Mom is out with her friends tonight for Salsa Saturday at some dance club. Once she found Richard snooping in my bedroom and snatching a pair of my underwear, she kicked his creepy ass to the curb. Now, she's been strictly going out with friends to have fun, and I love that for her.

Since Mom is out, I asked Mirko if Josie could join us for his Netflix and Girl get together. We've spent the last several hours hanging out and talking while we did each other's nails and hair. It was exactly the kind of escape I needed.

"It was fun, wasn't it? Maybe we should make it a monthly thing?"

"Oh, my God, yes! Maybe Sabrina can go—" Josie yawns. "Next time?"

"I'll discuss it with Mirko. Why don't you go get ready for bed while I take care of Jinxy?"

"K. G'night, big sis."

"Night, Jojo."

After tending to Jinxy and making sure all the doors and windows are securely locked, I head upstairs to my bedroom. Closing the door behind me, I cross my room to my desk and pick up the leather green sketch pad, the one Dylan gifted me for my birthday last month. Opening it up, I read the note he wrote on the inside cover.

> *To the future famous fashion designer.*
> *Don't ever stop chasing your dreams because I know you're*
> *meant for greatness. I'm just grateful to be along for the ride.*
> *Happy 18th birthday, Freckles*
> *Xo Dylan*

I run my fingers over his handwriting, tracing each letter as if I could somehow feel the connection between us through the ink on the page. I'll never admit I've read his note around a hundred times a day ever since I opened it, or that I had to tape plastic wrap over it because I was worried all the tears I cried would smudge the ink. I didn't want to erase the last piece of Dylan that I had.

Guilt eats at me that I never thanked him for his incredibly thoughtful gift. Is it still too late? I glance at the clock on my side table—11:10 p.m.

Dylan's birthday is in fifty minutes, and I'm sitting here debating if I should text him at midnight like we've always done. The thought of breaking that tradition makes my chest ache with a longing I've been trying desperately to ignore. But doing so would only confuse things more, wouldn't it? I've been working so hard to keep my distance, to respect the boundaries I set up. Texting him on his birthday would only muddy the waters. Right?

Lying on my bed, I open the sketchbook to my latest design, hoping it'll be a good distraction. But after going over the same section, I realize even sketching isn't helping.

Sighing, I place the sketchbook back on my desk and head to my window seat—my favorite place—where I've spent countless hours designing, reading, and daydreaming. It's been a while since I sat here, though, avoiding it so I didn't risk seeing him.

For the first time in a month, I open my bedroom curtains and peer across the yard into his window. His curtains are partially open, giving me a clear view of his bedroom. His light is on, and I see him moving around his room. He appears to be pacing, running his hands through his hair the way he always does when he's stressed about something.

I check the time again—11:23 p.m.

In the past, I would've texted asking if he was okay, and he may have denied that something was bothering him. Then I'd have to call him, allowing him to vent. Most people don't know Dylan suffers from anxiety attacks when things become too much. It's not bad enough for medication, but he goes to therapy for it, which seems to help. They started happening after Carver left for the military, and I'm fairly certain the two go hand in hand. Especially when Carver goes out on missions and they don't get to speak for an unknown amount of time. I can't imagine not being able to talk to my family for who knows how long and risking my life, but that has to wreak havoc on your loved ones' mental health.

My phone buzzes with a text, and for a brief, hopeful moment, I think it might be Dylan. But it's just Tristan.

TRISTAN

Hey, beautiful. Just wanted to say goodnight. I hope you had fun this evening with your friends. <3

I stare at the message, my thumbs hovering over the keyboard. We were supposed to go to dinner, but I couldn't bring myself to go and told him about the plans with my friends instead, how I needed time with them. He was completely understanding, even though it was the third time I've chickened out of a date. Tristan has been nothing but kind and patient with me, yet I can't seem to give him what he deserves—my full attention and affection.

MAISIE

Goodnight. Sleep well.

It's a lukewarm response at best, and I feel another pang of guilt.

Turning my attention back to Dylan's window, I notice he's now sitting on the edge of his bed, his head in his hands. He looks defeated, a far cry from the confident, golden boy everyone at school sees. This is the only Dylan I know—the one who carries the weight of expectations on his shoulders, who worries about letting people down.

Before I can stop myself, I reach for my phone and open our text thread—the one I haven't deleted despite everything. The last message was from him asking me to talk to him the day I ended our friendship.

11:42 p.m.

The minutes are ticking by, and I'm running out of time to make a decision. Do I reach out, or do I let another piece of our friendship slip away?

Taking a deep breath, I start typing a simple message:

MAISIE

I know we're not talking right now because of what I did, and I understand if you don't want to hear from me. But it's almost midnight, and I couldn't let your birthday start without saying happy birthday. I hope it's a good one, Dylan.

My finger hovers over the send button, my heart racing. Just as I'm about to press it, I see movement in Dylan's window. He's standing now, looking directly at my window, at me. Our eyes meet between the short distance of our houses, and for a moment, it's like nothing has changed—like we're those two kids again, signaling to each other with flashlights after bedtime.

Dylan types something in his phone seconds before my phone goes off. With our eyes still locked in place, he signals for me to look at mine, and I do as he asks.

DYLAN

> Words can't explain how happy I am to see you right now.

Tears prick at my eyes because he has no clue how happy I am to see him too.

I contemplate my response, deleting my previous message.

MAISIE

> I'm happy to see you too.

I watch as he reads the text, a small smile lifting on one side of his handsome face, the familiar dimple I love making an appearance. I'm about to send him a text to thank him for my birthday gift when a message comes through.

DYLAN

> I miss you, Freckles

Four simple words, but they hit me like a tidal wave. I haven't heard him call me that in a month, and I didn't realize how much I missed it until now. The tears begin to fall, and every ounce of heartache, of grief, pours out of me in that moment.

My phone begins ringing, and Dylan's name flashes on the screen. I look over at him and see the worry etched on his face. After taking a few deep breaths to calm myself down, I pick up my phone and place it next to my ear.

"Are you okay, Freckles?"

"Yes. No. I don't know." I laugh softly.

"Did I cross a line telling you I miss you? Is that why you're crying?"

"No, D. You didn't cross a line," I say as I look at him through the window and smile. "Because I really miss you too." More tears slip out, no doubt leaving streaks of mascara down my cheeks.

"You do?" His voice is soft, almost disbelieving.

"So much," I admit, my voice breaking. "Every single day."

There's a moment of silence between us, filled with all the things we haven't said since I broke us.

"Can I ..." Dylan hesitates. "Can I come over? Just for a little while?"

I look at the clock—11:52 p.m. "It's almost midnight."

"Exactly. It's almost my birthday," he says, a hint of his old playfulness returning. "And I can't think of a better way to start it than with you."

My heart races at his words, a sudden flutter taking over me. "Okay," I say, my voice barely above a whisper.

"I'll be over in a few minutes."

Hanging up, I rush to the bathroom, my hands trembling as I wipe away the mascara streaks. I splash some cold water on my face in hopes it will ease the puffiness from crying.

There's a soft knock on my window a few minutes later. I pull the window open, and there's Dylan perched on top of the white trellis that lines the side of my house—reminding me of the scene in *Romeo and Juliet*. The one I used to make Dylan reenact with me when we were in middle school since I was trying out for the role of Juliet in the play.

"This is a lot harder than it used to be," he says with a grin as he climbs in.

"Just don't break your leg like last time," I tease. He took a nasty fall and was stuck in a cast for about three months. I felt so horrible, but I made sure to help in any way I could to make up for it.

Once Dylan's inside, we stand facing each other, an awkward tension filling the space between us. He looks good—better than good—and I have to remind myself that we're just friends. He's with Charmaine and I'm with Tristan.

"Hi," I murmur.

"Hi," he says, his eyes never leaving mine.

"Happy birthday," I whisper as the clock on my nightstand changes to midnight.

A soft smile spreads across his face. "You remembered."

"Of course I did. How could I forget?"

He steps closer, his voice strained with emotion. "Because I thought you hated me, and that I wouldn't get another birthday message from you... ever again."

"I could never hate you, Dylan. I just ..." I'm unsure how to explain the mess of emotions inside me.

"I know," he says, understanding in his eyes. "I didn't get it before, but I do now."

We stand there, the silence between us charged with unspoken feelings.

"Your gift," I blurt out. "I never said thank you for it, and I just want you to know how thoughtful it was and how much I love it."

His smile widens. "I'm glad you like it, Freckles."

"I love it," I correct him. "I've also been using it every day since I filled my last one up."

"Can I see?" he asks, gesturing toward my desk where the sketchbook sits.

I nod, and he walks over and picks it up, carefully flipping through the pages. His fingers trace the lines of a dress I sketched just yesterday.

"These are amazing, Freckles," he says, genuine admiration in his voice. "You're so damn talented. I can't wait to see you take on the fashion world."

"I don't know about the fashion world. I was kind of thinking more along the lines of my own boutique. Something like Nonna's."

"Hey. Don't count yourself out. You could be a world-renowned designer with your own boutique shop wherever you decide to settle down."

"I'd love for it to be Bellwood. Or right outside of Bellwood." I smile. "How about you? You still planning to take over your dad's law firm?"

His face falls the moment I mention his dreams, and I feel a pang of regret. "What's wrong?"

"You know what? I should probably head back home." He charges for the window, but I pull him back and step in front of him.

"No-no-no." I raise my hands to cup his face. "Please don't leave, just stay. I'm sorry for whatever I might have said to upset you...just...I'm right here, D. You can talk to me. Let me in. I know I fucked up, royally fucked up when I hurt you, and if you don't want to talk to me, I'll understand. But I want you to talk to me. I want to fix this, fix us—"

Dylan's lips are suddenly on mine, catching me off guard. I'm stunned, unable to move for a moment before my body betrays me and I give in. His mouth claims mine, and he pulls me closer, deepening our kiss.

He lifts me in his strong arms, and my legs automatically wrap around his waist as he moves us to my bed. He lays me down, our mouths meeting in a soft, lingering kiss that speaks more than words ever could.

*Am I having one of my Dylan erotic dreams, or is this my reality?*

"What's a Dylan erotic dream?" Dylan pulls back, a smirk on his handsome face.

"I didn't say that in my head?" I ask, my face warming with embarrassment.

"No, baby. You definitely whispered that out loud. Care to elaborate for me?"

"Oh, god." I cover my face with both of my hands, horrified I exposed that dirty little secret to him.

I gently push on his chest, forcing him to let me up. "What are we doing, Dylan?"

"I ... honestly don't know." He looks around my room, at everything but me. Is he embarrassed? Ashamed?

I grab his chin, making him face me. "I don't regret what we just did. Do you?"

"Hell no," he says, his voice full of confidence. There's no hesitation or second thoughts, just him being as vulnerable as I am.

"Okay. Good."

He brushes a strand of hair from my face with a tenderness that feels different than anything else we've shared. "So, what now?" he asks, his voice a mix of curiosity and uncertainty.

I hesitate for a moment, then answer, my voice steady. "Well, you know about my feelings toward you."

"Do I?" He's looking less confident than he did a moment ago. "You told me how you felt before cutting me out, but I don't know about now. I mean, you're with Tristan. Do you lov—do you strongly care about him?"

"I'm not being fair to him. He's the one trying to make us work, and I find any excuse to pull away. Don't get me wrong, he's a great guy—"

"Hmph. Debatable," he mutters, and I gently smack his shoulder.

"Stop! You're saying that just because you don't like him now that I'm with him."

"No, baby. I'm jealous because he had the balls to ask the only girl I could ever give a damn about to be his girlfriend, not having any clue that you've always been mine."

"Yours?"

"From that day in the little bush when I moved in next door and saw you running from your house, the day those steely eyes looked up at me, I was gone for you. I may not have known it at six, and I may have been too much of a coward to man the hell up before, but I'm telling you now."

Dylan leans in and whispers, "You. Are. Mine" just before placing his lips on mine.

The moment our lips touch, I ruin the moment by blurting, "What about Charmaine?"

Dylan releases a snarl before pressing his forehead into mine. "Things with her are complicated."

Complicated. The same word he used at the lake. The one before I blew our world to pieces. I stand up from my bed, putting some distance between us.

"What's so complicated about you two?"

Dylan sighs, running a hand through his hair. "It's not what you think, Freckles."

"Then what is it?" I press, crossing my arms. "Because from where I'm standing, it looks like you're trying to have your cake and eat it too."

He sighs heavily, looking down at his hands. "I'm not with Charmaine because I want to be."

"What does that even mean?" My voice rises slightly before I remember Josie is sleeping down the hall. "Why are you with her?"

He sits on the edge of my bed, looking more vulnerable than I've ever seen him. "Her dad's on the alumni board at Harvard. With his connections and his promise to write me a recommendation, it would practically guarantee my acceptance."

"So you're dating her for a college recommendation?" I can't keep the disbelief from my voice.

"I know how it sounds," he says, his eyes pleading for understanding. "Believe me, if there were another way out of this, I would take it." He takes a moment before he continues. "I'm barely passing physics, and it's affecting my GPA, which could make me a hard pick. The letter will give me a better chance of getting in, and you know how much Harvard is my dream. I want to help people get the justice they deserve. And since Carver went the military route, I'll get to take over Dad's law firm when he retires and maybe even pass it down to my future children."

"But at what cost, Dylan?" I move closer to him, my voice softening. "Is it worth being miserable? Worth pretending to care about someone you don't? Is that what you want?"

He pulls me closer, resting his forehead against mine. "All I know is that I miss you. I miss us. And kissing you just now felt more right than anything has in a long time."

My heart races at his words, but my mind is still trying to process everything. "So, what happens now? You keep dating Charmaine for her father's recommendation while secretly seeing me on the side? I won't be that girl, Dylan."

"I would never ask you to be," he states. "I'm going to end things with her. I just have to handle her carefully."

"When?"

"After the alumni dinner next month. It will be in Boston where I'll meet with the admissions director. Once that's done, I'm out."

"Okay."

"Really? Just like that? And what about Tristan?" he asks, his jaw tightening at the mention of my boyfriend.

I sigh, guilt washing over me. "I need to end things with him. I can't keep leading him on when my heart is clearly elsewhere."

"Okay. Good." Dylan reaches for my hand, intertwining our fingers. "I'm sorry I didn't tell you the truth about Charmaine before. I was ashamed, and I hate myself for doing it. Just let me get all of this taken care of, and then I'll be all yours. I *promise*."

He presses a soft kiss to my forehead and wraps his arms around me, holding me close, as if to keep the world at bay. "Thank you for the best birthday present."

"What present?"

"You."

# Chapter 20

## Dylan

I still can't wrap my mind around Maisie being back in my life when she never should have been out of it in the first place. Now that I've experienced what life is like without her, I'll be damned if I ever let her slip away again.

It's been two days since we shared our first kiss, and I'm craving more. Every time I close my eyes, I feel her lips against mine, soft and tentative at first, then melting into something more profound.

Worse, she's refusing to kiss me in secret until she officially breaks up with Tristan this weekend. The guilt from our first kiss while she's still with him has left her feeling worse than she already did. So, I agreed. Breaking up with him this weekend after we show we're mending our friendship will make it less obvious than if both happen at the same time. Otherwise, people will talk, and my situation with Charmaine will get more complicated. If I didn't care so much about getting my foot in the door at Harvard, I would've never gotten back with Charmaine.

The hardest part is pretending nothing has changed when everything has. Watching her with Tristan in the cafeteria, seeing him with his arm around her shoulders while knowing she plans to end things with him soon, kills me. I hate that we're both stuck in these relationships we don't want, but I know it won't be for much longer.

For now, I settle for a quick glance and a secret smile as I pass by. She catches my eye and blushes slightly, tucking a strand of hair behind her ear in that way that always makes my heart skip. Damn, she's beautiful. And she's going to be *mine*.

After school, I head straight to football practice, grateful for the physical outlet for my frustration.

Coach Watson has us running drills for the first hour. All my wide receivers are nailing their catches, but Hollis? Something is in her head. It's unlike her to be messing up the way she is.

"Whitlock! Hit the bench and take five!" Coach Freeman yells. She follows his order, slamming her helmet down after she sits.

"What's up with Whitlock?" I ask Corrine, knowing the lady ballers, our nickname for the girls, seem to be getting close.

"Maisie mentioned something to do with her grandma, I think?"

"Why don't you go check on her." I nod in Hollis's direction. "She looks like she could use a friend."

Corrine simply nods, heading to go check in with her friend and teammate.

We continue with our passing drills when Colton stalls. "Hey. What's Brady doing here?" He tips his head to where Coach Watson is standing, along with Hollis and Brady Thomas. He was Bellwood's star player until last year when Payson Moore stole the show.

"No clue, man," Zion says.

"I don't know." I shrug.

Colton passes the ball to Zion, then Zion passes to me, and as I'm about to throw to Colton, Hollis storms past us like a raging bull, which makes Colton concerned.

"Hey, Coach!" he shouts as he jogs away.

"What do you think that's about?" Zion asks.

Before I can respond, Coach blows his whistle, calling us to gather around. "Listen up! We've got Lincoln Knights in three days, and their track record isn't that great, which should be an easy win for us. However, that doesn't mean we can slack off. We need to be ready." He begins outlining our strategy, but my attention drifts to where Maisie stands with the defensive line.

She's nodding along to whatever Coach Wells is saying, her face serious and focused. Unlike the past month, she doesn't avoid looking in my direction, and when our eyes meet, there's a small, almost imperceptible smile that sends a surge of warmth through me.

"Myers!" Coach Freeman's voice snaps me back to attention. "You with us?"

"Yes, Coach," I say.

"Good, because I need your head in the game."

Practice continues with scrimmage drills, the offense versus defense. When it's my turn to lead the offense, I'm acutely aware of Maisie across the line.

After a particularly good play where I evade her and complete a pass to Colton, I can't help but flash her a grin. She rolls her eyes, but there's no malice in it—just the playful competition we've always had.

We run through a new drill we learned several times, with Maisie trying to break through my offensive line to sack me. She's fast and determined, getting past my protection more often than not. Each time she tackles me, there's that moment of contact that sends electricity through my body.

*Do not get a boner in practice.*

When practice ends, I head to the locker room and rush through my shower so I can catch Maisie before she leaves. As I exit the building, I spot her walking toward the parking lot, her gym bag slung over her shoulder.

"Hey," I call out, jogging to catch up with her. "Good practice today."

"Thanks," she says, glancing around to make sure no one is watching us too closely. "You too. That throw to Colton was pretty impressive."

"Only because I knew you were coming for me," I tease, resisting the urge to touch her. "How are you doing, you know, with everything?"

"I'm okay." She sighs. "This weekend can't come fast enough though."

"I know what you mean," I say, glancing around. "Do you have any plans? Maybe we could meet up somewhere?"

"As much as I would love that ... I can't. I've got to go help Nonna tonight. Homecoming season is in full swing and she needs my help."

"Oh. Okay, it's cool." I try to keep the disappointment out of my voice but fail.

"Awe, don't be sad," she taunts. "Why don't I message you when I'm heading home and we can meet in the window and talk? Kind of like when we were kids?"

"I'll take what I can get. For now, at least."

"I promise to make it worth your while." She winks as she walks past me and heads to her car, leaving me to wonder what exactly she means by that.

# Maisie

Nonna and I managed to sew two complete homecoming dresses this evening before calling it quits by nine. As promised, I messaged Dylan to let him know I was on my way home. I skipped dinner and rushed straight to my room.

"Everything okay, MJ?" My mother appears at my bedroom door.

"Yeah, yeah. Everything's fine! I just have an assignment to do before I can go to bed, and I don't want to be up too late. Beauty rest and all that."

"Speaking of. I'm off to bed for some beauty rest myself. Good night!"

"Night, Mom!" I watch as she goes down the hall into her bedroom. The moment I hear her door click, I close mine and lock it. In my closet, I snag the black box sitting on top of the shelf, nerves slowly creeping in.

After setting the box on my bed, I pull out the two-piece satin set I purchased on my birthday. I wanted something that felt mature, something adult like. A tattoo was out since I'm afraid of needles, and there's no election to vote in, so I figured buying a sexy lingerie night set was next best. Not to mention, I was feeling extra vulnerable.

The thin, spaghetti strap top is baby pink, with black lace lining the bustline. The matching shorts are just as soft in color and cut incredibly short, with black lace trimming the leg openings, giving them a cute, cheeky, booty-short look.

I stand in front of the mirror, admiring my curves in the night set. My soft belly is slightly exposed, the top snug over my ample breasts, and the way the shorts give my butt a lift? I feel every bit the sexy, confident woman I know I am.

As I finish the braid in my hair, my cell phone chimes with a text.

DYLAN

**Are you coming to the window?**

I smile, amused by his impatience.





If someone had told me Dylan Myers wanted to be with me, I would have laughed in their face and thought they were crazy.

I grab my black silk robe and wrap it around me, ensuring every bit of the night set is covered. Going by the door, I take one quick listen, making sure my house is asleep before calling Dylan.

He wastes no time answering his phone. "Picking up on the first ring? Someone's a little eager," I purr.

"You have no idea," he whispers. "I miss you."

"I miss you too. Are your parents asleep?"

"Yeah. They went to bed about thirty minutes ago. Are you at your window?"

"Of course I am. Just needing you to join me."

I smile even though he can't see me, and make a show of slowly opening my curtains to tease him a little before opening them completely.

"Damn, baby." He jumps up, pressing his body into the glass of his window. "You're incredibly stunning."

"That's not even the best part." I give him a wink and slowly untie the string on my robe and glide the silky fabric off my shoulders until it drops on the floor.

"Jesus!" Dylan groans, putting his hand to his mouth to bite down on his knuckle. "I take it back. You are so fucking sexy. You going to turn around for me so I can see all of you?"

"Sure thing, handsome," I say in my best sultry voice. I twirl, my body moving to imaginary music, until my backside is on display for him. I lean forward and give a little booty shake just to torment him.

"God, I want to bite your ass right now," Dylan growls out, and I feel myself getting wet.

Who knew a growly voice could be so sexy?

"You want to know a secret?"

"Tell me."

"I'm not wearing a bra. Or panties."

"Fuck. Me."

I take a seat on the bench, admiring the man I'd dreamed I'd be the object of his fantasies.

"I'd love to, but we kind of have ourselves a situation, don't we? It's bad enough you get me worked up, taunting me in my dreams."

"The erotic ones?"

"Precisely the ones. Now, I think it's my turn to get you worked up."

"Baby, I'm fucking hard as hell since you opened those damn curtains, standing there like a seductress."

"Pull it out. Let me see it." Dylan follows my command, wasting no time pulling his beautiful dick from his sweatpants, gripping it in his hands and giving it a quick stroke. "You listen so well."

"You can tell me to do anything, and I'll do it. I'm at your command." He strokes himself, his groan echoing down the line, and the sound goes straight to my clit.

"I'll keep that in mind." Dylan casually strokes himself, and my mouth waters to pleasure him.

"You hungry for my cock, baby? I can see the hunger in your eyes from here."

"God, yes." A small moan slips out, and Dylan does the same. I place myself on the window seat, my back against the wall, and drag my hands gradually down my body toward the apex of my thighs. Slipping my fingers under the shorts, I touch my sensitive little bud, pressing gently and going in a circular motion.

"Do you have any idea how sexy you look touching yourself for me? Are you wet for me, Freckles? Is your cunt weeping for my dick?"

"Damn. I think your dirty mouth is hotter than when you call plays in the game." He lets out a soft chuckle before another groan slips past his lips.

"Just wait until this dirty mouth goes down on that delectable body of yours, kissing every inch of you as I work my way to your pussy, devouring you until you scream my name from those pouty lips."

"Yes … I want that," I moan out, doing my best to keep quiet. "Tell me more."

"I want to bend you over, right there on that seat, and smack your ass, then watch it jiggle from impact before I slowly glide in behind you, making you feel every inch of my cock."

Another moan escapes, this one a little louder.

"Shh … you don't want to wake your mom and sister, do you?"

"The door's locked, for safe measure," I pant out.

"Tell me about one of those dreams you been having about me. Maybe we can reenact it when we can finally be together."

I sift through the many dreams until I remember one in particular. "You're dressed in a suit, with a briefcase, and when you opened this briefcase, there was a pair of handcuffs."

"Go on," he grunts, and I chance a look, seeing lust fill those blue eyes.

"I make you remove every piece of clothing, but you have to leave the tie on. You do as you're asked, and I tell you 'Such a good job, my pet' before making you get on your hands and knees. I'm on the edge of my bed. You attempt to crawl, but I put my foot up to your chest, stopping you. I reach for the end of your tie, pressing my breasts in your face."

This time, Dylan releases a moan that's a little too loud. "Fuck. Keep going, baby. I need to hear more."

The way my heart skips at hearing him call me baby, I could melt.

"I gently tug on the tie, although this one is a little longer than usual, and tell you to crawl to me very slowly as I admire every inch of your naked body."

"Then what?"

"When you reach me, I tug your face to mine, kissing you deeply, before demanding you to eat me out." My fingers begin to move faster, my orgasm building. "Oh god."

"Are you close, baby? Because I'm getting there, just thinking about how good you'll taste coming on my tongue. Dreaming what you'll feel like as you come all over my cock."

"I'm so close, D. I'm almost there."

"I want us to come together," he grunts out. "And when you do, I want to hear *my* name come from those pouty lips."

The pressure builds and builds until I finally reach the precipice, a wave of pure pleasure rippling through me like a tidal surge, and Dylan's name leaves my lips. At the same moment, my name is being moaned from Dylan's.

I look over in time to see ropes of cum shoot out of Dylan's cock, some of it landing on his window.

I do my best to smother the laugh that dares to creep, but Dylan hears. "You find that amusing, do you?"

"I do. I hope cum is easy to clean off. Otherwise, I'd like to be a fly on the wall when you have that conversation with your mom."

"I clean my own room, thank you very much." He shoots me a look, one that says he is a grown man capable of cleaning up after himself. "Be right back. I need to go clean ... this ... all up."

He disappears for a few moments, then returns with a rag to clean his window before chucking it somewhere in his room.

"So—" Dylan clears his throat. "I wasn't, exactly, planning on that happening. Are you okay?"

"Hey, look at me." When his eyes lock with mine, I see the hesitancy in them, and I hate that he worries he messed up, or if I had to guess, worried I may leave him again. "I wanted to do that with you. With only you."

"Just need to be sure, Freckles. I don't want to mess this up."

"You won't, Dylan. You already have me. You've always had me."

His eyes soften, the weight of doubt lifting off his shoulders, and he lets out a soft sigh. "Then that's all I need."

# Chapter 21

## Dylan

It's Friday, my favorite f-word, next to football and family. Since Maisie and I had our little window rendezvous, I've been counting down the days for the weekend to get here. In a matter of hours, she will break Tristan's heart and no longer be his girl.

She will be one step closer to being mine, the way it was supposed to be.

"You seem different," Zion says, taking his seat across from me at lunch. "Something happen I should know about?"

"No idea what you're talking about," I say, but I feel the smile I'm trying to suppress.

"Uh-huh," he says. "And that's why you've been staring at Maisie all week like a lovesick puppy?"

"That obvious, huh?"

"Only to someone who knows you," he assures me. "So ... you two have been talking?"

"We're... working things out," I half admit, rubbing the back of my neck. "I finally came clean about everything with Charmaine."

"About damn time," he says, launching his straw paper at me with a smirk. "You're doing the right thing, man."

"I just hope it all works out, you know? Get into Harvard, make things official with Maisie..." I trail off, the weight of it all pressing on my chest. That would be the dream. But dreams come with choices—and if it came down to it, I already know what I'd choose. Or rather, *who*.

Zion and I are discussing tonight's game against the Lincoln Knights when Principal King approaches. "Mr. Myers?"

The cafeteria dies down when students see our principal standing beside the table full of football players. "I need you to get your stuff and come with me, please."

Zion and I share glances, uncertain as to why the principal needs me. I haven't done anything to land me in trouble, but something about this feels serious. I chance a look at where Maisie sits just as lost and confused about what is going on.

"Yes, ma'am," I say, grabbing my tray to discard my lunch before following Principal King. She escorts me to my locker, which I find odd. "Am I in some kind of trouble?"

"I am not at liberty to say. Just that you are needed at home. I'll escort you out to the parking lot once you have all your things."

I simply nod, gathering my backpack and anything else I may need before I'm ushered to my car. The whole way home, my mind races, trying to figure out what could be happening and why I was sent home in the middle of a school day.

As I approach my house, an all-black SUV catches my eye, parked ominously at the curb. My parents' cars sit in the driveway—right where they usually are when they're home. But they're *not* supposed to be home. They should be at work. A sinking feeling coils in my stomach, slow and heavy, like my body knows something my mind hasn't caught up to yet.

I rush inside, finding Dad pacing back and forth and my mother on the couch, her eyes red and tears pouring down her face.

"Mom? Dad? What's wrong? What's going on?"

"Dylan!" Mom jumps up and rushes me, pulling me into a tight hug, afraid to let me go.

"Have a seat, son. These officers have something to tell us."

That's when I notice the two gentlemen dressed in military attire in the corner of the living room. Mom drags me with her over to the couch, pulling me down with her, my father taking the seat on the other side of me.

"Afternoon, Myers family. I'm Sergeant John Ford, and this is Sergeant Joseph Harris, and we are both here as casualty notification officers."

Casualty officers? Army? Fuck.

"We regret to inform you that your son, Carver Myers, a Night Stalker with the 160th Special Operations Aviation Regiment, is currently listed as MIA. His team was involved in an attack overseas and at this time, we do not have confirmation of their whereabouts. We assure you we are going to do everything we can to find your son and his comrades."

"So there's a good chance our son is still alive?" my mom chokes out. "He may not ... be ..."

"We are hoping and praying so, ma'am. At this time, we are still gathering all information about the specifics of the incident, but we will keep you updated as soon as we have more details."

Carver is missing? He was in an attack? Or he could actually be dead.

The air feels thick, like it's pressing all around me. My chest tightens, and every breath I take feels shallow, strained, like I can't get enough air in. A fluttering sensation starts deep in my stomach, quickly spreading into my limbs, making them feel heavy and unsteady. My hands become clammy, and I grip them together, trying to keep control, but it feels like everything around me is closing in. My heart pounds loudly, too fast, echoing in my ears, and the world around me seems to blur, as if I'm detached from reality. The walls feel too close, and my throat tightens with a dry, scratchy feeling, and I know I'm seconds away from losing it.

"Dylan? Dylan?" My mom's voice sounds distant, like she's submerged in water.

All of a sudden, my head is being shoved between my legs, someone telling me to breathe in deeply and exhale. So I do what they say and take several slow, deep breaths until I feel my heart calm down, my muscles relax, and my breathing return to normal.

When I lift my head, my parents and both officers are surrounding me.

"You all right, son?" Dad asks, his voice low and steady.

I nod, swallowing hard. "Yeah. I'm good."

"Do you normally have panic attacks?" one of the officers asks me.

"Sometimes. Rarely any as bad as the one I just had." I'm grateful for that too. I can't imagine having these frequently.

The officer nods. "Your family will be assigned a Family Liaison Officer who can assist you with any questions or concerns you may have. We also have counselors available for emotional support, should you need them." He glances at me before continuing. "We understand this is incredibly difficult news to hear but please know that the Army will provide support throughout this process. We are here for you, and we will help you all through this difficult time."

My father goes to each man to shake their hands before escorting them to the door. "Thank you, gentlemen. We appreciate it."

When he returns, his eyes are glistening with tears that desperately want to fall.

"It's okay to cry, Dad. You don't need to hold back." As if on cue, the tears fall, and my father, a man I've always seen as strong and brave, crumbles to the floor, with cries of sadness and pain I've never heard escaping him. Mom and I go to him, wrapping our arms around each other in a tight hug as the three of us cry for a member of our family. A son. A brother.

No way can my big brother be gone. He can't leave us, leave me. Twenty-two is way too young, and I refuse to believe my brother is gone for good. He has to be out there. He has to come home.

He just has to.

# Maisie

We make our way onto the field, being booed by Lincoln Knight fans decked out in their black and silver.

Heading to the away team side, Coach Watson gathers us around for his pregame speech. "Listen up. We are without two of our key players tonight. Miss Whitlock and Mr. Myers."

Dylan's not coming? Does this have anything to do with Principal King showing up at lunch?

"Parker Malone, you'll be our quarterback. You're going to have to step up and lead tonight. I need you guys to remember what we worked on in practice. We are not overconfident, but our game plan is solid, so let's go out there and win. Eagles on three. One, two, three."

"Eagles!" we shout in unison before taking one side of the field to stretch and warm up. As the team breaks from the huddle, I pull Zion aside.

"What's up with Dylan? Is he okay?"

"I don't know. Principal King took him out of lunch, and no one has seen him since. I've tried calling him when school let out, but it goes straight to voicemail, and he's not responding to any of my texts."

My stomach twists with unease. "That's not like him."

"I know. I'm *really* concerned."

"What about Hollis?" I ask, changing the subject to distract myself from the worry. "She hasn't been to practice all week."

"Coach pulled her to take some time off and get her head right," Coach Brady answers, coming to our side.

The former Bellwood High star quarterback joined the coaching staff recently, specifically to help with the quarterbacks, but he also assists with the offense when need be.

"Some time off will do her good. Why don't you guys go stretch. It's almost game time."

The game begins with the Knights receiving the kickoff. Alora and Zealand make the stop, forcing the Knights to start from the ten-yard line. Our defense takes the field, ready to put up some blocks.

The first play, I shove past their tackle and nearly have their quarterback when I collide with one of my teammates. On the second play, two of their defenders hold me back and the wide receiver for the Knights gains twenty yards. Five minutes in, the Knights score their first touchdown, and their fans go wild.

Shit. We are not looking too good. Hopefully, our offense can bring us back.

Offense takes the field, and our misfortune seems to continue. Colton dropped one too many passes, ones he should have caught, but his head clearly isn't in the game; his thoughts must be with Hollis. Corrine took a nasty hit, so she's sitting on the bench, per concussion protocol. Tristan catches a pass, getting us near the goal line before one of our running backs fumbles the ball, giving it back to the Knights.

*Dammit!*

On defense, we stop the Knights at the fifty-yard line, forcing them to punt and giving us the ball back. In the next two plays, Tristan scores the first touchdown for the Eagles, lifting our spirits and giving our team hope we can turn this game around.

I try to focus on the game, but my mind keeps drifting to Dylan—how much I wish he were here, rallying the team, pushing us toward a win.

There's this gnawing sense of foreboding, like something's happened ... something bad. But I force myself to push it down and keep playing.

By halftime, we're trailing by seven points, and it's clear that while Parker has talent, he's not yet ready to lead the team. Coach isn't happy with our playing, and the sentiment is felt among my teammates, myself included. This isn't like us. We don't make this many mistakes.

In the second half, it's clear there was a momentum change. Our team manages to score two more times, tying the game at twenty-one.

We're down to the final two minutes with our defense on the field. Their quarterback has the ball, and I'm pushed back by their lineman, doing my best to break his hold. The ball is handed off to a Knights running back, who charges down the field, gaining fifteen yards before being tackled by our linebacker, Kroy Jennings.

The Knights continue to run with the ball, chewing up the play clock in an attempt to win. I'm hoping like hell we put a stop to their run game, which would lead us to a tie and give us the opportunity to beat them in overtime.

It's third down. I watch the offense closely, pinpointing who I believe the next player is to receive the ball. The ball gets snapped and handed off to the one I targeted. I push off my opponent and bypass him before he has the chance to stop me, charging at the one carrying the ball. My arms wrap around the Knights player's legs, and I bring him down, forcing the stop.

Fourth down.

Knights can either attempt the field goal to try to win the game or take a knee, putting us into overtime. They could still send us into overtime with the missed field goal, but from what I've learned, the team usually goes for the kick.

Knights call out their kicking team, setting it up. There's only three seconds left on the clock. The ref blows the whistle, the ball is snapped, and ready for the kicker. I jump as the ball is kicked, hoping I can reach just high enough to deflect it.

The ball soars over our heads, all eyes watching as it flies through the air between the yellow goal posts, ending the game.

By the final whistle, we lost twenty-four to twenty-one. It's a loss that should have been a win, but I can't bring myself to care about that right now.

On the bus ride home, the mood is somber. Some of my teammates have their headphones in, drowning out their postgame loss with their playlist. Others sit back with their eyes closed, exhausted and defeated.

Once we arrive back at school, Coach Wells gives us a brief talk about learning from defeat before dismissing us to go home.

"Corrine, do you need a ride home?" I ask, concerned about her driving with the hit she took.

"Yeah, that would be great."

The two of us walk toward my car when Charmaine's shrill voice approaches.

"Porkenstein!"

Not who I want to deal with right now. I turn to face the pompous Barbie, giving her a saccharine smile. "Yes, Charmin?"

Charmaine gets in my space, her expensive perfume suffocating. "When did you last talk to Dylan?"

I keep my expression neutral. "Football practice?" Like hell I will tell her we talk every day and night.

She narrows her eyes. "So you don't know why he's ignoring my calls and texts? His phone goes straight to voicemail."

I shrug, though I'm not surprised. If Dylan's really sticking to his plan—waiting it out until the dinner for the sake of the letter—he'd still have to talk to her. But maybe he's finally done playing nice.

Charmaine suddenly snaps, her voice sharp and demanding. "Give me your phone!"

"Excuse me?" I say, brows lifting.

"Give it to me!" she snaps, eyes wild. "If he won't answer me, I *know* he'll answer for you."

I cross my arms tightly over my chest, grounding myself. "And what makes you so sure of that, Charmaine? Did you forget our little fallout? Or are you just hoping I'm still dumb enough to play along?"

We glare at each other, our distaste for the other clear as day.

"Maisie ..." Corrine's soft voice cuts through. "Just call him and put it on speaker phone. If he hasn't answered Zion, it has to be worth a chance."

I look at Corrine, an almost carbon copy of her sister. Her eyes pleading because like the rest of us, she's worried too.

"Fine!" I relent, reaching into my pocket for my phone. I quickly go to his contact, not risking Charmaine seeing how recently we talked, and dial Dylan, then put it on speakerphone.

"The person you are trying to reach is unavailable right now. Please leave a message after the tone."

I hang up the call. "See? He's not even answering *my* calls. Happy now?"

The lie settles uneasily on my tongue, but I'm relieved. *So* relieved. If he'd answered—if he'd said *"Hey, baby"* or anything close—Charmaine would've lost it. And knowing her, she wouldn't have just made a scene. She would've gone nuclear and destroyed whatever future Dylan's still trying to hold onto.

"Very." She gives me a smug smile. "Let's go, Corrine. Mommy wants you to get home and rest. She's got the doctor stopping by tomorrow."

"Bye, Maisie." Corrine waves, taking off after her sister.

I try calling Dylan two more times, both my calls going directly to voicemail.

MAISIE

Heyy. Is everything okay? No one can get in touch with you, and you're worrying us. Please reach out. I'm here for you. Just say something. Please?

As I pull up to my house, I see his car, along with his parents' vehicles, parked in the driveway. They're all home?

If Dylan is home, there is a good chance he could be in his room.

Grabbing my football gear, I hurry inside.

"How was the game?" Mom asks from the couch, her and Josie watching some trashy reality TV show.

"We lost, sadly."

"Oh. I'm sorry to hear that, sweetheart."

"Eh, we can't win them all, now, can we?" I shrug. "I'm going to go shower because I smell of sweat and defeat."

"Pizza's in the kitchen if you're hungry," my mom calls out as I quickly climb the stairs.

As soon as I make it to my bedroom, I rush to the window, all hopes of seeing him dashed when his curtains are closed.

"What?" I whisper, taken aback.

Why would his be closed? He hasn't closed them all week since we talked—and kissed.

I take a seat, Jinxy hopping up in the window beside me, and wait. Hoping for some sign of life.

"He's got to be in there, right, Jinxabelle?" I whisper to my cat.

After five minutes of sitting with no change, I decide to go get cleaned up. It's almost ten, and we usually talk to each other when our families go to bed. There's still a chance, I hope.

So I go clean up, enjoy a few slices of pizza with my mom and sister, and watch one episode of their incredibly dramatic show while constantly checking my phone before calling it a night.

*One last check*, I tell myself.

Peering out into the dark, across the yard, Dylan's bedroom is still obscured from view. For a moment, light trickles through the gaps before immersing back to darkness.

With exhaustion tugging at my eyes, I decide to let it go—for tonight. I'll give him the space he clearly wants. But tomorrow? There's no escaping me.

# Chapter 22

## Maisie

The next morning, I wake up to beams of the morning sunshine blasting me in the face, and feeling groggy from a fitful night of sleep. Tossing and turning, I kept waking up to check my phone for any messages from Dylan, but there was nothing. I even got up several times to peek through my window, hoping to catch a glimpse of movement in his room. The worry gnawing at my stomach seems to only have intensified overnight.

After I get dressed, I make my way downstairs and peer through the living room window on the side facing the Myers home. All their vehicles are still there, parked in the driveway.

I hurry through tending to Jinxy, ensuring she's fed and has fresh water, before grabbing my sneakers.

"Where are you off to?" Mom appears from the kitchen.

"Going next door. Something's up with Dylan, and I just need to make sure he's okay."

"I wonder if it has anything to do with the vehicle that showed up yesterday. Barb said a dark SUV was there for a while."

"Dark vehicle?"

Barb is the nosiest neighbor on the block, but she comes in handy if you ever need to find something out about anything on this street.

"Yeah. Said it looked serious." Mom glances at her watch. "Shoot. Josie, we need to leave, or you're going to be late for dance!"

"I'm coming!" my sister shouts from upstairs.

"I shouldn't be too long," I call out as I head out the door and dash to the neighbor's house.

Taking a deep breath, I approach the front door of a place that felt like a second home to me growing up, and knock a few times. Mrs. Myers answers the door, her eyes red and puffy as if she had been crying for awhile.

"Maisie," she says, pulling me into a tight hug. "Oh, sweetie, I'm so happy to see you."

"What's wrong?" I ask, my worry spiking. "You've been crying."

"It's Carver," she says, her voice cracking. "His unit was attacked, and he's... he's missing."

My hand flies to my mouth as a gasp escapes. "Oh my God. I'm so sorry."

I pull her back into my arms, hugging her even tighter—trying to pour all the strength and love I have into her as tears sting my eyes.

"How's Dylan doing with all of this?" I ask, pulling back to swipe a lone tear.

"Dylan's been stuck upstairs. He hasn't come down since the officers left yesterday afternoon. It's like he refuses to leave his room. You're more than welcome to go up there to try to talk to him. I think he could really use a friend right now."

I nod, squeezing her hand before heading up the familiar stairs in a house I used to run around in with both the Myers boys.

As I take each step, I look at the photos lined perfectly parallel with the staircase. So many pictures of Dylan and Carver at different ages, from cute chubby babies all the way to their awkward pubescent stage.

Looking at Carver's pictures, especially the one from his military graduation, I feel the sting in my chest.

The thought of Carver never coming home grips me like a vice. It's too painful to even imagine. This can't be real—can't be happening. Not to Nora and Wade. Not to Dylan. They don't deserve this kind of heartbreak.

I climb the last few stairs, my heart heavy as I reach Dylan's door and knock gently. "Dylan? It's me." No response. I try again, a little louder this time. "D, please. I know you're in there."

Still nothing.

Taking a deep breath, I turn the doorknob, relieved when it opens. The room is dim, curtains drawn tight against the morning light. It takes my eyes a moment to adjust before I spot him sitting on the floor at the foot of his bed, back against the mattress and knees pulled to his chest. He's staring at something in his hands.

"Hey," I murmur, closing the door behind me.

Dylan doesn't look up or acknowledge my presence at all. I cross the room and carefully lower myself to sit beside him, our shoulders touching. He's holding a framed photo of him and Carver, his grip so tight it's like letting go would mean losing his brother.

For several minutes, I sit there with him in silence, letting him know he's not alone.

"I can't lose him, Freckles," he finally whispers, his voice raw and broken. "I just ... I can't."

"I know," I say softly, reaching for his hand. His fingers are cold when they lace with my mine, trembling. "Your mom told me what happened."

Dylan doesn't look up. His eyes stay fixed on the photo, his thumb gently tracing over Carver's face like it might bring him back. "He always promised he'd come home," he says, voice cracking. "'Don't worry, little brother. I always come back.' That's what he'd say every time."

He swallows hard. "But what if this time he doesn't?"

The pain in his voice breaks my heart. I've never seen Dylan like this—so vulnerable, so lost. The usual spark in his eyes is gone, replaced by a hollow ache that steals the air from the room. I wrap my arm around his shoulders and pull him close, hoping my presence can offer even a sliver of comfort in the middle of his storm.

"You can't think like that, D. Carver is strong and smart. If anyone can make it through this, it's him."

Dylan leans his head against mine, a shuddering breath escaping him. "I had a panic attack when they told us. First one that bad in awhile."

My heart clenches. "Of course you did," I say gently. "Anyone would've. That kind of news... it would knock the air out of anyone."

"I should have called you," he admits. "I wanted to, I really did ... but I just ... I couldn't talk to anyone. I couldn't make it real by saying it out loud."

"Hey," I whisper, brushing his arm gently. "It's okay. I'm here now, right?"

He nods, his eyes glassy. "Thank you."

"You're welcome." I press a soft kiss to his head, and just hold him there, letting the silence wrap around us like a blanket. There's nothing else to say, at least not right now. All I can do is be here, steady and unshaken, while the world tilts beneath his feet.

We sit like that for a while, the heaviness of it all settling over us. His eyes are rimmed with exhaustion, dark circles shadowing the skin beneath them. His hair is a mess, sticking up in places where he's clearly been dragging his fingers through it over and over.

"Have you slept at all?" I ask softly.

He shakes his head. "Every time I close my eyes, I see him out there somewhere hurt or ..." He doesn't finish his sentence, but he doesn't need to.

"Come on," I say, standing up and gently tugging his hand. "You need to get some rest."

To my surprise, he doesn't resist as I guide him to his bed. He lies down, still clutching the photo frame, and I pull the covers over him.

"There you go." I start to move away, but his hand grabs mine, stopping me in my tracks.

"Stay with me?" He pleads.

"Yeah. Of course I will." I climb into the bed next to him, draping an arm across his chest as he wraps an arm around me.

We lie there together, not talking. Just the sounds of our breathing and Dylan's heart beating beneath my ear. After a few moments, Dylan drifts off to sleep. I linger, waiting until I know he's deep in sleep before removing myself from his side. A task much more difficult than it should be.

I creep out of his room and down the stairs, finding his parents sitting together in the living room.

"How is he?" his father asks when he sees me.

"He's really torn up about this whole mess. Afraid, as anyone would be in your situation. I did get him to lay down, and he's sound asleep, which I think will help him."

"Thank you for coming over, for checking on him. Nora and I appreciate it."

"You're an angel, Maisie," his mother says, pulling me into a warm hug.

"If you guys need anything, please don't hesitate to reach out. I'm here for you guys." I give his parents extra hugs, knowing it's the only source of comfort I can provide. "I have to go help Nonna finish my dress, but I can come back when I'm finished, if that's okay?"

"You know our door is always open for you."

After another hug, I leave the Myers home, my heart aching for their pain. I hope that Dylan is able to get some rest and wake with a sense of clarity, even if it's just for a moment.

"Are you ready to see it?"

"Girl, come on! I've been dying to see this dress since you sketched it! Now bring that beautiful ass out here!" Alora shouts from the waiting area.

"Language, nipote femmina!"

"Sorry, Nonna." Alora winces like she's heard that warning a hundred times.

I laugh at their banter and pull back the curtains and step up on the platform, giving Nonna and Alora the full 360 view.

"Shut. Up!" Alora's jaw drops, her eyes wide. "This dress is so freaking stunning! And you designed this!?"

"All me. With Nonna's help of course!"

"Oh! We need to take a picture!" Nonna says, reaching for her phone. We take several photos from different angles, ensuring to capture every detail of the dress.

"How do you feel about it, Rossa?"

"I love it," I say, smoothing my hands over the silky fabric. "It's everything I imagined when I sketched it."

"The color complements your skin and hair beautifully. You're going to be the belle of the ball," Nonna says proudly, adjusting one of the cap sleeves.

"Oh, it's so gorgeous! Do I really have to take it off?" I shoot Alora a pouty look. She laughs, but her smile quickly fades as she picks up her phone.

"Uh ... you're going to want to change," she says, showing me a text from Corrine.

> Hey. Party at Davenport mansion. Dylan showed up a little bit ago, and he's getting super drunk. You may want to tell Maisie because my sister looks like she's up to no good.

"Quick, help me unzip the back," I tell Alora. She pulls the zipper all the way down, and I quickly change out of the dress and back into the clothes I came in.

"Nonna! Maisie and I need to go. Are you okay for the evening?"

"You girls go. I'll be all right. Ti amo!"

"Ti amo, Nonna! I'll call you later, okay?" Alora leans in to kiss her cheek before grabbing my hand and heading for the door.

We get in my car, and I drive as fast as one can without getting pulled over by the police.

The Davenport mansion is precisely what you'd expect from one of the wealthiest families in Bellwood—a massive, modern estate with floor-to-ceiling windows and a grand entrance. Music pulses from inside, growing louder as we approach the massive house.

I scan the cars for any sign of Dylan's but come up empty. There has to be like a hundred cars lining the circular driveway, the overflow spilling into the street.

"You ready?" Alora asks, giving my arm a reassuring squeeze.

"As I'll ever be," I state, taking a deep breath.

We push our way inside, the smell of alcohol and sweat hitting us immediately. Bodies press against each other in the massive foyer, dancing to the beat of some hip-hop song, with red cups in hand as they sway to the music.

"Let's find Dylan," I shout over the music, already scanning the crowd.

We weave through the throng of partygoers, checking the main rooms on the first floor—no sign of him. I'm about to suggest we check upstairs when Zion and Corrine appear in front of us, relief washing over their faces.

"Thank God you're here," he says, pulling me into a quick hug. "He's out back by the pool."

"Maisie, he's really messed up," Corrine adds. "I've never seen him like this before."

My pulse quickens. "And Charmaine?"

"Practically glued to his side." Corrine grimaces. "She's been feeding him shots for the past hour."

My blood boils at the thought of Charmaine taking advantage of Dylan's vulnerable state. "Thanks for texting us."

"How bad *is* he?" I ask, following Zion as he leads us through the house.

"Really bad. I've never seen him like this, Maisie. It's like he's trying to drink himself into oblivion—like he doesn't care if he wakes up tomorrow."

The words hang in the air between us, thick with dread. My stomach turns, my heart racing as I try to brace myself for whatever I'll find when we reach him.

We step out onto the expansive patio where several people are swimming despite the cool night air. Others are gathered around a fire pit, laughing and talking loudly. And there, sitting at the edge of the pool with his feet dangling in the water, is Dylan.

Even from here, I can see he's a mess. His hair is disheveled, his shoulders slumped, and he's clutching a bottle of something dark—whiskey, most likely. Worst of all, Charmaine is next to him, her hand on his thigh, body pressed into his side as she whispers something in his ear.

I can feel my pulse quicken, the anger rising in my chest like a furnace.

"I've been trying to keep an eye on them," Zion says, his voice strained. He doesn't look at me, but I can tell by the way his jaw tightens that he's just as pissed off as I am. "She's been all over him since he got here."

"Of course she has," I mutter under my breath, my blood boiling with every second that passes. The image of her touching him, using his brokenness, is unbearable. The protective urge inside me flares up, desperate to pull him away from her.

"Want me to create a distraction?" Alora offers, already eyeing Charmaine with disdain.

"No, I've got this," I state, straightening my shoulders. I march over to where they're sitting, my heart pounding with each step, and ignore the curious glances from people we pass.

As I get closer, I can hear Charmaine's sugary-sweet voice.

"Why don't we go somewhere more private, Pookie Bear? I know just what you need to forget all your problems." Her fingers slide up his thigh, dangerously close to his groin.

Dylan doesn't even seem to notice her advances, his gaze fixed on the water, lost in his thoughts as he takes another long swig from the bottle.

"Dylan," I call out, my voice firm but gentle.

His head snaps up at the sound of my voice, and for a moment, there's a flash of recognition, a spark of life returning to his eyes.

"Fffrrrreckles?" He blinks as if he can't quite believe I'm standing there.

Charmaine's expression darkens the moment she sees me, her usual sneer instantly taking over, like it's been carved into her face. "What are you doing here, Porkenstein? This is a private party, invitation only."

"I invited her." Corrine steps forward, coming to stand beside me, her stance protective, a silent declaration that she's not backing down.

Charmaine shoots her sister a venomous look, her tone sharp as a blade. "Of course you did."

"I'm here for Dylan," I say, not bothering to look at her. "He needs to go home."

"He's fine right where he is," Charmaine snaps, tightening her grip on his arm. "Aren't you, baby?"

Dylan's gaze shifts between us, confusion clouding his features before settling back on me. "Carver," he mumbles, his voice cracking. "They can't find him, Freckles."

"I know," I murmur, kneeling in front of him so we're eye level. "That's why you shouldn't be here right now. You should be home with your parents."

"What is he talking about?" Charmaine demands, her perfectly shaped eyebrows furrowing.

I ignore her, keeping my focus on Dylan. "Come on, D. Let me take you home."

"Can't you see he's busy?" Charmaine hisses, clutching his arm possessively. "We were just about to go upstairs."

"Nooo, we werrenn't," Dylan says. He yanks his arm away from her, nearly losing his balance again. My arm shoots out instinctively, as the fear of him stumbling into the pool floods me.

"Dylan, please. Let me take you home," I plead.

"Home," he repeats, as if testing the word. "Can't go home. Too quiet. Too many memories."

"Then you'll come to my house," I say, reaching for the bottle in his hand. "I have a feeling Jinxy will be happy to see you."

A ghost of a smile touches his lips at the mention of my cat. He allows me to take the bottle from him, which I promptly hand off to Zion, who approaches from the other side of Corrine.

Charmaine stands up, putting herself between us. "Back off, Porkenstein. He's *my* boyfriend, and I'll be the only one taking care of him."

"By getting him more drunk?" I shoot back, my voice hard with disbelief. "He's hurting, and the only thing you're doing is taking advantage of him."

"Oh please." She scoffs. "Like *you* know what he needs."

"I know he doesn't need this." I gesture to the bottle in Zion's hand. "And he definitely doesn't need you trying to get him into bed when he can barely stand up."

Charmaine's face contorts, her eyes flashing with fury. Her hands ball into fists at her sides as her lips curl into a sneer. "Listen to me, obesity Ariel," she spits, her words dripping with venom. "He's not going anywhere with you. Not now, not ever."

The words hit like a slap, but I don't flinch.

Dylan looks at her, then back to me, his expression clearing slightly. "I want to go with Maisie," he says, his words still slurred but his intent clear.

"What?" Charmaine's voice rises, drawing attention from nearby partygoers. "You can't be serious!"

"He is," I say, addressing her directly. "And if you cared about him at all, you'd let him go without making a scene."

"You fat bitch. You think you can just waltz in here and take him?"

"I'm not taking anything," I snap, my words sharp as a knife.

*Especially when he was never truly yours.*

# Chapter 23

## Maisie

With the help of Zion, the two of us get Dylan upright, draping his arms around our necks. Corrine and Alora step in when Charmaine attempts to reach for Dylan.

"Oh, I don't think so, bitch," Alora spits out. Before anyone can react, she shoves Charmaine into the pool with a swift, practiced motion.

The sound of splashing water echoes through the air, followed by a shocked silence, then an eruption of laughter from the onlookers. Some pull out their phones, recording the chaos, their faces lit up by the flickering screens, as if this were some kind of sick performance for their amusement.

"Wait. Where's his shoes?" I ask, noticing his bare feet.

"I've got them!" Corrine shouts from somewhere behind me.

Ensuring we have all of Dylan's belongings, we make our way through the house, weaving through the sea of bodies. Just as we reach the door, Tristan steps in front of us, blocking our exit.

"Where do you think you're going?" he asks, his eyes narrowing as they shift from me to Dylan, suspicion and brewing in his gaze.

"Not now, Tristan," I say, my tone tight with barely-contained irritation as we try to maneuver around him. "I need to get Dylan home."

His jaw tightens as he blocks our path again. "So you're the one taking him?" His voice carries an edge I've never heard before. "Interesting choice, considering he's the one who's been ignoring your existence for weeks."

"Not the time, man," Zion warns, adjusting his grip on Dylan's waist.

"Was I talking to you, Weedon?" Tristan snaps, his eyes never leaving mine. "I believe I was talking to my girlfriend."

Dylan's head lifts at the word "girlfriend," his glazed eyes finding Tristan's face. "Ssshe's not your girlllfriend."

"What the fuck did you say?" Tristan steps closer, his voice low and dangerous.

This time, Alora steps forward, placing a hand on Tristan's chest, giving him a shove. "Back off, Tristan," She snarls. "Can't you see Dylan's in bad shape? All we're trying to do is get him home."

Dylan straightens slightly, swaying as he tries to stand more upright. "Listen to my friend. She's smart."

"Fine," he says after a tense moment, stepping aside but catching my arm as I pass. "But you and me? We need to talk."

I meet his eyes, unflinching. "Actually, Tristan? Let me save you the trouble."

"Maisie ..." Alora's voice cuts in, low and tense, a warning laced with concern. She knows me too well—knows I'm standing on the edge, ready to push him over it if he gives me one more reason. Her eyes plead for restraint, but the fire in my chest is already lit.

"No, Alora," My voice is steady, despite the storm brewing inside me. "I'm done pretending—done hiding how I really feel."

I meet Tristan's eyes, ready to be completely honest with him. "You're a good guy, Tristan. And you've been a decent boyfriend. But I can't keep faking my happiness with you, not when my heart's never really been in it to begin with."

His expression flickers, but I push forward. "The truth is … I've only ever loved one person, and that person isn't you. I wanted to give you a chance, I really did. But the reality is … you became a distraction from my heartbreak, not a cure for it."

I swallow hard, the weight of my words finally settling between us. "It's not fair of me to keep pretending, to drag this out like it might somehow fix itself. For that, I am truly, deeply sorry for letting you believe otherwise. So go ahead. Say whatever you need to say, but it won't change anything. I'm breaking up with you, Tristan."

I step back, giving us both some much-needed space, then pause to add, "I just hope we can put this behind us when we're on the field. For the good of the team."

I glance over at Zion, nodding toward the door. "Let's go."

As we pass, Dylan mumbles something that sounds suspiciously like "She's mine," but it's too slurred for any of us to make out.

We finally make it outside, the cool night air a welcome relief after the stifling heat of the party.

"Your car or mine?" Zion asks.

"Mine's closer," I reply. "Keys are in my pocket."

Zion fishes them out and hands them to Alora. "You get the car door, and I'll help get him in the back."

"I can walk," Dylan protests weakly, though he's still leaning heavily on us.

"Sure you can, buddy." Zion humors him as we carefully maneuver toward my Honda.

Once we reach my car, Alora unlocks the doors, and Zion and I work together to get Dylan into the back seat.

"Are you sure you can handle him from here?" Zion asks once we get Dylan settled.

"Yeah, I've got it. Thanks for your help."

"Anytime. Call me if you need anything." He gives my shoulder a squeeze before stepping back.

Alora walks up, arms crossed. "That was quite the exit scene. You want me to come with you?"

"No, I think it's better if it's just me." I look to Zion. "You think you can give this one a ride home for me?"

"Yeah. I've got Lewis twin number one." Zion says, gently shoving Alora.

"As long as you know I'm number one," Alora retorts.

"Hey, don't forget his shoes," Corrine says, passing me Dylan's white Air Force Ones.

"Seriously, you guys. Thank you." I give them each a quick hug before sliding into the driver's seat. Dylan's head is lolled against the window, his eyes half closed.

"Let's get you home," I mutter, as I start the car.

"Not home," he mumbles. "Don't wanna see their faces. Too sad."

"No, not your home. My home. Is that okay?" I ask, looking in the rearview mirror.

He nods slowly, and I pull away, heading toward my house. The drive is quiet, with Dylan drifting in and out of consciousness. Every few minutes, he'll mutter something about Carver or let out a shaky breath that breaks my heart all over again.

## Dylan

Everything's spinning.

Sounds are muffled, lights too bright, and my thoughts are a jumbled mess swirling through my alcohol-soaked brain. The only thing that feels real is the crushing weight in my chest—Carver is missing. Or my brother could be dead.

I vaguely remember showing up at the party, desperate to drown out the thoughts of my brother, to numb the pain that's been eating me alive since those officers showed up at our door.

Charmaine was there, pushing drinks into my hands, whispering things in my ear that I couldn't care less about. All I wanted was to stop feeling, to prevent the constant loop of worst-case scenarios playing in my head.

Then Maisie was there. My Freckles. Like an angel cutting through the fog, her voice broke through the haze of alcohol and misery.

I feel the car stop, and through half-lidded eyes, I see we're at her house.

The porch light is on, casting a warm glow that beckons me inside.

"We're here," she murmurs, turning off the engine. "Can you walk, or do you need my help?"

"I can walk," I say, though I'm not entirely sure that's true. I fumble with the door handle, eventually pushing it open. My bare feet hit the cold pavement, and I stand, the world tilting dangerously around me.

Maisie is at my side instantly, her arm wrapping around my waist to steady me, supporting my weight. "Easy there, quarterback."

I lean into her, grateful for her strength. "Sorry," I mumble, embarrassed by my state. "Shouldn't have to ... take care of me like this."

"Shh," she soothes, guiding me toward her front door. "Let's get you inside."

We make it to her porch, and she helps me lean against the wall while she unlocks the door. The house is quiet and dark—her mom and sister must be asleep.

I stumble over the threshold, nearly bringing both of us down.

"Easy," she whispers, her voice low and gentle.

"I'm sorry," I mumble, not entirely sure what I'm apologizing for—showing up at that party, getting wasted, or being a burden to her now.

"Hey. It's okay. I'm here and I got you. We just need to be quiet," she whispers, helping me inside and closing the door softly behind us. "Mom and Josie are sleeping so we don't want to wake them. Can you do that for me?"

I nod, trying my best to move silently as she leads me up the stairs to her bedroom. Every step is a challenge, my body heavy and uncoordinated, but eventually, we make it.

"Here we go," she says, helping me sit on the end of her bed. I sink onto the edge of it, the room still spinning slightly.

"Freckles," I say, my voice cracking. "I messed up."

She kneels in front of me, her steel-blue eyes filled with concern. "You didn't mess up, D. But getting drunk isn't going to help Carver."

"I know," I admit, hanging my head. "I just ... I couldn't stand being in that house for another minute. Watching my parents try to hold it together. The silence. It's suffocating."

Maisie rises, sitting beside me on the bed. "I understand. But there are better ways to cope than drowning yourself in whiskey."

"Bourbon," I correct, a pathetic attempt at humor.

She rolls her eyes, but there's a hint of a smile. "Let's get you out of these clothes. They smell like booze."

I try to unbutton my shirt, but my fingers feel thick and uncooperative. Maisie gently pushes my hands away and does it for me, her touch sending sparks across my skin despite my intoxicated state.

"Arms up," she instructs, and I comply as she pulls my T-shirt over my head.

"This feels familiar," I murmur, remembering all the times we've taken care of each other over the years.

"Except usually I'm not peeling you out of alcohol-soaked clothes," she replies, setting my shirt aside. "Do you think you can manage your jeans, or do you need help with those too?"

Even in my drunken state, I can see the blush creeping up her cheeks. "I got it," I say, fumbling with my belt.

She turns away, providing me some privacy. "While you take care of that, I'll be right back."

Once I'm down to my boxers, I take a seat back on the bed.

Moments later, Maisie returns with a glass of water and some pills. "Aspirin," she explains, placing them in my palm. "Trust me, you'll thank me in the morning."

I take the pills from her hand, swallowing them with a large gulp of water. My throat feels parched, and I drain the entire glass before handing it back to her.

"More?" she asks, and I nod gratefully.

When she returns with a refilled glass, I drink half of it before setting it on her nightstand. The room has stopped spinning quite so violently, but my head is still foggy, my thoughts scattered. She's right about the aspirin—my head is starting to throb, a preview of tomorrow's hangover.

"You should get some sleep," she says, pulling back her covers. "We can talk more in the morning."

As she turns to leave, I reach out, catching her wrist.

"Stay with me?" I ask, my voice barely above a whisper, suddenly afraid to be alone with my thoughts again. "Please?"

She hesitates for a moment before nodding. "Let me just change first."

I slide under her covers and watch through heavy eyelids as she grabs clothes from her dresser and disappears down the hall. When she returns, she's wearing a pair of sleep shorts and an oversized T-shirt I recognize as one of mine.

"You kept that?" I ask, a small smile tugging at my lips despite everything. "I thought it got up and ran away from my closet."

"Shut up," she mumbles, but there's no heat in her words. She slides into bed beside me, careful to maintain a small distance between us.

I immediately reach for her, needing her close, and inwardly smile when she comes willingly, settling against my side.

For a few moments, we lie there in silence, the only sounds being our breathing and the occasional jingle of Jinxy's collar from downstairs. Despite the alcohol clouding my system, I'm acutely aware of her presence, the warmth radiating from her body.

"He has to come back, Freckles," I whisper into the darkness. "I can't lose him."

"I know you can't," she says, her hand finding mine beneath the covers. "None of us can. But especially not you."

"What if they never find him? What if he's gone forever?"

"No what-ifs," she says firmly, squeezing my hand. "We have to believe he'll come home. He needs us to believe that."

Maisie props herself up on one elbow, looking down at me. "And if they don't find him? Then you'll get through it. Not alone, but with your parents, with me, with everyone who loves you. But let's not go there yet, okay? There's still so much hope."

I nod, though the lump in my throat makes it hard to speak. She settles back down beside me, her head resting on my chest, her warmth seeping into my skin.

"I'm sorry about what happened at the party," I say after a while, my fingers absently playing with her hair. "With Charmaine."

"You have nothing to apologize for," she assures me. "The fact she was taking advantage of you is appalling."

"I heard what you sssaid to Tristan," I admit. My words are still slurred but clearer than before. "About only ever loving one person."

Even in the darkness, I can feel her tense slightly against me. "You heard that, huh?"

"Did you mean it?" I ask, needing to hear it again, to know it wasn't just the alcohol playing tricks on me.

She's quiet for so long, I think she might have fallen asleep, but then she shifts, her face turned up toward mine even though we can barely see each other in the dark room.

"Yes," she whispers. "I meant every word."

I pull her closer, pressing a kiss to the top of her head. "I love you, Freckles. I always have."

"I love you, too," she murmurs against my chest. "Now get some sleep."

# Chapter 24

## Maisie

What a crazy few days it has been since I rescued a drunk Dylan from that party.

As I expected, he was horribly hungover the next day, but I did what I could to help make the experience less sufferable for him.

As much as he protested, I convinced him we had to tell his parents about what happened. They deserved the truth, but more importantly, Dylan needed help before he risked going down a much darker path. It was painfully clear he was unraveling under the weight of the news about his brother.

So, once he was sober enough to walk, I took him home, and the two of us sat down with his parents and told them everything.

To their credit, Nora and Wade didn't explode. They listened. And in the end, they agreed—this time, the punishment didn't fit the crime. The brutal hangover, the guilt, the grief... he was already paying the price. What he needed now wasn't discipline. It was support.

Thankfully, with the Army's support for families of soldiers who are missing or killed in action, Dylan was able to start therapy right away. His parents, too, reached out for help—both of them recognizing that they couldn't navigate this kind of grief alone. They've each begun seeing therapists to help them process the overwhelming grief and uncertainty that comes with not knowing if their son is ever coming home.

There have been no updates on Carver, but now that word has spread through Bellwood, our community has come together in support of the Myers family. Neighbors delivering meals, running errands—doing whatever they can to ease the weight of the unknown. Church members have included an extra prayer into morning services, praying for Carver and his team to be found alive and brought safely home.

It's incredible, really—walking through town and seeing posters for fundraisers and prayer services taped to windows and bulletin boards. Bellwood is holding on to hope, refusing to let go of one of its own. The community has so much faith, and I hope it's enough for Dylan and his family to keep pushing through the days ahead.

This week, the tension at school has been palpable, with everyone on edge as tomorrow marks the big rivalry game against Wimbleton High.

"Corrine, are you cleared to play tomorrow night?" Hollis asks as Corrine joins our table for lunch.

"Should have the final okay this afternoon, especially since I didn't have any symptoms."

After Saturday's incident, Corrine has been sitting with us for lunch. She's gradually learning to stand on her own, pulling away from her sister's toxicity—and I couldn't be more proud of the courage that takes.

"Good! We need *all* of us girls out on that field," Hollis replies.

"Yeah, I don't want a repeat of the Lincoln game," Alora says with a dramatic shudder. "Felt like someone put some bad voodoo magic on us or something,"

I laugh softly. "Is Nonna putting weird ideas in your head again, Lor?"

She grins, unbothered. "Always."

"Speaking of Nonna…" I lean in a little, eyes gleaming. "Please tell me you all have no plans after practice tonight?"

"I'm free," Corrine says.

"Same," Alora chimes in.

"I'm pretty sure I have work," Hollis mumbles. "Sorry."

"Okay, well, then we are going to have to think of something," I say, buzzing with excitement. "Because Nonna and I have a surprise for all of you."

"I hate surprises," Hollis mutters, sitting back in her seat, her arms crossing over her chest.

"You hate a lot of things, grump-a-lump."

"You're not wrong," she deadpans.

"Wait … she's my Nonna. How did you two sneak a surprise by me?"

I just shrug, fighting back a smile as I look at Alora. "We have our ways…"

There's a flicker of mock betrayal on her face, but it quickly melts into amusement. She knows Nonna's always had a soft spot for me—probably because she sees right through both of us. Honestly, the two of us scheming together? It was only a matter of time.

After football practice, Corrine, Alora, and I head to Thread & Thimble for a surprise I have been dying to share since it was finished on Saturday.

"Nonna!" Alora calls out.

"Come to the fitting area!" Nonna shouts from the back of the store.

In the back, Nonna has three fitting rooms for customers, and I made sure she placed the dresses we designed for my friends in each of them.

"I hate that Hollis has to miss this so you both have to swear you won't tell her!" I finger-point to each of them. "Buuutttt …your surprise awaits you behind these curtains. Nonna and I designed and handmade each of your homecoming dresses. We just need you to try them on so we can make sure they fit."

"What!?" Alora exclaims.

"You're joking?" Corrine's eyes nearly bug out.

"No joking. Your friend wanted to do something special for you ladies, and she's put in a lot of hard work," Nonna states. "Your dresses are already in your fitting room. Alora, yours is in room one, Corrine, yours is in room two."

My friends run to their prospective fitting rooms, their excited screams echoing through the small boutique, loud enough to be heard from Main Street.

After a few moments, they emerge at the same time, looking stunning in their beautiful dresses I got to design specifically for them.

"Oh. My. God!" Alora gasps, completely at a loss for words.

"I'm speechless, Maisie! This dress ... it's absolutely stunning!" Corrine exclaims.

Alora's dress is a long black satin mermaid gown with a sweetheart neckline and delicate, thin straps. Intricate red beading traces the neckline—a choice I made knowing it would complement her olive skin and subtly nod to her Italian heritage. The bodice mimics a corset, but instead of traditional fabric between the boning, I chose sheer black material for a bold, modern twist.

For Corrine's dress, I chose a shorter style to suit her petite frame—she's about five three, maybe five four. It's a blush pink, A-line halter dress, sleeveless, with a delicate white lace floral pattern that flows from the neckline down into the skirt. At the waist, we added a silver-beaded belt to accentuate her figure, and in the back, a lace-up corset allows her to adjust the fit as needed.

"You really like them?" I ask, trying to keep my voice casual, but there's a flicker of uncertainty beneath the words.

"Like them? Are you kidding? This is incredible! I absolutely am in love with it!" Corrine rushes to me, wrapping me up in a hug. "Thank you, Mase!"

"You're welcome!" I beam, relieved by her comment and happy I could make this happen. "You want to know the best part?"

"You're getting us shoes to match?" Alora asks.

"Ha! In your dreams," I laugh. "Do I look like I'm made of money?"

"Keep making dresses like these and you will be swimming in it," Corrine says, checking her reflection in the mirror as she twists and turns in her dress.

"You guys! The dresses have pockets in them!"

"Shut up!" Alora exclaims.

"Seriously? You thought of everything!" Corrine adds.

Nothing excites a lady more than finding out your dress has built-in pockets. Trust me.

Wimbleton game day is finally here, and the air is thick with anticipation as fans of both teams fill our stadium.

The girls and I are all getting suited up in the girls' locker room, excited and maybe a little on edge for our first rivalry game.

I glance over to Hollis as she makes work with her hair. "You nervous, Holls?"

"Nope. If anything, I'm ready to stomp all over those fuckers."

"Got a lot of animosity against your old school, do you?" Alora questions.

"You have no idea," she states.

"Anything we should know about these guys before we head out?" Corrine asks.

"Yeah. Watch their hands when it comes to tackling. They'll use any excuse to cop a feel," she warns us. "But if you really want to get under their skin? Just use your badass athletic skills against them. They really don't like it when a female can one-up them."

"Good to know," Alora says with a sly smirk. Alora is always down to put some guy in his place. Ask her brother Anthony.

After our cleats are tied, our hair is pulled out of the way, and our gear is on, we head out to the field to meet with the rest of our team. The stadium is packed, not a single empty spot can be seen in the bleachers.

"Mase!" I hear someone shout from the stands, and to my surprise, Josie and Mom are in attendance, my sister waving at me enthusiastically.

"What are you guys doing here?" I ask, confused but smiling. "I thought you didn't like watching sports?"

"Yeah, well, everyone says what a total badass you are, so I thought it was time to come cheer you on for once."

"Josie Mae, language," Mom admonishes my little sister, before turning to face me. "It's a big game and we wanted to come support you."

"Thanks, Mom. That means a lot." I pull them both into a quick hug before leaving them to meet with my team.

As I head over to the group huddle for the pregame speech, I can't help but feel touched that they came. They're here—for me. Which means I need to really kick ass tonight. If my sister is hearing I'm a badass on the field, then badass is what she will see.

"Alright, team, this is it. Our biggest game of the season so far. Wimbleton may be our rivals, but tonight, they're just another opponent standing in our way. I know you've all worked your asses off to get here, and I expect nothing less than one hundred and ten percent effort out there. Whitlock, are you ready to show your old school what they're missing?"

"You bet, Coach." She nods firmly.

Coach continues addressing the whole team. "Remember what we practiced. Stick to the game plan, watch each other's backs, and play smart. Myers, I'm counting on you to lead this offense. Wallace, lock down that secondary. And ladies"—he looks at the four of us—"show these boys what you're made of."

We all nod, determination written across our faces. If there's one thing the four of us love doing in this sport, it's proving we are just as good as they are.

"Alright, bring it in," Coach calls.

After we all shout "Eagles," we get ready for kickoff. The coin toss goes in our favor, and we elect to receive. The kicked ball soars through the air, and Alora catches it cleanly at the five-yard line. She's been begging Coach Wells for a shot at kick returns, and now that he's finally giving her the chance, she's got a lot to prove.

Alora takes off running, following her blockers as she weaves through Wimbleton's special teams. She breaks free around the thirty-yard line, picking up speed as she races down the sideline. Logan Putterman, a defender on Wimbleton, is closing in fast. Just as he's about to make contact, Alora cuts back sharply, leaving him grasping at air as she sprints the final twenty yards into the end zone.

"Alora Lewis with the touchdown!" the announcer shouts into the microphone, and the crowd goes wild!

Hollis, Corrine, and I jump up and down, cheering our friend on. She did that!

The kick for the extra point is good, which means it's time for our defense to put in the work.

We meet our opponents on the line of scrimmage, and I can feel the adrenaline pumping through my veins. The Wimbleton quarterback barks out his cadence, and the ball is snapped. Their running back takes the handoff, cutting to the left, but I get to him, wrapping him up for a minimal gain.

"Nice stop, Jorgensen!" Coach Wells shouts from the sideline.

From the stands, I hear a loud and proud "That's my sister!" and pride blooms in my chest, hearing Josie's voice in the crowd.

I didn't think it would matter to me if they came to my games, but I was wrong. Having them here matters more than I will admit.

On second down, I break through their offensive line, forcing their quarterback to throw early. The pass falls incomplete, bringing up third and long.

"Keep the pressure on, forty-eight!" Dylan shouts from the sideline, his eyes locked on me with a mixture of pride and intensity that makes my heart skip a few beats.

Third down is another incomplete pass, forced by our cornerback's tight coverage, and Wimbleton has to punt the ball.

The game is intense with both teams trading touchdowns. Wimbleton's offense is tough, but my fellow defenders and I are making key stops when it counts. By halftime, we're up twenty-one to seventeen.

The third quarter starts off strong.

Their quarterback, number twelve, sets up under center. He's tall, with broad shoulders that fill out his pads impressively. Doesn't mean he will be hard to bring down.

"Blue forty-two! Blue forty-two! Hut!" he calls out.

The ball is snapped, and their offensive line pushes forward. I engage with their tackle, using my speed to try to get around him. He's strong, but I'm quicker. All the running Coach makes us do is paying off. I slip past just as their quarterback steps back to throw.

I charge forward, my eyes locked on my target. Their quarterback sees me coming and tries to scramble, but I'm too quick. I launch myself at him, wrapping my arms around his waist and driving him to the ground with a satisfying thud.

"Sack by number forty-eight, Maisie Jorgensen!" the announcer calls out, and our fans erupt in cheers.

We hold off the Wildcats and force the ball back to the Eagles.

# Dylan

Defense is killing it tonight on the field, but they're not as impressive as my girl. Damn, I am loving the way she is manhandling our rivals. I'd dare someone from their school to start talking shit so I can brag how a strong woman, *my* strong woman, kicked their team's ass.

As defense comes off the field, I strap on my helmet, pausing by Maisie.

"Did I mention how sexy you are taking down other men?"

"No," she says as she removes her helmet, "but I'll keep at it. Just for you." She winks before taking her well-deserved water break as I make my way onto the field.

On the first play, I fake a handoff to Hollis, and the Wildcats' defense takes the bait. By the time they realize she doesn't have the ball, it's too late—Corrine's already scored.

"Corrine Summers is in the end zone for another Eagles touchdown!" The announcer exclaims, and our fans cheer.

With the extra kick, we are now up twenty-eight to seventeen.

The rest of the game is a back-and-forth battle. Wimbleton scores again, closing the gap to twenty-eight to twenty-four. With just under two minutes left, we need to run out the clock to win the game.

It's now third down. I make a pass to Colton, but just as Colton goes to catch the ball, he's hit excessively hard by one of their defenders. That was definitely an illegal hit, and I can only hope these refs make the proper call.

When the refs throw their yellow flags, whistles are blown, and we all take a knee for our injured teammate.

"Folks, it looks like number eighty-two, Colton Reynolds, has been injured on the play."

The stadium falls quiet, all of us watching with bated breaths as our coaches and medics surround Colton.

Damn. This isn't looking too good. *C'mon, Colt! You gotta get up.*

A few moments later, the crowd claps when Colton stands and is able to walk off toward the sidelines.

"It appears the ruling on the field is a personal foul, unnecessary roughness on Wimbleton's number sixty-one, Logan Putterman. The result is a fifteen-yard penalty."

Cheers echo from our fellow blue and gold while boos ring out from the opposing side.

"Maybe they should learn how not to play dirty." Zion shouts at a few of our opponents, his voice sharp with anger. One of our linemen quickly pulls him back, not wanting to risk a fight—or worse, a penalty that could cost us the game.

With Colton out for the rest of the game and only a minute left on the clock, Coach Watson calls a timeout so we can regroup. As we huddle up on the sidelines, I can see my teammates are worried.

"Alright, listen up," Coach says. "We're still up, but it's too close for comfort. We need one more first down to run out the clock and seal this win. Whitlock, you're our best option right now. Think you can handle it?"

"Absolutely, Coach."

"Good. We're going with Jet Sweep Left on my signal. Offensive line, I need you to hold that block for just a few seconds. Give Whitlock the room she needs. Dylan, I need a clean handoff. Whitlock, you get that ball and run like hell. Got it?"

We all nod in understanding.

"Alright, let's finish this. Eagles on three. One, two, three!"

"Eagles!"

We head back out on the field and take our positions. This is it. If this all works out, we seal the win for us against one of our longest-standing rivals.

*Carver, my brother, wherever you are, this one's for you.* I kiss my hand and point it to the sky.

The ball is snapped, and I fake the handoff to Zion before turning to hand it off to Hollis as she sweeps across. She clutches the ball tightly to her chest and sprints down the left sideline.

Holding my breath, I watch as Hollis books it down the field, with that defender who illegally tackled Colton right on her heels.

*Let's go, Whitlock. Come on!*

The Wildcat defender, Putterman, wraps his arms and takes her down, but where she lands is hard to tell from my position. The refs blow their whistle, before one of them strides forward, turns to face the defensive end zone, and thrusts his arm out, signaling the first down.

"Hell yeah!" Zion and I run toward each other, jumping up to bump chests.

With only a few seconds left, there's no way Wimbleton can beat us now.

"Offense! Offense! Let's go!" as I call them to the line of scrimmage. Chase snaps the ball, and I take a knee. We repeat the play and stake our win.

# Chapter 25

## Maisie

After our kickass win and the usual postgame speeches by our coaches, I set out to find my mom and sister.

"Holy cow! You were absolutely incredible!" Josie shrieks as she comes running toward me. "I may not like sports, but I'll definitely be coming to watch you play, sis."

"You have no idea how much I would love that, Jojo."

I look at our mother and am surprised to see her eyes are red, like she's been crying. "Mom, are you okay?"

"Maisie," my mom starts, taking my hand, "I owe you a huge ass apology."

"For what?"

"For being the most god-awful mother on the planet." She swipes away a few tears, her voice breaking. "I scrutinized your body, your size, and what you wore. I compared you to your smaller friends, and that was incredibly harmful and toxic of me. And I'm so, so very sorry for it.

I allowed the pain and the trauma of what your father did and the things he said about me and my postpartum body to blind me. I let that pain spill over onto you, and I see now how unfair and damaging that was. You didn't deserve any of it."

She looks to the sky, taking a moment. "Honey, watching you out on this field just savagely taking on these boys like you did? Do you even know how empowering that was to see? You … you are a warrior, and you didn't give a shit you were taking on these boys. I overheard some of those things they were saying about you and your girls, but the four of you just proved the magnitude of a woman's power. That was incredibly beautiful. You, my Maisie Janine, are beautiful and perfect just the way you are."

Tears are now coming down my face as I embrace my mom, soaking in her love and her apology. "You're so forgiven. I'm just sorry Dad was a shitty person and never saw your beauty, never appreciated the woman you are and what you did for our family."

We pull away, happy smiles and streaked mascara down our faces, but in this moment, there is healing.

""Hey!" Alora jogs up to us, eyeing our red, splotchy faces with a raised brow. "Okay... what did I miss?"

"A broken generational trauma bond." I smile.

As the girls and I make our way to the locker room to get our stuff before heading home, a conversation stops us in our tracks.

"I still can't get over how gullible he is."

I'd recognize that annoying voice anywhere.

Charmaine.

Without a word, Hollis pulls out her phone and opens the voice recorder app. Of course she does. Hollis always knows when something might come back to bite us—or save us. It's like she has a sixth sense for when the truth needs a receipt. In moments like this, she doesn't hesitate. She just acts.

"He really thinks Daddy is writing him his letter of recommendation."

"Wait. So your dad's not writing it?"

"Come on, Tessa. Do you really think I can get two minutes of Daddy's attention? The man is always working."

"So … the dinner in Boston with the admissions person?"

"A big ass ploy. A ruse, if you will. I know Dylan fawns over Miss Piggy. I don't know what he sees in her. But as long as Dylan believes I'm helping him get into his precious Harvard, I keep those two apart. And when we leave for Boston after the homecoming game, I'll just use the excuse that Daddy will have to catch a later flight due to work. And once we get to that hotel room, I'm going to pop one of these little pills into his drink. I'll be damned if that fat bitch gets to claim Dylan's virginity before me!"

What. The. Fuck.

Hollis quickly ends the recording, and we take off to the girls' locker room, not wanting to get caught eavesdropping.

"Holy shit," Hollis states.

"Dylan's a virgin?" Alora asks, sounding surprised.

That makes two of us. I thought for sure in the four years they dated, they'd had sex.

"Now, you know why my sister cheats," Corrine just casually throws into the conversation.

"What!?" Hollis, Alora, and I shout in unison, heads snapping toward her like we just got whiplash.

"A part of the reason why Charmaine kept me from you guys was because of all the dirt I have on her. Knowing that I'm not a confrontational person and practically break out in hives at the mere thought of going off on another person was a weakness she preyed on.

Honestly, playing football with you three? It's because of you guys and this sport that I was able to take back my power and am not allowing her to control me anymore."

"I think I need therapy," Alora says, taking a seat on the bench.

"Join the club," Corrine says. "Hollis, if you can forward that recording to me, I'd like to know what my father thinks of his golden daughter now."

"But wouldn't your dad just get rid of it?" Hollis asks, and she makes a fair point. If Charmaine is his favorite, according to Corrine, then he would do what he can to make sure she doesn't go to prison.

"Who said I was taking it to my father first?" She quirks her eyebrow. "She's basically confessing to date rape, and I think the proper authorities need to be involved. You guys, let *me* handle my sister."

"Damn. Well, okay, sister girl." Hollis gives her a high five. "Got to watch out for you silent types."

Corrine turns to me. "Dylan needs to know the truth. He deserves to know he's being played, and my sister's done enough damage coming between you two. She was never the right girl for him, and deep down, she knew it—no matter how hard she tried to deny it. It's always been you, Maisie. Maybe he was drawn to her at first, but there's no doubt in my mind Dylan has always loved you."

Alora leans in, her voice softer but no less certain. "Corrine's right. This? This is your moment, Maisie. Go remind him who's really been there all along."

# Dylan

FRECKLES

Hey. We need to talk.

If there was ever a phrase that could make a man panic, it's those four words.

DYLAN

Did I fuck up?

FRECKLES

No. I promise.

It's good news.

Well, bad but also good news.

Is she trying to trigger a panic attack in me?

DYLAN

Which is it?

FRECKLES

Just meet me downstairs.

Downstairs? She's here?

After the game, everyone headed home to shower and freshen up before we meet at Munson's Diner. Beating Wimbleton is definitely cause for celebratory milkshakes.

I spritz on some cologne and hurry downstairs for whatever this conversation will be, surprised to see not just Maisie but Corrine too.

"Hey, Dylan, can you come here please?" my dad calls out from the dining room.

"What's going on?" I ask, a bit confused, trying to make sense of the situation.

"You're going to want to sit down for this," Maisie states, and the way she says it, a sense of dread creeps up my spine. She pulls out a chair at the table, and I hesitantly take a seat.

Sensing my unease, Maisie quickly takes the seat beside me.

"Whoa, whoa, hey. Baby, breathe. I'm sorry, I wasn't thinking. I should have said that differently."

Did she just call me baby?

"Are you okay?"

I stare into her gorgeous eyes, how the lighting in here makes them look almost like sparkling silver. "Yeah. I am now."

"Good." She pulls my hand to her lips and presses a soft kiss to the back of it.

"Son, Maisie and Corrine have something they need to share with us, regarding Charmaine."

"What about her?" I grit out, wanting nothing more than to detox myself from her.

My father looks at the girls, his arm outstretched. "Ladies, the room is yours."

"Thank you, Mr. Myers," Maisie starts. "So, after the game tonight, the girls and I were heading back to the locker room to get our stuff. As we were walking past the bleachers, we overheard a disturbing conversation between Charmaine and Tessa."

"Hollis had the smart idea to record the conversation, and honestly, without this, no one would believe what we overheard," Corrine adds. "May I play the recording?"

My dad and I both nod. Corrine sets her phone down and presses play, Charmaine's voice coming through.

The recording doesn't last long, but the details are horrifying.

"Does your father know about this?" my dad asks Corrine. They're both lawyers and know each other reasonably well. As for whether they actually get along, that's another story.

"No. I wanted you to hear it first, to have the evidence you need in case you'd like to press charges. My father tends to favor my sister, and I have no doubt she would have gotten away with this. That is just something I cannot live with. Blood or not."

"I appreciate that, Miss Summers." He shifts his gaze to me. "You were going to get a letter of recommendation from Lucian Summers?" My dad sounds slightly hurt by that information.

"It's nothing against you, Dad. I just wanted it to come from someone who isn't related to me, to give me a fair shot."

"When you put it that way, I can see the logic." He takes a few moments. "Miss Summers, would you kindly forward that recording to my work email. I will happily handle this situation."

"Are we pressing charges?" I ask, hoping he does.

"You bet your sweet ass we are," my father growls. Lucian Summers has no idea the wrath he's just invited. When it comes to his sons, his family, you don't mess with Wade Myers. That's a line you simply don't cross.

"I'm so sorry for putting this on your family, especially with everything you're going through," Maisie says, her voice full of empathy and care.

That's the complete difference between Maisie and Charmaine. Where Charmaine is ignorant and selfish, Maisie is thoughtful and selfless—always thinking of others, even when she has every right to fall apart herself.

"Maisie, I'm grateful you brought this to my attention. I'm sure it wasn't an easy decision, but it was the right thing to do. At least I will have somewhere to displace my anger."

He gives her a warm smile. "Now, how about you kids go out and celebrate that win?"

"Thank you, Mr. Myers," Corrine and Maisie say in unison.

The three of us walk outside into the cool October night. "I'm actually going to head home. There is an important conversation to be had with my father." Maisie and I watch as she climbs into a black car waiting out front of my house and disappears into the night. For the first time, I see a look on Corrine I'm not sure I want to see again.

"When did Corrine grow some balls?"

"Dylan!" Maisie smacks me in my chest.

"What? I mean, come on. Who was that girl?"

"That's a girl who's finding her voice and standing on business." Maisie beams with pride. "Thanks to football."

"Soo ..."

"Sooo ..." Maisie repeats. "I have something I need to confess."

"Should I be worried?"

"I don't think so." She chuckles. "So, you know when I was a bitch and cut you out completely?"

"Yeah, one of the worst fucking days of my life, Freckles."

"And I'll never forgive myself for hurting you the way I did." She takes a moment for herself. "The reason I was so angry at practice that day was because, as I was coming to the field, you and Charmaine were coming out from behind the bleachers, adjusting your clothes. I assumed that the two of you ..."

"Had sex? Behind the bleachers?"

"Yeah..."

"Freckles, she claimed she had to talk to me about her dad before she accosted me. She wanted to give me a blow job, but I literally had to fight her off. Nothing physical happened with her. I swear to you."

"And I believe you. I guess I just felt used ... or played. It was like the only way I could have you was by loving you in silence while you were with someone else. And that's torture. That's why I broke our friendship pact."

"You know why I never crossed the line, no matter how tempted I was?" I push her red hair behind her ear. Cupping the side of her head, I gently pull her closer. "I wanted you to be my girlfriend for so long, but the biggest fear was if we broke up, how much that would have killed me. I never want to imagine a life where you are not in mine."

I lean down, pulling her face to mine, claiming her mouth.

The world fades away, and it's just us, the heat of the moment, and the rush of everything we've held back. I could drown in this feeling, in the soft press of her lips against mine.

Maisie pulls back, and I groan at the loss of her mouth. "I want you, Dylan," she pants out.

"Where's your mom and sister?"

"Crap. Probably in the living room watching their reality TV show."

I glance at her house, then along the side where her bedroom window is, an idea coming to mind.

"We could just play *Romeo and Juliet*," I say, flashing her a devilish smile.

"Meet me in five?"

I lean down, pressing a kiss to her lips. "Five minutes. That's all you get to be ready."

With a quick kiss, we part ways.

As Maisie makes her way to her house, I rush back to my bedroom to grab a condom from a box that's yet to be used. I rush back down the stairs to head for the trellis.

"Dylan?"

"Sorry, Mom, forgot my wallet." I lie like a rug.

"Oh. Well, have fun and be safe!"

Ironically enough, that's precisely what I plan on doing.

Grabbing onto the sturdy rails, I pull my body up and make my way to Maisie's window. Keeping my balance so I don't fall, I tap on the window to let her know I'm outside.

Seconds later, the window is shoved up and her beautiful face greets me.

"If it isn't my own Romeo."

"Does my Juliet allow me entry?"

"She does." She grabs my hand and pulls me through. I step on the bench and into her room, closing the window behind me.

"At last, we meet again." I stare into those eyes, seeing the love reflected back at me. I brush her hair back, letting my hand settle at the nape of her neck as I pull her close, her soft curves molding perfectly against the hard lines of my body.

Our mouths crash together. The kiss is heated, years of want and tension exploding between us, our teeth gnashing as we taste one another with desperate intensity.

I move my lips along the column of her neck, enjoying the little gasps she releases.

"Clothes. Off. Now!" My little vixen seems to be impatient.

"Make me, Freckles," I command, pressing a kiss and smiling against her lips, knowing how those three words will rile her up.

"You asked for it" is all the warning I get before she shoves me onto her bed.

I sit on the edge of her bed as she stands before me, the moonlight peeking through the window and bathing her in its light.

She grabs the hem of my shirt and slowly lifts it over my head, the cool air of the room sending goose bumps all over my heated skin.

Her fingers trail down my chest, leaving a path of fire in their wake. Her touch is both gentle and demanding, exploring every ridge and plane of my torso with a curiosity that makes my breath catch.

"You're beautiful," she whispers, and I can feel the heat rising to my cheeks. No one's ever called me that before.

I pull her between my legs as my hands find the hem of her shirt. "May I?" I ask, and she nods, lifting her arms to help me remove it.

The sight of her in her bra nearly stops my heart. The pale moonlight casts shadows across her skin, highlighting the constellations of freckles scattered across her shoulders and chest. I've dreamed of this moment for so long, but reality is far better than any fantasy.

"You're staring," she says, a hint of vulnerability in her voice.

"Because you're breathtaking," I say, my hands finding her waist and bringing her closer. "I want to memorize every inch of you."

With a shy but pleased smile, she leans down to kiss me again. This time it's slower, deeper, as if we're both savoring the moment. My hands slide up her back, finding the clasp of her bra, but I hesitate.

"Is this okay?" I ask against her lips.

"Yes," she breathes. "Please."

With fumbling fingers, I undo the clasp, and she lets the straps fall down her arms before tossing it aside. I lean back slightly, taking in the sight of her bare chest, and my mouth goes dry.

"You can touch me," she murmurs, taking my hands and guiding them to her ample breasts.

The weight of them in my palms feels perfect, like they were made for my touch. I brush my thumbs across her pink nipples, and watch as they harden, delighting in the soft gasp that escapes her lips.

"Lie back," she commands, and I comply, scooting farther onto the bed as she climbs on top of me, straddling my hips.

The feeling of her weight on me and the sight of her above me in the moonlight is almost too much to bear. I reach up, cupping her face and hauling her down for another kiss, needing to taste her.

"I love you," I whisper against her lips, my words trembling with the weight of years spent holding them in. "I've always loved you, more than you'll ever know."

"I love you too," she says, her voice thick with emotion, her breath catching. "So much … I've always loved you too."

Our hands explore each other's bodies with reverent curiosity, learning what makes the other gasp and moan. When my fingers find the button of her jeans, she nods eagerly, lifting her hips to help me slide them down her legs.

Our clothes discarded, our bodies pressed together, skin against skin. The heat between us is intoxicating, and I can feel myself trembling with want and nervousness.

"Are you sure about this, baby?" I ask, my voice husky with desire but tinged with caution. "We can stop if—"

"I've never been more sure of anything," she says, pressing a kiss to my lips. "I want you, Dylan. All of you."

"I want all of you too, Freckles." I reach over to where I dropped my jeans and fish the condom from my pocket. Maisie takes it from me, her fingers brushing mine, sending a spark through me.

"Let me," she says, her voice a seductive whisper that sends shivers down my spine.

I nod, watching as she tears open the golden packet with trembling fingers. There's something incredibly intimate about the way she slips the condom on me, her touch both tentative and determined, as her soft palms squeeze my cock.

A moan sneaks past my lips, relishing her touch.

As Maisie straddles me once more, I place my hands on her delectable hips, guiding her slowly onto my hardened cock, and revel in the heat of her cunt squeezing me. As our bodies join, we both gasp at the sensation. Her eyes flutter closed for a moment before opening to meet mine, eyes filled with love and wonder.

"You okay?" I ask, barely able to form words through the overwhelming feeling of being inside her.

"Perfect," she breathes, leaning down to kiss me as she begins to move.

We find our rhythm together, slow and gentle at first, then building in intensity. Her soft moans and the way she whispers my name drive me wild. I've experienced nothing like this—the physical pleasure amplified by the emotional connection between us.

"Dylan," she gasps, her movements becoming more urgent. "I'm close."

I slip a hand between us, touching her where she needs it most, and watch in awe as she comes undone above me. The sight of her in ecstasy sends me over the edge, and I follow her into bliss as our bodies tremble together.

For a moment, we lie together, my arms wrapped tightly around her, relishing this new depth of intimacy. Our unspoken understanding speaks louder than words ever could.

Maisie stands and reaches for her robe.

"What are you doing?"

"Bathroom. It's important for a girl to use the restroom after sex. Also, I thought I could dispose of this." Her hand gently brushes against my dick, and I shutter at how sensitive I am.

"Right," I say. I stand, not wanting to make a mess on her bed, although the idea of my cum on her sheets does something to me. I gently pull the condom off and tie it before placing it in her hands. Before she can move, I pull her into me for another kiss, savoring every one I can get.

"We may have a problem," I mumble against her lips.

"Oh yeah, what's that?"

"I might be addicted to kissing you." With another quick kiss and swat on her ass, I watch her disappear through the door and return a few moments later.

I pull back her bedding, the both of us crawling under the covers. We lie tangled in her sheets, her head on my chest as I trace lazy patterns on her bare back. The silence between us is comfortable, filled with unspoken happiness.

"Was it worth the wait?" she asks, looking up at me with a playful smile.

I laugh softly, pressing a kiss to her forehead. "Beyond worth it. Though I do believe we have some catching up to do."

"I like the sound of that," she murmurs, snuggling closer.

As we drift toward sleep, I think about all we've been through to get to this moment—the years of friendship, the misunderstandings, all the heartache. And now, finally, we're where we're meant to be. Together.

Whatever challenges come our way—Harvard, my brother, or anything else life throws at us—I know we'll face them together. Because some loves are worth fighting for, and what Maisie and I have? It's the real deal. The kind that lasts forever.

"I love you, Freckles," I whisper into her hair.

"I love you too, Dylan," she replies, her voice heavy with sleep. "Always have, always will."

And in that moment, everything feels right in the world. Well, almost everything.

# Epilogue

## Graduation Day

## Dylan

"**W**ho in the world thought it would be a fun idea to streak at a high school graduation?"

Maisie and I look at each other, fighting back our laughs. I still can't believe Colton actually went through with it or that Hollis allowed it to happen. No way would Maisie want me streaking and allow other girls to see what belongs to her. And vice versa.

"Do you think they caught him?" Clara, Maisie's mother, asks.

"Can't say for sure," Coach Wells says. "I'll be back, okay, baby?" He leans down and presses a kiss on Clara's cheek as he makes his way toward the food table. Maisie is still trying to wrap her head around her mother and Coach Wells dating, but something tells me watching her daughter play football wasn't the only reason Clara Jorgensen showed up to every football game after the Wimbleton one.

Colton's family offered to host a post-graduation party, complete with a tasty array of food and ice-cold, sweet tea.

The Lewis twins with their mother, Hollis and her grandmother, Maisie's mom and sister, as well as Zion's family are all in attendance.

Even though she's not a graduate this year, Corrine came with only her mother, the fallout from Charmaine's arrest still hanging over their heads. Charmaine was taken into custody in the cafeteria just before homecoming weekend, charged with attempted sexual assault, conspiracy to commit a crime, as well as drug-related offenses—all thanks to the audio recording Hollis had gotten. It was the evidence they needed to convict her, and now she's facing anywhere from five to fifteen years.

*Good riddance.*

Maisie's mom quickly swipes at her eyes. "I just can't believe our babies are growing up."

"I know, right?" Mrs. Lewis chimes in, dabbing at her eyes with a napkin. "Feels like just yesterday Alora was throwing mud pies at the neighborhood boys."

Maisie laughs beside me, her fingers intertwined with mine. "Some things never change. She's just traded mud for football tackles."

My parents stand a few feet away, talking with Mr. and Mrs. Weedon. Dad has his arm around Mom's shoulders, and I notice how they both look lighter these days, more at peace. The dark circles that had taken up permanent residence under their eyes have faded, replaced by genuine smiles that reach their eyes.

"You good?" Maisie whispers, giving my hand a gentle squeeze.

I nod, pulling her closer to my side. "Never better."

And it's true. After everything we've been through this past year, we've come out stronger on the other side. Not just Maisie and me, but all of us.

Carver's return home three months ago was nothing short of miraculous. After being held captive by insurgents for weeks, he and two other soldiers were rescued during a special ops mission. He's still recovering—both physically and mentally—but having him home has brought life back into our house. The therapist says he's making remarkable progress, and seeing him laugh again is the best graduation gift I could have asked for.

"Hey, little brother!" Speak of the devil. Carver limps over, his cane flattening the grass. The physical scars from his ordeal are still visible—the healing gash across his left cheek, the slight limp from the bullet wound in his leg—but his eyes are clear and bright.

"I was just telling Mom and Dad how proud I am," he says, clapping me on the shoulder. "Harvard-bound with a football scholarship. Can't beat that."

"Couldn't have done it without my personal letter of recommendation writer," I say, nodding toward our father. After the whole Charmaine debacle, Dad stepped up and wrote me the most heartfelt recommendation letter I've ever read. It turns out that having a respected criminal defense attorney, as your father, holds weight with the admissions board.

"And don't forget your tutor," Maisie adds, playfully poking my side. "Someone had to make sure you actually passed physics."

"How could I forget?" I press a kiss to her temple. "My amazing, beautiful girlfriend, the genius."

"Who's also headed to Boston I hear," Carver points out with a wink. "Convenient, huh?"

When Maisie got her acceptance letter to the Harborview School of Fashion, it felt like the universe was finally aligning everything for us. One of the brides she helped with a last-minute dress alteration—Penelope—just so happened to be on the school's board. She was so impressed with Maisie's work that she put in a quiet recommendation. I'd like to think that gave her application just the boost it needed.

The school's close enough that we'll still get to see each other regularly, but far enough that we'll each have space to grow—separately, but hopefully not apart.

Maisie is my endgame. No one holds a flame to the woman she is and how happy she makes me.

"You two are disgustingly cute," Zion says, approaching with a plate piled high with food. "Save some romance for the rest of us single folks."

"Like you're going to stay single for long," Alora snorts, appearing with her own plate. "I'm sure there will be a plethora of LSU sorority girls lining up for you on your first day."

"Not my type." Zion shrugs, popping a grape into his mouth. "I need me a smart, bookish girl."

"A book girl?" Hollis asks. "Like the educated, schoolbooks type?"

"Nah. The ones who are reading those romance books with the sex in them. Have you read the scenes in those books? It's the quiet ones you gotta watch out for," Zion explains.

"Oh, we know. Right, Corrine?" Maisie elbows her friend, who is now sporting some darker locks.

"I don't know what you're talking about." She smiles mischievously.

The sun is setting, casting a golden glow over the backyard. Someone has strung fairy lights in the trees, and they're beginning to twinkle as dusk approaches. In this light, surrounded by everyone I care about, I can't help but feel overwhelmingly grateful.

"Picture time!" Mrs. Reynolds announces, waving her camera. "All the graduates get together!"

We gather under the oak tree, arms around each other's shoulders. Maisie stands beside me, her graduation cap slightly askew, her smile radiant. I adjust her cap, admiring the way she looks up at me with those eyes that still make my heart flutter wildly.

*I love you, Freckles*, I mouth.

*I love you, too*, she mouths back.

The camera flashes, capturing this perfect moment—the seven of us on the edge of our futures, ready to take on the world.

## *Four Years Later*

# Maisie

"Dylan, where are we going?"

"It's a surprise, Freckles. It won't be much of one if you see where we're going now, will it?"

"I'm not sure how I feel about surprises. Maybe Hollis had a point in disliking them."

"Oh, but I think you will like this one. In fact, I am about a thousand percent positive that you are going to love it."

"We'll see, won't we?"

Dylan and I are recent college and design school graduates. We decided to come home to Bellwood to spend time with our families and enjoy no longer having exams, essays, and all the madness that comes with getting a higher education.

We are renting a room at the Bellwood Hotel, foregoing staying with our families because ... well, we like to have sex when we want. And where we want. The last thing we want to do is get caught in an awkward situation by one of our family members.

Dylan woke me this morning, first with his mouth between my legs, followed by hot shower sex, before we *finally* got dressed. He told me he had something special planned, so I had to dress nicely.

Going for a simple, pink floral sundress in this South Carolina summer heat was the best option.

Also, easy access in case the mood arises.

Before we left the hotel, Dylan blindfolded me and told me to just "trust" him.

And I do. I've trusted him for as long as I've known him.

He helped me into our car, and we drove around for what felt like a few minutes before the car comes to a stop.

"Do not remove the blindfold!" Dylan commands me, sending a shiver through me that goes right to my core.

*Oh, he's going to pay for that when we get back to the room.*

He knows precisely what that commanding tone does to me.

The door clicks open and big, strong hands grab onto mine. "Alright, be careful as there is a sidewalk. Alright, baby?"

I nod, stepping out of the car carefully, feeling for any uneven edges beneath my feet.

Once I'm situated on flat ground, Dylan removes the blindfold, and I'm instantly taken aback.

White rose petals create a delicate pathway leading to my old fairy bush, which is adorned with pink and white calla lilies. An assortment of vases filled with more lilies are elegantly arranged in front of the bush, enhancing the scene with their soft, vibrant hues.

Somewhere in the distance, music begins playing, and the first gentle notes of Ed Sheeran's *"Perfect"* drift through the air, wrapping around the moment like a memory I never want to forget.

"Dylan ... what is this?" I whisper, breathless, my heart racing.

He says nothing, just takes my hand and leads me to the center of the petal path.

"Maisie. The first time I laid eyes on you, you were running from that house"—he points to my childhood home—"into this very bush. I was in the middle of helping my family move our things in when it looked like you needed a friend."

Tears start to prick the corners of my eyes, my mind taking me back to that day.

"It was this very bush that I crawled in after you, wanting to make sure you were okay. The moment you lifted your pretty face to look at me, was the day you stole my heart without even knowing it."

"Oh, Dylan …" A tear escapes, and I curse, hoping it doesn't streak my makeup.

"Do you remember what I said to you that day? When you were scared?"

I think back to the day, on the front porch, his mom's gentle hands, and the way she bandaged me up.

"I'm sorry, baby. I don't."

"It's okay." He leans in and presses a gentle kiss to my lips. "I squeezed your hand and said 'Don't worry, Freckles. I got you.' It was that day that our story began, the day that the girl next door and the boy next door became best friends. Best friends who grew up, hormones got added, and feelings began to change into something more."

Dylan drops to one knee, pulling out a small blue box, and opens it. The most beautiful pear-cut diamond with a matching diamond band sparkles in the bright sun, nearly blinding me. My breath catches in my throat as I try to take it all in, the weight of the moment settling over us both. He looks up at me, his eyes full of hope and love, as if he's already made his decision.

"Maisie Janine Jorgensen, I have loved you since we were children, and I will love you until my last breath. You have been there for me in my darkest times. You helped me get through my brother missing, tutored me so I could pass a class, and supported me even when you disagreed. You have been with me through my highs and my lows, and I know, without a doubt, you're the only woman for me, have been the only woman for me. Will you do me the honor of taking my last name, to become Mrs. Maisie Myers?"

*Fuck the makeup.* Tears stream down my face at his words, at the love and commitment he has put into us, for us. This man, who values me and respects me, worships the ground I walk on and loves me just the way I am. How could I say no to him?

"Yes, a million thousand yeses."

I pull this handsome man off the ground and kiss him as if I am deprived of oxygen and he is the air I need.

Behind us, cheers erupt, pulling me away from Dylan's lips with a startled laugh. I turn to see our families and friends emerging from between our old homes, clapping, whistling, and grinning from ear to ear.

Hollis and Colton. Alora. Zion. Corrine glowing beside her handsome, tattooed fiancé.

My mom is dabbing at her eyes with a tissue, and next to her, my former football coach—now stepdad—stands with his arm around her shoulders, beaming with pride.

"You planned all this?" I ask Dylan, my voice still shaky with emotion.

"I might have had some help," he admits, sliding the ring onto my finger. It fits perfectly, catching the sunlight and sending prisms dancing across my skin.

"Your man has been planning this for months." Alora comes up and squeezes me in a bear hug. "I told you that the two of you were soulmates."

"You *did* say that." I laugh. "Just like I knew there was something more between you and LJ."

"Guess we both called it." She grins, a blush creeping into her cheeks. I'm just happy my best friend has found someone who treats her the way she deserves.

One by one, my friends hug me tightly, their voices filled with excitement as they gush over the stunning ring on my hand.

I watch the man I love celebrate with our family and friends, his happiness radiating like sunlight.

"Let me see the ring!" Josie squeals, grabbing my hand. "Holy shit, Dylan! You did good!"

"Language," my mom scolds my sister, but she's smiling as she examines the ring herself. "It's absolutely beautiful, sweetheart."

"Dylan picked it out himself," Nora Myers says proudly, joining us. "Though he did call me about fifty times asking for opinions."

"Only because I wanted it to be perfect." Dylan defends himself, sliding an arm around my waist. "For my perfect girl."

He leans in and kisses me softly, mindful of the fact that our moms are watching.

"I'm just happy you actually listened to me for once," Dylan's mom says with a smile.

"What are you talking about? I always listened to you and Dad!"

"That's debatable," she laughs, gently smacking Dylan's shoulder. Nora faces me, taking my hands in hers. "You've always been like a daughter to me, Maisie, and now... I'm just so happy to welcome you into our family officially."

Her voice trembles slightly, eyes shining with emotion. We pull each other into a tight embrace, holding on as if words alone could never capture what this moment means. Nora and Wade have always felt like bonus parents to me growing up. Now, in the very near future, they will officially be my in-laws.

Carver, no longer in need of a cane, raises a champagne bottle with a grin. "I think this calls for a celebration!"

Corrine and the newly married Mrs. Hollis Reynolds follow right behind him, carrying the champagne flutes and handing them out to everyone.

Wade Myers, Dylan's father, begins pouring champagne into the glasses until each one is filled with the bubbly golden liquid, except for my eighteen-year-old sister, of course. She gets sparkling cider.

When everyone has a filled glass, Carver raises his.

"To Dylan and Maisie," he says, a smile tugging at his lips. "Two souls who grew up side by side and ended up finding their way to forever."

"To Dylan and Maisie!" everyone echoes.

As I take a sip, I catch Dylan watching me, his eyes filled with so much love it makes my heart ache.

"What are you thinking about?" I mutter.

He tucks a strand of hair behind my ear. "I'm thinking about how lucky I am that you crawled into that fairy bush all those years ago."

"And I'm thinking how lucky I am that you followed me," I state.

# Acknowledgements

First and foremost, I must thank my wonderful husband. From the moment the idea of becoming an author first touched my heart, he's been by my side, making sure I saw it through every step of the way. His unwavering love and support, and the way he's been my rock when I needed it most, mean more than words can express. Whenever I doubt myself or question whether this dream is truly worth the struggle, he's always there—reminding me that it will all pay off, and that I should never let anything convince me to give up. Having a supportive partner like him is everything, and I'm endlessly grateful he's mine.

To my four, beautiful children ~ If there is anything I want you to take from watching me write my books, it's this: go chase your dreams. Never let fear hold you back or the doubts hinder what you are capable of. With patience, hard work and support, you can do anything.

To my family and friends ~ Thank you for all the love and support you have shown me on this newfound journey of mine. Whether you are telling people about my books, reading them or just buying my work to support me, I am so appreciative that you are showing your love for me and it does not go unnoticed.

To Maria ~ Thank you for the All Write Well program and your always positive feedback as I stepped foot into the writing world. I would not be turning this dream into reality if it wasn't for you and the program you have created. I hope I make you proud! I will continue to use what I learned from AWW to help me build this author dream of mine.

To my editor, Dee Houpt ~ Thank you for your time and work that you put into editing my manuscripts. Thank you for always being so positive, understanding, reassuring and always giving your honesty. I knew the moment I saw your website, you were the person I wanted to work with and I'm so glad I took the chance. This book wouldn't be what it is today without you. Thank you truly doesn't seem to be enough!

To my book cover designer, Dee Garcia ~ You always have the magic touch when it comes to designing book covers. When I feel like I can't fully express my vision, you somehow manage to put together my visions and make them reality. The number of compliments I get in regards to the covers make me proud to showcase your talent for the world to see. Thank you for the amazing work you do!

Finally, to the readers who took the time to read this book. Thank you for taking a chance on a new indie author. It means the world to me that you chose to read my story. Whether you loved it or felt it could have been better, I appreciate you and thank you! If you could leave an honest review on Amazon and any other social platform, I would greatly appreciate it! Reviews help indie authors such as myself get our books out to more readers.

# About the Author

Dev Hahn is a new indie author who is ready to bring her notebook of story ideas to life and share them with the world. Reading has always been an escape for Dev when her depression became too much or when she just needed to escape reality for a few chapters. She hopes she can do the same for anyone willing to take a chance on her books. Besides reading romance and falling for fictional characters, Dev enjoys watching American football, singing karaoke with her family, iced lattes all year round, and spending quality time with the people she loves most. She's a stay-at-home mother who writes around her children's schedules. She resides in Maryland with her husband, two fur babies and their four children who make life fun, chaotic and entertaining.

# *Also By Dev Hahn*

**<u>Standalones</u>**
Beyond Broken Colors


**<u>Bellwood Lady Baller Series</u>**
Coming Out on the Sidelines
Catching Feelings in the End Zone
Tackling Temptations on the Line
Opposing Hearts on the Field, *Coming Fall 2025*

# Connect With Me

Be sure to follow me on my socials for updates and new releases!

**Bookbub:** bookbub.com/profile/dev-hahn
**Facebook:** facebook.com/authordevhahn
**Goodreads:** goodreads.com/author/show/47750634.Dev_Hahn
**Instagram:** instagram.com/authordevhahn/
**Pinterest:** pinterest.com/authordevhahn
**TikTok:** tiktok.com/@author.dev.hahn
**Threads:** threads.com/@authordevhahn